ENSORCELLED HEARTS

"You're not making any sense," Ravyn snapped. "I'd give anything to find and stop this maniac. I don't know what you're accusing me of, or why. *Why?*"

Nick sighed and shook his head. "Damn it, I don't know. I don't know."

She put a hand on his arm. "I'm sorry, Nick."

He gave her a small, humorless smile. "Sorry for what? Are you sorry Kayne is a dangerous fanatic? Or are you sorry that I can't stop thinking about you, can't stop wanting you? Sorry that my desire for you is stronger than it ever was for my dead wife?" He grabbed her once more and pulled her to him. "Do you have any idea how crazy that is? How it makes me feel? I want you every second of every day. Even with people dying around me, even with the frustration and guilt of not being able to stop this murdering psychopath, I still want you. It's . . . it's like I'm under some sort of spell."

Heart
of the
Witch

ALICIA DEAN

LOVE SPELL   NEW YORK CITY

To my extraordinary, beautiful, precious children,
Lana, Lacey, and Presley. You are my world.

To my best friend, Paige—a truly exceptional person—
and her girls, Kyleigh and Alexandra, who I love as
though they were my own.

LOVE SPELL®

December 2009

Published by

Dorchester Publishing Co., Inc.
200 Madison Avenue
New York, NY 10016

Cover art by Anne Cain.

ISBN 10: 0-505-52826-6
ISBN 13: 978-0-505-52826-1
E-ISBN: 978-1-4285-

The name "Love Spell" and its logo are trademarks of Dorchester
Publishing Co., Inc.

Printed in the United States of America.

10 9 8 7 6 5 4 3 2 1

Visit us online at www.dorchesterpub.com.

ACKNOWLEDGMENTS

I believe the one thing that has surprised me most in my journey as a writer is the genuine encouragement and support my fellow authors have shown. I've been fortunate enough to make the acquaintance of so many wonderful people along the way: My OKRWA chapter, my critique group (The Sooner Writers), Judith Rochelle and her magic wishing well, and the fantastic men and women I've met through the Wild Rose Press and online loops such as Contest Alert and ProOrg. But of all the amazing people I've come in contact with in the writing world, none can compare to the generous and remarkable Sharon Sala. Thank you so much for being the catalyst that made this happen. For that, and all of your other exceptional qualities, I love you. You'll always be very special to me.

Also, I'd like to thank my mentor, Mel Odom. Without his teaching and inspiration, I would never have had the confidence to finish that first book. I would also like to thank Jordan Dane for all she's done. I am awed by her success and the fact that she's still willing to reach out to assist aspiring authors. Thanks to my friend, Rhonda Penders, for her unfailing help and belief in me, even though she's not into the "eerie" stuff I write. Thanks to Faith V. Smith and Martha Kopcienski for reading my book and offering insightful suggestions.

I want to thank my family for a lifetime of love and support. My mother, Eva Robertson, for being the most giving and loving mother I could ever hope to have. My father, Dean Robertson. Although he's no longer with us, I will always carry the memory of his gentle love and encouragement.

My loving and supportive sister and friend, Ruth, and her husband, Tom, whose greatness as a brother-in-law is surpassed only by his perfection as a husband. My sister, Sheri, who I adore and who is always there for me, and who I think has been more excited throughout this process than I have, and her husband, Larry. My kind, loving, sister, Janis, and my brother, Brett. To my beautiful nieces and nephews. To Madison, even though I'm not able to see you, not a day goes by that the kids and I don't think of you and miss you, and our love for you will never change. Thank you, Liz, for being my lifelong friend. And her beautiful children, Preston, Kandis, and Nathan, who will always have a special place in my heart . . . love you so much.

My terrific agent, Meredith Bernstein, who hung in there with me. And my fantastic editor, Chris Keeslar, who believed in my book enough to take a chance.

I have been truly blessed with a tremendous network of friends and family and I am honored beyond measure to have them beside me as I see my dream come true. I can't possibly name everyone, it would take me more pages than my actual book, but I hope that you know who you are and that I've told you along the way how much you mean to me. If not, I'm telling you now.

Heart

of the

Witch

Chapter One

If she didn't wake soon, he'd have to cut her. He wasn't ready to do that. Not yet.

Moonlight filtered into the cabin through sheet-covered windows, casting a patchwork of shadows on her face. She was a beauty. In the brief moments before she lost consciousness, he'd seen her eyes: a deep, rich green with flecks of amber. Never in his life had he seen eyes that color. He'd been so captivated, he'd nearly forgotten the chloroform.

Her hair was the color of midnight with streaks of crimson, and it fell in glossy waves around her shoulders. Dark lashes lay on her pale cheeks. She had full lips, with a slight overbite. Soooo sexy. She had full breasts, rounded hips, long shapely legs. Her feminine curves were the kind that drove men wild. She wasn't emaciated like so many women these days. It was sickening, the way they starved themselves to skin and bones, leaving nothing a man could hold on to—or sink a blade into.

A cracking noise sounded, and he lifted his head. Had a hunter wandered too close? At this time of year in southeast Oklahoma, hunting was almost a religion. He ran a high risk of detection by some redneck with more firepower than brains. That didn't matter, though. The risk only added to the thrill.

The sound came again, and this time he recognized it: a log popping in the fireplace. He let out a relieved sigh.

The risk might add excitement, but he was in no hurry to be discovered by Billy Bob Redneck and his hillbilly buddies. There was too much yet to be enjoyed. Some pleasures shouldn't be rushed.

The girl—Ravyn, he'd learned from her driver's license—groaned. He felt a swelling in his loins, and his arousal pressed against his zipper. The groan was just the beginning. The groan meant she would soon be awake, that she would soon be a witness to the pleasures he took with her body. He always waited until they were awake. Without consciousness, there was no fear. Without fear, there was no satisfaction.

His heart raced. He'd never been this excited before. He hoped to make this woman last longer than the others. "Time to wake up, my lovely," he whispered. His spine tingled with anticipation. Soon. *Very* soon.

The ecstasy had begun the first time he lost a patient in surgery. Even though it hadn't been on purpose, her death had given him a thrill beyond measure. He'd discovered that the power to take a life was more exhilarating than the ability to save one. Since, taking lives had developed into a pleasure beyond imagining.

This exquisite creature strapped to the bed was his sixth victim, and she was the most stunning of all. Nearly perfect. He always chose perfection, because that was more satisfying to destroy. Seeing the look in the eyes of a beautiful woman who knew her life was in his hands, seeing her realize that her beauty couldn't save her . . . that was a thrill beyond words.

When little boys choose to be naughty little bastards, they must suffer the consequences!

What the . . . ? He whirled as the voice echoed through the cabin. The room was empty. He looked back at the girl. Still unconscious. It hadn't been her.

Of course it wasn't her, you stupid little fuck. Don't you recognize your own mother's voice?

A chill coursed through his body, settled in his groin. He shivered, and his dick shrank as if trying to crawl inside him. He was losing his mind. His mother had been dead for years. She couldn't hurt him anymore, could no longer control him.

The girl moaned again, and he forgot about his mother's voice. He sucked in a breath as the girl's eyelids fluttered open. God, she was magnificent. Her eyes looked almost black in the light from the moon, but he recalled their incredible shade, those rich emerald irises flecked with gold. He couldn't wait to see them colored with fear.

"Hello. I've been waiting for you. Do you remember me?"

The girl shook her head. With his handkerchief lodged in her mouth, she couldn't speak even if she wanted.

"I saw you at the restaurant. You were with two other women. Celebrating an engagement, I think?"

Her eyes held confusion but no fear. Yes, the disorientation was always there first. The fear would come soon. The fear always came shortly after the blade appeared. Then the questions. Then the begging. Finally the screams.

"Tell me, are you the bride?" She didn't respond, so he continued. "If so, congratulations are in order." He allowed himself a secret grin. If she was the bride, somewhere there would be a very disappointed groom.

He took off his dinner jacket and tossed it onto the foot of the bed. Walking to the fireplace, he pulled his knife from its sheath. "It's okay that you don't remember me. After tonight you will." He didn't add she wouldn't remember him long because she wouldn't *live* long. No need to cause all-out panic. Not just yet.

He held his knife blade in the flame until it glowed red, then walked back to her side. Her gaze traveled to the knife, and then to his face. He saw anger but still no fear. Damn. He gripped the neck of her red dress and yanked until it tore down the front. A sheer red bra barely covered tantalizing breasts that were, yes, perfect. Her eyes showed more anger. She began to mumble behind the gag and struggle against her bindings.

"Don't fight. You can't win." Smiling, he pressed the hot steel against her stomach. A guttural cry tore from her throat, and the smell of burning flesh filled the room.

There, that was better. He looked into her eyes. Pain. But still no fear. Who the hell did she think she was?

"You're a tough one, huh?" He slowly lowered the blade again and watched as her eyes followed his movement. He grinned. *Let me see that fear.*

Her expression began to change, but there was still no fear. Instead, her face showed something different, something he couldn't explain. The amber flecks in her irises began to glow, casting light of their own. Her eyes burned brighter and brighter until they were golden pools of fire. They became a blaze of scarlet, the color of blood.

He stepped back, rubbed his eyes. A tremble of fear wormed through him. When he looked again, her eyes still blazed crimson. Around the gag, her lips stretched into a sneer, and for the first time in his adult life, *he* was the one afraid.

No, not afraid. He was terrified.

A strangled shriek wrenched loose from his throat. His mind told him to run, but he couldn't move; it was as if his feet were mired in quicksand. He shook his head from side to side, emitting small whimpers from between clenched lips. His knife slipped from his hands and clattered to the floor, seemingly a useless toy. His bowels clenched, then loosened, but the humiliation of soiling himself was lost in the awfulness that followed.

His groin warmed. It heated to the point of being uncomfortable, even painful—excruciating pain like he'd never felt before. An animalistic scream reverberated through the room as his genitals burst into flame.

Chapter Two

Flashes of red and blue stroked the treetops above Ravyn Skyler's head. She lay on a stretcher while the paramedic applied ointment to her burn. "You're sure you won't go to the hospital?" he asked, his young face scrunched in disapproval.

"I'm sure. I'll be fine."

He puffed his cheeks out and heaved a sigh. "You'll have to sign a release."

She nodded. "Okay."

"All finished," he said, pulling her tattered dress over the injury. "You can sit up now. I'll be right back with the release form."

Ravyn rose to a sitting position and pulled the blanket she'd been given around her shoulders. She wore nothing except her torn dress underneath—just another humiliation added to an already horrific night.

Sheriff Whitehall, who'd arrived immediately after the ambulance, appeared at her side. He pushed his cowboy hat back, revealing a large forehead and a receding hairline. Crevices lined his sunburned face. His stomach hung over his belt, and an unlit cigarette dangled from his mouth. His eyes looked sleepy, as if maybe he'd just gotten out of bed. Since it was the wee hours of the morning, he probably had.

"Ms. Skyler? The ambulance driver's gonna let you stay right where you're at while we chat. Mind tellin' me what the hell happened here?"

Ravyn looked around. The cabin in the wooded area bore no resemblance to the last place she'd been: the parking lot of the Caribbean Nights restaurant in Oklahoma City.

"Where am I?"

His thick gray eyebrows drew together. "You're outside . . . on a stretcher . . . 'bout a mile and a quarter east of Cotton, Oklahoma. I'm not sure what yer askin'. You all right?"

"Cotton? How far is that from Oklahoma City?"

"'Bout fifty miles. You from the city?"

Ravyn nodded. "I need to get home."

"Your sister should be here before long." The sheriff had let Ravyn call her from his phone, and Sorina was en route. "I need to ask you some questions while we wait."

Ravyn managed a weak smile. "Sure."

"Oh, by the way. Don't fret about this." He pointed to the cigarette. "Throws folks for a loop these days, but I never light it 'cept in the cruiser. I reckon anybody that winds up in there deserves to have a little smoke blown at 'em. Ya know what I mean?"

Ravyn nodded. She didn't give a damn about the cigarette. She just wanted to go home.

The paramedic returned with the release form. Ravyn signed it and he walked away, shaking his head.

"Now." The sheriff crossed his arms and narrowed his eyes. "You wanna tell me what happened?"

Ravyn sighed. She wrapped the blanket more tightly around herself and without looking at the sheriff began to speak. "I met my mother and sister for dinner. After we finished, I walked to my car. As I was about to open the door, someone grabbed me from behind. He put something over my mouth, and the next thing I remember I was waking up in that cabin."

Ravyn closed her eyes. In her mind's eye she could see her captor. Not just his features, which were rather ordinary, but the evil pleasure on his face, especially as he pressed the hot blade to her flesh.

She opened her eyes and the vision disappeared. Swallowing, she continued. "After he burned me with the knife, I screamed. The guy ran. I heard a car take off. Then those boys—hunters, I guess—came in and found me. They called nine-one-one."

"Did you know the man?" the sheriff asked.

"No."

"Can you describe him for me?"

This was where it got tricky. Ravyn didn't want to tell the authorities what the man looked like. If they found him, he would tell them what he'd seen. What she'd done. How she'd set him on fire.

"It was dark. I was drugged."

The sheriff blew out a breath and was silent for a moment. At last he said, "Ms. Skyler, I think the man who attacked you was the Tin Man. He's murdered at least five women. You would've been his sixth. Why do you reckon he let you go?"

Ravyn shrugged. "Probably because I screamed. I guess it scared him."

"All of his other victims were gagged. Weren't you?"

Ravyn looked down at her hands. Anything to avoid the lawman's piercing stare. "Yes. But I managed to dislodge it," she said, lifting her gaze.

Sheriff Whitehall rolled his cigarette around in his mouth and shook his head. He clearly didn't believe her. Had her story sounded as implausible to his ears as it had to hers?

"Can you at least give me some kind of idea what he looked like?"

Ravyn hesitated. She was afraid for them to find him, but she was also afraid they wouldn't. He'd kill again. If she hadn't finished him, she was sure he wasn't finished.

She let out a breath and said, "He was of average height. Brown hair. Beard. That's about all I can remember. He wore a dinner jacket and slacks. A dark color, maybe black or navy."

The sheriff nodded thoughtfully. "Mighta been a customer, then, eating in the same place. Probably watching you. We'll need to check the restaurant's receipts for the night."

"He was," Ravyn recalled. "He mentioned that he saw me dining with my mother and sister. He was there."

"Okay, then. What about scars, tattoos, jewelry of any kind . . . ?"

"No. I didn't notice anything like that."

"Was there anything familiar about his voice? This is mighty important, Ms. Skyler. Anything you can remember might help."

She shook her head. "I'm sorry. I'd like to help, but I can't. I've told you everything." Well, *almost* everything. In spite of the ointment, her wound throbbed. She just wanted this to be over with. "Can I go home?"

"Ravyn! Dear God! Are you okay?"

Ravyn looked up and the sheriff turned as Ravyn's sister descended on them. Taller than Ravyn, blonde, vivacious and striking, Sorina was the kind of woman men devoured with their eyes. Whitehall was no exception.

"I'm fine," Ravyn said as her sister bent and enveloped her in a Versace-scented hug.

"What happened?"

"Ms. Skyler was attacked by a man that coulda been the Tin Man," the sheriff answered.

Sorina's face paled. "Oh, my God! No! Honey . . . !" Her eyes filled with tears and she hugged Ravyn again. "How? When Mother and I left you at the restaurant, we thought you were leaving right behind us. We assumed you'd gone home."

"He grabbed me in the parking lot." Ravyn shifted uncomfortably and glanced at the sheriff from under her lashes. She didn't like the way he hung on her every word.

"And I just went home!" Sorina wailed. "I left you there alone."

"You didn't know. Don't blame yourself," Ravyn assured her.

Sorina lifted a trembling hand and brushed a tear from her porcelain cheek. She turned to Sheriff Whitehall. "The Tin Man is the serial killer, right? The one I read about in the papers? He mutilated those poor women. He was the one who did this? Are you sure?"

The sheriff shrugged, his gaze on Ravyn as he answered. "The guy got away, and your sis here can't tell us much about him."

"I gave you a description," Ravyn replied.

The sheriff peered at her, his brow furrowed. "Not a very detailed one."

"How did you manage to escape?" Sorina asked.

Lying to her sister was more difficult than lying to the sheriff, but Ravyn couldn't admit to Sorina what she'd done. "As I told the sheriff, I screamed, he ran. Some hunters found me. Can we please go home now?"

Her sister took her hand and squeezed. "Are you sure you're telling him everything?"

A cold shiver seeped through Ravyn from deep inside her body, from inside her soul. Icy trepidation trickled outward and traveled over her flesh.

Death is coming, said a voice.

Ravyn looked at her sister, then the sheriff. They apparently hadn't heard; the voice had come from within. Not really a voice. More like a premonition. A warning. But did this feeling mean that someone close to her was in danger, or was it simply because she'd encountered a monster who wore murder like a cologne?

Chapter Three

Local residents claimed the building on the eastern out-
skirts of Oklahoma City was haunted. It had once been a
nightclub, but business quickly declined following the af-
ter-hours rape and murder of one of the barmaids back in
the sixties, right in the center of the dance floor. The bar
closed within the month. Through the years other com-
panies had taken over, but none stayed for long.

The building sat vacant for close to ten years before
Nick Lassiter bought it at an outrageously reasonable price.
He purchased it with the lump payout he'd received when
he "amicably" severed all ties to the police force. The space
was converted into two offices. Nick leased one to an accountant named Marvin. Nick's side held a scarred desk
and a black vinyl chair. His PI certification and an auto-
graphed photo of Pete Rose hung on the wall. On top of
the desk were an ashtray, a notepad, a pen, a bottle of
whiskey and a phone with a blinking message light.

Nick ignored the light, reaching instead for the whiskey. A force inside his head pushed against his temples like
the beating wings of an eagle struggling to be set free. He
unscrewed the lid from the bottle of Old Crow and lifted it
to his lips.

The cheap whiskey didn't burn the way it once did,
which showed a man could get used to about anything.
There was a time when it would have been Crown Royal.
Of course, back then he wouldn't have been drinking it at
the office. Definitely not at ten o'clock in the morning.

Hell, give yourself some credit. It's been a while since you've made it in by ten in the morning.

His stomach protested the whiskey's assault. Acid rolled deep in his gut, working its way up his throat. He took another swallow. "Hair of the dog, you know." As he wiped the back of his hand over his mouth, a golden retriever lifted its head and stared at him.

"I wasn't talking to you, Dog. And don't look at me like that. The only reason you're even here is 'cause it's raining and I didn't want to leave your whiny ass outside all day."

The mutt had wandered into Nick's yard last year. Nick supposed the dog belonged to him now, since no one had come looking for it.

"Maybe I should give you a name," Nick told the beast. But he knew he wouldn't. He'd been saying that for months, and he still just called the dog Dog.

Nick took another drink from the bottle. The pungent smell of the whiskey temporarily overpowered the odors of wet canine and stale cigarette smoke. His stomach was starting to accept the liquor a little better. Today might not be so bad after all.

Dog stood and ambled to the door, wagging his tail and looking mournfully at his master. Nick got up and let him out into the hallway. There was a doggie door in the front lobby. The mutt would go back out into the rain, get soaked all over again and stink the office up even more. Perfect.

Nick returned to his desk and punched the play button on the answering machine.

"Hey, Nick. It's me, Phil Bodinski. Listen, I was wondering if you had anything for me." Phil's voice trembled with the next words. "I know I just called yesterday, and I don't mean to bother you, but . . ." Phil cleared his throat, trying to choke back the tears before he continued.

Hell, did the guy think he was the only one in the world

whose wife had died? Yeah, sure. Phil's wife was killed by *somebody*. He had someone to blame. He wanted Nick to find the Tin Man. Wanted him to find a serial killer who had managed to elude the police for two years. At least Phil had someone to punish. The only person Nick had to punish was himself. Not for his wife's death, but because of where he'd been when it happened.

"Anyway." Phil regained his composure and his voice came back through the speaker. "Give me a call. Even if you don't have anything. You know, just to check in. Well . . . bye."

Nick took another pull from the bottle of whiskey. He lit a cigarette and watched the smoke dance into the light fixture above his head.

Mentally he reviewed the evidence on the Tin Man case. There wasn't a lot. Five victims. The fourth one was Phil's wife—twenty-eight years old, a good-looking blonde, taken as she left work one evening. Missing four days before her body was found along I-35. Nude, tortured and stabbed, with burn marks all over the corpse. Forensics concluded the burns were more than likely made by the heated blade of a knife. The words *Tin Man* were written in blood down her legs, virtually the only place on her body unmarked enough for the psycho's signature.

There had been no identifiable DNA, no fingerprints, no witnesses. The police were baffled. Nick was baffled, and there wasn't a damned thing he could do about it. Yeah, sure, he wanted the murdering bastard stopped. Wanted him to pay with his worthless life. But not enough to really *do* anything about it. Even if he could. Which Nick couldn't.

So, that left him taking Phil's money for nothing. Giving the guy half-assed reports a few times a week that amounted to not a goddamned thing. When Nick was on the force, it had been a different story. Back then he cared. Back then he thought he could make a difference.

Back then he'd had Annie.

He tilted his chair back and closed his eyes. What time had he gone to sleep last night? He couldn't remember, but he knew it was more like this morning than last night. Maybe he should have stayed in bed.

The phone rang, the noise piercing the silence of the office. Nick's body jerked and he nearly tumbled from the chair. He smelled something burning. What the . . . ? Shit. He must've dozed. His cigarette was on the carpet, starting a fresh hole among the older ones.

He stood and stomped on the smoldering butt as he picked up the receiver. "Lassiter Investigations," he answered automatically.

"Nick? Hey, Phil Bodinski here." The man's voice was filled with excitement. Nick started to tell him he didn't need to use his full name when he identified himself. It wasn't necessary, since ol' Phil was his only client.

"Did you hear?" Phil asked.

"Hear what?" Nick was only half-listening. His foot rubbed at the burn even as he lit another cigarette.

"There's a survivor."

"A what?"

"One of the Tin Man's victims got away."

Nick's foot stopped. He stubbed out his fresh cigarette, this time in the ashtray, and plopped down in his chair.

"No kidding?"

"Yeah. Joe called me this morning."

Joe Smothers was a retired lieutenant Nick had once worked with. Joe and Phil played golf together. Joe had sent Phil to Nick, God only knew why. Phil should try solving this thing himself. He seemed to know a hell of a lot more details of the case than Nick did.

"What happened?" Nick was curious in spite of himself. A shot of adrenaline buzzed through him, something he hadn't felt since he'd turned in his badge.

"Can I come in? I have her name and everything."

"How'd you get her name?" Joe wouldn't have given Phil that even if he'd known it.

"This reporter friend of mine. He said they weren't allowed to print it, but he told me."

"Shit." Phil was an attorney. He'd made a lot of "friends" along the way and gotten a shitload of people out of trouble. Now he was collecting on old favors.

"You know, there's usually a reason they keep that stuff confidential. It's really not a good idea for you to be snooping around a case like that."

"Yeah, I know. You're the one who should be getting the information."

Ouch. Okay, Phil had him there. Nick wasn't exactly doing an ace job, but what the fuck? If the cops couldn't find the guy, how the hell was he supposed to? Nick lit another cigarette and absentmindedly rubbed the scar on his chin. The bottle of Old Crow sat on the desk, staring at him. Enticing him. If he scheduled Phil later this afternoon, he could have a few more drinks and still disguise the smell before the guy got here.

"Can you come in at two?"

"How about now?" Phil's usual passive demeanor had changed. He was like a barracuda with a goldfish.

Nick looked longingly at the bottle, then sighed. "Fine. Come on in."

"Be there in half an hour."

After he hung up, Nick put the bottle of whiskey in the drawer, rinsed his mouth out with Scope and shrugged a brown corduroy jacket on over his tattered, once-white T-shirt. He rubbed a hand over his jaw, thinking he should have shaved this morning. Or at least this week. He sat down and swiveled his chair around, looking out the window as he smoked and waited for Phil.

Sheets of rain slapped against the glass. It had rained like this five years ago on the day they'd buried Annie. At least, he assumed it had, since rain always made him think of Annie's death. He didn't remember much about that day. He'd gotten pretty drunk at the start of it and had stayed that way for over a week.

The overcast sky and the downpour blocked his normal view of the convenience store across the street. The window was like a mirror. The image that stared back at him revealed dark circles beneath bloodshot eyes. Nick turned away, telling himself the dampness he saw in them was just a reflection of the rain.

Chapter Four

The first thing Jay Haleck noticed was the smell of Betadine. When he opened his eyes, he saw the brass ceiling fan with the frosted globes. He was in his bedroom. Or maybe he was dead and just *thought* he was in his bedroom.

A face materialized in the center of his vision: Marshall Weindot, the gay doctor from the hospital. The man had made it clear he had a thing for Jay. So what the hell was Jay doing with *him*?

Suddenly, Jay remembered. He had called Marshall after the incident, just before passing out.

Marshall gazed at him out of striking gray eyes framed by thick eyelashes most women would kill for. A lock of dark hair fell over his tanned forehead. He was almost too pretty to be a man. If Jay *were* a homo, Marshall was the type he'd go for.

"How do you feel?" Marshall's voice was the most masculine thing about him—oddly deep, in spite of his effeminate appearance.

"Not sure," Jay grunted. Then he knew. Pain seared deep inside him, ripping him apart. That bitch. She'd done this to him. But how? "Hurts. God, it hurts."

"I know. I'm sorry. I'll give you some morphine. It's only been a few hours since the last dose, but with that injury—" Marshall broke off and walked away. He came back with a syringe.

"How long have I been out?" Jay asked as Marshall prepared the injection.

"A couple of days. You called me in the wee hours on Saturday morning. Today's Monday. I called the hospital. Told them you had an emergency and they'd need to have someone cover for you."

"Thanks," Jay whispered. Instant relief coursed through him as the needle sank into his vein. He floated on a sea of pleasure.

"You feel like talking? Like telling me what the hell happened to you?"

What *had* happened? Jay didn't know. But even as he figured it out, he knew he couldn't say. He remembered the agony of the flames, the terror rendering him immobile, fleeing the cabin, dropping to the ground to put the flames out. Then, the rustle through the woods. Someone was coming. He'd jumped into his car and fled, then . . . That was it. Next thing he knew, he was calling Marshall.

His hand went to his face as for one terrified moment he remembered the beard. It was gone. Yes. He'd removed it while he waited. Even in his pain-racked nightmare, he'd thought of that.

"It's . . . uh . . . a little embarrassing." His voice sounded thick, slurred. As if his mouth was filled with oatmeal. "I was with a . . . friend. She likes it a little rough. Know what I mean?"

Marshall nodded, and Jay saw the jealousy in his eyes. Maybe he should have told him he'd been with a guy. Marshall still might be jealous, but at least he'd think they both swung from the same side of the plate. Jay needed him right now. Needed his medical expertise and his discretion. But it was too late to change the story now.

"We were playing around. She tied me to the bed. There

was a candle. The bedsheets . . . I don't know. It all happened so fast."

"You were alone when I found you. You called me. She didn't even bother to help you, call nine-one-one? Why were you in your car?"

So many questions. Damn. He couldn't think straight. "It's all a blur. She freaked. I freaked. I guess I took off. She was probably scared she'd get into trouble."

Marshall crossed his arms and shook his head. "And well she should. She nearly killed you. Those burns . . ."

Jay saw a delicate shudder move over the other man, who was clearly repulsed. And who could blame him? No telling what the damage looked like. If nothing else, this should cool his ardor. The guy probably wouldn't be so enamored of him now.

Jay slowly nodded. "I know."

"You really should go to the hospital. I've done all I can, but it's bad."

"Surely you understand why I can't do that? My reputation, my career . . ." *My freedom, my life* . . . but he couldn't say that out loud. "I can't."

Marshall shrugged. "I'll do the best I can, but you're in bad shape. Your penis was . . ." He looked at the ceiling, took a deep breath. "You won't have the same function you had before. Urination will be about all you can manage, and that will be difficult. You need treatment."

Jay choked through the ball of fear in his chest. "I'll be okay."

Marshall stood looking down at him for a few moments, then mercifully left him alone with his morphine-filled body and thoughts of the woman.

Ravyn Skyler. What in blazing fuck did you do to me? And how did you do it?

That was just it, though. She couldn't have done it. No

possible way. So, what had happened? Had he simply stumbled into the fireplace? Lost his balance and fallen?

Yeah, right. Happens all the time. *Not*.

Besides. He remembered. Those eyes. Jesus Christ, those eyes! A whimper tore from his throat. Terror raced through his body, leaving tremors in its wake. Sweat beaded on his flesh. She was a demon. A demon sent from hell by his mother.

But that couldn't be. *He* had found *her*. She hadn't come after him. So, what was she? The question burned like the flames that had nearly devoured him.

It was a question he would get an answer to as soon as he recovered. He would ask the bitch face-to-face.

Chapter Five

Ravyn clenched the phone against her ear and closed her eyes as Sheriff Whitehall fired questions at her. She'd regretted answering the call the moment she heard his voice.

"No, I haven't thought of anything else. No, you can't drive up and see me. It won't do any good. Yes, I heard they figured out he abducted women from all over the metro area and took them to the cabin in Cotton. No, I have no idea why he chose me." *But I bet he regrets it almost as much as I do.*

Whitehall said good-bye after extracting a promise from her that she'd call if she thought of anything. He also issued a warning that he wasn't giving up.

She replaced the receiver and sighed. Normally she enjoyed the solitude of her lake house, but tonight loneliness pervaded her soul. Dusk crowded the windows, bringing with it her favorite time of day: nightfall, when her secret seemed safer. Though lately nothing felt safe.

Afghans, handmade by the grandmother she barely remembered, adorned the black leather furniture, vivid splashes of bright color among the mostly black and red decor. The flames from several candles danced in the shadowy room, giving off the warm scent of cinnamon. The candles were the only source of light. Her upstairs bedroom loft, an open floor above the living area, was steeped in darkness. A red sheer curtain billowed with the cool breeze drifting in through the open window.

Ravyn curled her bare feet beneath her in the black pa-

pasan chair. Resting her head back, she closed her eyes. The Tin Man's face appeared on the inside of her eyelids. Her eyes snapped open and the image disappeared.

You have to stop him before he talks to someone.

Once again she felt the pain of hot steel on her flesh, and she shuddered. No. She couldn't face him again. But if she did, if she ever had the chance . . . Rage sank deep and sharp, a knife in her heart. The bastard should pay—not only for what he'd done to her but also for what he'd done to the others.

She hadn't taken much notice of the newspaper articles about the murders. Not beforehand. She seldom concerned herself with anything outside the small scope of her own world. But now she recalled the stories. The horrible things he'd done to those women.

Maybe he'd stop now. After what she'd done to him, how could he ever kidnap a young girl again? Also, there was a chance he had died from his injuries. But if that was true, she'd broken a law of her people: under no circumstances shall any member of the coven willfully take the life of another, be they witch or mortal.

A shudder ran through her. The truth was, he wasn't dead. She could feel him out there. Could sense his evil. *The evil I allowed to escape.*

I could go back, touch the room he held me in, see what kind of vibes I get.

But she couldn't do that. She needed to actually touch the person, to connect with their heart.

Sometimes it works without touching them. Sometimes you can just touch where they've been. . . .

Needing a distraction from these tormenting thoughts, Ravyn uncurled her legs and stood. She opened the back door and stepped outside, breathing deeply of the fresh air. She walked across the yard, her bare feet sinking into the lush, damp lawn. Crickets chirped, harmonizing with the

nearby sounds of laughter and rock music from late-season
campers. They were probably on the other side of the lake,
but sound carried quite a distance across the water.

Ravyn stood at the back of her property and stared out
over the lake. The moon shone behind a narrow bank of
clouds, a starkly white orb in a blanket of black. Large oak
trees bent toward the water, the leaves glinting from the
reflection of moonlight. She closed her eyes, lifted her
arms to the heavens. The slow steady rhythm of her heartbeat calmed her mind.

An owl hooted, barely registering on her consciousness.
A breeze pushed from the lake, caressing her skin. She
could smell a campfire from across the way, mingling with
the scent of moist earth. Behind that pleasant smell was
the odor of something dead. She ignored it, concentrating
instead on the healing scents nature provided.

"O gentle Goddess, bend to me thine ear. My thoughts
are not one with our teachings. I have anger in my heart.
Death has touched me. Be with me now. Cleanse me. Heal
me. Ease my rage."

She stood silently, not moving. Time became something separate from her world. She had no idea how long
she waited, but finally lightness filled her heart as peace
settled around and inside her.

Opening her eyes, she squatted and plucked a handful
of grass from her yard. She sprinkled the grass into the
wind. A few errant blades blew against her lips. She flicked
out her tongue. The grass tasted of earth and moon. Content for the first time in days, Ravyn murmured a prayer of
thanks and turned to head back inside.

She caught a movement from the corner of her eye,
someone just on the other side of her fence.

It's him.

The peace she'd found in her ritual left her like air from

a punctured tire. She whirled toward the movement, her steps rapid and determined.

."Come out! I know you're there."

Her heart thumped in her chest as she ran on unsteady legs. The flicker of movement came again but quickly disappeared around the corner of her property. Ravyn quickened her pace.

Opening the gate, she stepped through just in time to see a figure disappear down the dirt road. A small figure. Much too small to be *him*. Ravyn recognized the intruder now—a strange old woman who lived down the road. They'd passed at a distance from time to time. Ravyn had caught the woman's gaze upon her more than once and thought she might be mentally challenged, because she always just stared and never said a word. Until now, Ravyn had never caught the woman on her property.

Why had the old woman been watching her like that? Ravyn didn't know. Maybe she needed to keep a better eye out. The woman might just be a harmless old busybody, but if she became too meddlesome, she might discover things she shouldn't.

Ravyn went back inside. She paced the length of her living-room floor, then back again. When she passed the bookcase for the second time, her gaze fell on the top shelf. It wasn't the row of books on display that caught her attention, but what she knew was behind them.

She pulled a worn copy of *Gone with the Wind* from the shelf, revealing a burgundy leather-covered book behind. It wasn't with the other books, because this was something she wouldn't want anyone else to see, something she shouldn't see herself. Kayne had given it to her just before he left the coven. Just before he'd been *driven* from the coven. She'd refused to go with him, refused to go along with his sudden conversion to the dark side.

He'd been angry with her—so why had he given her this gift? Maybe because he knew it was a gift she couldn't use. Maybe because he knew there would be no turning back if she did use it.

She shoved the volume back toward its hiding place but stopped. *You could at least look through it. At least see what your options are.*

Taking the heavy tome down, she sat at the rolltop cherrywood desk in the corner of her living room and stared down at the book. *Invocations of Shadows* was emblazoned on the leather cover.

The skin on Ravyn's fingers tightened as she flipped through the pages. As if knowing what she needed, the book opened to a section on retribution. She stared at the words, not reading them but just looking at the blurred, Old English lettering.

She was unaware that she'd begun reading, but the words suddenly jumped at her from the page:

This incantation is most powerful while in the presence of the one you wish to harm. It is also effective while holding a personal possession belonging to the enemy.

Light a black candle and send your mind to the soul of the cursed one. This must be done in the black of a moonless night.

"*By the flame of the dark pillar,*
O Horned One!
We call thy name,
O Ancient One!
We invoke thee, beseech thee, to hear our cry.
Come to us this night,
shed your dark light,
our enemies will cry out,
their torture echo . . ."

A gust of wind much stronger than the earlier breeze whipped through the room, sending a Tiffany lamp crashing to the floor. Ravyn jumped, fear hammering through her veins. Goose bumps shivered along her flesh. She slammed the book shut and rushed over to close the window.

The cold air bit at her skin, billowing her black gown around her. The creaking frame split her eardrums as she slid the window shut. She quickly flipped the latches, then jerked the curtain closed.

Slowly, her fists held tightly at her sides, she turned and walked toward the desk. A gasp escaped her clenched lips. The book was open again. And while she wanted to believe the wind had blown it open before she shut the window, the pages were turned to the exact place she'd been reading.

She reached out but stopped before touching the book. *Let it go. He won't hurt you again. He won't hurt your people as long as you let it go. There's no reason for him to come after you. Not as long as you leave him alone.*

But she couldn't convince herself of that. He was all she could think about. She could not forget what he'd done to her and what he'd done to those other women. What he might be doing to someone right now.

She slipped back into her chair. Glancing around the room, she considered turning on the lights but discarded the idea and instead bent her head back over the book, reading as if compelled. She was deeply absorbed in the words when she felt a tickle in her throat. Her hand went to her neck. The tickle became a pressure, tighter and tighter until she couldn't breathe. She gasped and pushed back from the desk, struggling with the effort to draw air into her lungs—

The feeling dissipated and she could once more breathe as normal. But this was not the first time it had happened—suffering the sensation of having the life choked out of her as if she were suspended by a rope from a tree just before her body was set ablaze. Was it a memory from another life, or just a manifestation of unreasonable fear? She didn't know, and it haunted her both in dreams and when she was awake.

Ravyn looked down where her fingers rubbed the scar on the inside of her right hand. She still remembered how that had felt, how the fire had singed her skin and burnt the tender flesh from her palm. She lifted her gown and looked at the burn on her stomach. The one *he'd* given her. She could still smell the sweetish odor of melted flesh. Her own flesh. It smelled the same way it had twenty years ago, when Ravyn's mother had placed the flame of a candle against the hand of her eight-year-old daughter.

Chapter Six

Ravyn clasped her hands together beneath the table, her thumb massaging the scar on her palm. Her stomach seemed to have a lead ball suspended in its center. She swallowed—a gulping, desperate sound, like a scuba diver sucking air through a mouthpiece.

Her gaze flittered over the stark interview room. Her eyes took in the battered metal table and straight-backed chairs. The glare from the austere lighting bounced off of a large window taking up half of one of the yellow walls—a two-way mirror, most likely. Was yellow supposed to calm, or to cause anxiety? She couldn't remember which. Maybe there was no significance to the color of the walls. Maybe her thinking that was just an indication of her growing paranoia.

Dread suffused her at the prospect of the upcoming interview. The detectives had phoned and offered to come out to speak with her, but she didn't want them at her house. She didn't want to talk to them at all, but she knew she couldn't refuse. So she'd offered to come in to the police department.

The Oklahoma City police wanted to follow up on Whitehall's questions. It made sense. All of the Tin Man's victims had been kidnapped here and taken to that cabin.

The more she talked to the police, the more questions she answered, the more likely they were to find him. That's what she wanted, wasn't it? She wanted them to stop him?

Yes! But she didn't want them to know what she'd done. Didn't want her coven to know.

Ravyn took a sip from the bottle of water that had been provided, and looked up as the door opened. A tall Latino officer and a shorter, balding cop with a mustache entered the room.

The Hispanic man stuck out his hand. "I'm Detective Carlos Mungia, and this is my partner, Detective Scott Harris. Thanks for coming in."

Ravyn nodded and shook his hand. The other cop eyed her with a mixture of contempt and suspicion. He smoothed the sparse hair on top of his head before extending the same greeting.

The moment she took his hand, Ravyn's whole body tensed. She wanted to release it immediately, but her grip held tight, almost as if she were suffering a spasm. Nausea rolled from her stomach and up her throat. Her eyes fluttered shut, and images flashed across her mind.

An evil leer on the detective's face. A woman was screaming and cowering, arms over her head as if warding off a blow.

The scene faded to a darkened road. *Detective Harris was standing behind an open trunk, accepting a wad of cash and handing a long package to a tattooed, burly man with mean eyes and greasy hair.*

And there was another flash:

The same man, Harris, inside a rundown apartment. A young girl, maybe twelve or thirteen, eyes round in fear, blood dripping from her nose. There was swelling beneath her left eye.

"Miss Skyler, are you okay?"

Ravyn wasn't sure which detective had spoken, but her eyes snapped open and she was staring into Scott Harris's face. His skin had lightened a few shades, and lines pinched the corners of his mouth. He tugged his hand free and the images disappeared. Ravyn shuddered in relief.

Mungia took a seat in the chair next to her, but Harris stood slightly behind him and to the right. His hands were shoved into the pockets of his brown slacks. Those pants were already a size too small, and his stance emphasized that fact to an unflattering degree.

Mungia opened a folder and glanced down at it. "Miss Skyler, I know you spoke with the uniforms and Sheriff Whitehall, but we'd like to do a follow-up interview, just to make sure nothing was missed."

Ravyn returned to her palm massage beneath the table and said, "I don't see the point. I told them everything I know."

"I understand." Mungia smiled kindly, and she noticed his eyes were an appealing shade of velvety brown. They were caring eyes, unlike those of his partner. "But sometimes witnesses remember extra details after a few days, when the shock has worn off. If you would, please tell us your version of that night step-by-step, and take your time."

Ravyn did, speaking slowly as she recounted her story, hoping she repeated her earlier description of events verbatim. She didn't want any inconsistencies that might raise a red flag.

The whole time she spoke, Detective Mungia glanced back and forth from Ravyn to the paperwork in front of him. Once in a while he would nod or scowl a little, as if a thought had occurred to him. When she was finished, he looked up and gave her a reassuring smile.

"Well, that's pretty much what we have here. You haven't remembered any more about the man? Maybe some physical characteristics you didn't recall the night of the attack?"

Ravyn shook her head and opened her mouth, but before she could answer, Harris spoke. "Can you perhaps tell us how you managed to get away, when the other vics weren't quite so lucky?" His voice was laced with contempt.

She looked up at him, hoping to keep the loathing out of her eyes. "As I said, I screamed. That must have scared him away. Or maybe the boys who found me were nearby, and he heard them. I don't know exactly how I escaped, but I'm very grateful. It was terrifying, and my heart breaks for the poor girls who weren't as lucky."

Harris's lip twisted in a sneer. "Yeah. I bet."

Ravyn didn't want to get into a fight with the jerk, but it took all her willpower to control her temper—and her magic.

The situation was quickly defused by Detective Mungia. "I apologize for my partner's insensitive remarks, Miss Skyler. This case has been very hard on all of us. We're under a lot of stress, a lot of pressure to catch the killer, so we'll attribute his bad behavior to that." His gaze swung over to Harris. "I'm sure Miss Skyler would appreciate an apology."

Harris stared mutinously at Mungia, his lower lip protruding in a childish pout. After a moment, he turned to Ravyn. "I apologize. I meant no disrespect."

Though the words of contrition were clearly grudging, Ravyn gave a slight nod and turned back to Mungia. "Is that all, Detective?"

"Actually, we'd like you to get with our artist. We'd like a composite sketch of the man who attacked you."

Reluctantly, Ravyn nodded. "Sure. Okay."

"Wait right here."

Ravyn's eyes flew to Harris, afraid Mungia would leave them alone, but both detectives left the room. In moments, Mungia and Harris returned, followed by a man who looked to be in his fifties. He had a ruddy complexion and thin, graying hair.

"This is James Coloran. I want you to describe the suspect for him," Mungia said.

Ravyn did, and the artist sketched quickly. She watched the paper as he drew, correcting him a few times on the size of the nose and thickness of the beard. When he was done, Ravyn stared at the drawing. It was strange, but she was realizing that her image of the killer was really more of an impression. Maybe this was a combination of the drugs and the trauma, but she couldn't get a clear picture in her head. This drawing *could* be him. But it could be almost anyone.

"Is that all?" she asked Mungia after the artist left.

"Yes. For now. Please contact us if you think of anything else," the cop replied.

"I'll do that," Ravyn promised. Then she shook Mungia's hand one final time, pointedly ignoring Harris.

As she left the police department, she found herself shivering. She was almost as disturbed by what she'd learned about Harris as by her time with the Tin Man. The detective couldn't be trusted. He was almost as evil as the monster he was hunting. She would have to take matters into her own hands.

Chapter Seven

Ravyn stood in the clearing outside the home of the coven's high priestess, Vanora. The power was greater here, in the secret place where the coven held rituals and cast spells. Her coven practiced white magic, using their powers for good, for healing and protection. Even though the outside world wasn't aware of it, many disasters were averted and people were helped due to the incantations of covens like Ravyn's, which were scattered throughout the world.

The other coven members didn't know she was here now; this was something she had to do on her own. She would invoke a spell to track the killer and . . . then what? Confront him? Capture him? Kill him? No, of course she couldn't kill him. But if she could figure out who he was, she could let the police know. They would take the matter into their hands, then, and she would have no more reason to feel guilty. She would have done her part.

Or maybe she could just render him paralyzed. The rule said she couldn't *harm* anyone. But paralysis didn't hurt, right? She'd start with his tongue, so he couldn't tell people what she'd done.

She shook off the thought. Paralyzation wouldn't work. She knew what she had to do, even if she didn't want to do it.

On the ground a cauldron bubbled, and the scents of sage, rosemary and other herbs tinted with the fragrance of sweet alyssum wafted in the air. Ravyn lit two black pillar candles and two purple ones, placing them on the altar. She closed her eyes and began to chant. The words tumbled from her mouth, and she beseeched the goddess to reveal the killer's identity. A shiver ran through her as the enormity of what she was doing sank in. Never before had she been touched by such evil. Never before had she used her magic to bring her close to someone so vile, so reprehensible.

The Tin Man's face filled the blackness behind her closed eyelids, and her body began to shake violently. It was as if she were in a dark room with the man. As if he were standing so close she could reach out and touch him. Subconsciously Ravyn leaned back, as if trying to get distance.

Pushing away her fear, she concentrated on his features, tried to connect with him, tried to come up with a name, an address, anything to help her find him. But before the information could come, the evil visage in her mind became larger, his face splitting into a grin. His gaze bored into hers as they connected. Their minds met, and his evil presence filled the space around her. It was horrible and suffocating and—

Her eyes shot open and the vision disappeared. She was trembling, cold. The flames of the candles were burning very low, and the steam from the cauldron had dissipated. The Tin Man's spirit had been here. Her magic hadn't been enough to discern the information, but it had been enough to summon his evil for a visit.

She stood in the clearing for several moments, watching the flames of the candles as they flickered in the darkness, her heart hammering loudly in her chest. She'd failed. The madman was still out there, a stranger to her, unknown. And yet . . . he was so close, so intimate, she could practically feel him inside her.

She felt something else, too, something she'd heard, or

perhaps sensed, when the maniac had her captive. He fed on the fear of others, but he had an inherent fear of his own.

Mother.

It was more than just fear. The mind-numbing terror consumed him. *Naughty little bastard . . . Evil little fuck . . . You'll burn in hell . . .*

A shudder ran through her, and she banished the thoughts—that voice—from her head. Quickly she gathered the items she'd brought with her and on trembling legs left the clearing.

Haleck thrashed in bed. Even the cool, soft sheets hurt him. Colors—some bright, some dull and murky—undulated in the darkness of his sleep. In his ears was an echo, a pounding, booming echo. Behind the pounding were sharp, terrified screams. Those screams were a balm. His body relaxed, and even in his unconscious state he smiled.

Faces began to float through the darkness of his drug-induced slumber. He was on the verge of waking but really didn't want to. He was reliving his past victories, his moments of triumph.

The first had been a blonde. He'd snatched her from her front step, forced her into his car at midnight and driven her to the cabin. She'd screamed, oh, she'd screamed and begged, her eyes beautifully insane with fear. Then came the others, one magnificent scene after another.

His mother was here, too. She was watching and shaking her head, that beehive hairdo sticky with hairspray, her grim mouth tight with disapproval. Words were flowing from her lips, even though they were closed.

Just as I thought. You're an evil little bastard. Never could beat it out of you. You'll burn, Jay. You'll burn in hell.

The bitch had died in a car accident, and he'd been

freed at the age of eighteen. His only regret was that he hadn't been the one to kill her. Now, *that* would have been a thrill.

He moaned as a searing pain shot through him, from his groin clear up to his jaw. His eyes flew open and the moan turned into a screech. *Make it go away, make the pain go away, please.* But Marshall was gone; he remembered that. And with Marshall went the morphine injections. He'd been left a bottle of oral morphine, but that didn't cut the pain as well.

Tears surfaced in Haleck's eyes and ran down his cheeks into his pillow. Sleep—he needed to sleep and let the dreams come back.

He fumbled around the nightstand for the bottle of pills. Swallowing two, he washed them down with the water Marshall had left. Then he lay back and closed his eyes, willing the pain away, willing the return of blessed sleep and his beautiful dreams.

Clenching the bedsheets in his fists, he took deep, calming breaths, waited for the drugs to work. Waited in agony. Slowly—too slowly—the pain ebbed, and he felt himself drifting, drifting into oblivion. The dreams. The dreams would return. He would see again his beautiful victims, hear their beautiful screams.

Suddenly he was jolted, as if someone or something had reached out and grabbed him. His eyes flew open and a shriek tore from his throat. Another vision came, this one even more terrifying than the others had been calming. It was a woman with flowing hair and fire in her eyes. Demonic fire. And she was searching for him.

Chapter Eight

The afternoon sunlight crept between the forest green curtains, spilling shafts of light across the hardwood floor, but Ravyn's mind was on darkness. She couldn't stop thinking about the Tin Man. Couldn't stop wanting to hurt him. Couldn't stop wanting to hurt him even more than she already had.

Studiously untangling the silver and onyx necklaces in the jewelry display at her store, she tried to force him from her mind.

"Are you sure you're okay?" Sorina's voice startled her. She had been so deep in thought, Ravyn hadn't realized her sister had walked up beside her.

Sorina's blonde hair shimmered in the rays of sun spilling past the curtains. The salmon-colored shirt she wore, although not revealing, clung to her curves, giving her an unconscious sex appeal that was all the more attractive because it was unintentional.

"I'm okay," Ravyn replied, looking away from the question in her sister's eyes.

"You haven't thought of anything else to tell the police?" Sorina asked.

Ravyn released a breath and shook her head. "I told them everything I could." Which really wasn't a lie. She'd told them everything she could without risking them finding out what she'd done. Them and the coven.

Sorina glanced over her shoulder. Ravyn followed her

gaze. Two customers were browsing the store. One was a heavyset woman who was sniffing the jars of candles. Occasionally her nose would turn up, and she'd hurriedly replace the jar on its shelf with a horrified look. The other patron was a scruffy, dark-haired man perusing the jewelry in the case near the front door.

Neither of them was within earshot, but Ravyn's sister still lowered her voice. "I know you don't trust mortals, but you have to help the police find this guy. What he did to those women . . . What he could have done to you . . ." She broke off. Tears pooled in her eyes.

"This has nothing to do with how I feel about mortals," Ravyn whispered. "And I *am* trying to help."

Sorina took her hand. "I thank God you survived, Ravyn. If it had been me, I know I wouldn't have been as brave as you. For you to escape without using your powers . . . ? It's unbelievable. I'm so proud."

Ravyn couldn't meet her sister's eyes. "It was all over so quickly," she said.

"I'm just glad you're okay. I don't know what I would have done if I'd lost you."

Ravyn forced a cheerfulness into her tone that she didn't feel. "Hey, you don't need to worry about this stuff right now. You have a wedding to plan."

A grin eased the quivering from Sorina's lips. "I know. And thanks for pretending you're excited about it."

Ravyn smiled in return, if inside she was a bit melancholy. "Well, as far as mortals go, Justin isn't that bad. I guess if you have to get married, you could've done worse. Much worse." *As I almost did.* She didn't say the last words aloud. Her sister knew all about the fiasco with Kayne, and the two of them never spoke about it.

"If I *have* to get married? You're such a bummer sometimes." Sorina rolled her eyes, but happiness glimmered in their depths. "You'll know someday. When you find the person you want to spend the rest of your life with, you'll know. Love makes everything better. Even with the problems, you have that glow inside, the assurance that no matter what, everything will be okay. I want that for you someday. I want you to know the bliss of love."

"Don't hold your breath," Ravyn muttered.

Sorina snorted, but she didn't respond to the softly spoken cynicism. Instead she suggested, "Justin's going away on a business trip for a few days. Why don't you come stay with me while he's gone?"

Ravyn could see the concern in her sister's eyes, but she wasn't sure whom it was for. "I can't stay at your place with your cat," she reminded her.

Sorina laughed and shook her head. Still speaking in a whisper, she grumbled, "A witch who's allergic to cats. There's one for the record books."

Ravyn shrugged. "Why don't you stay with me?"

Sorina turned up her nose and gave a delicate shiver. "At that primitive hovel you live in?" A smile softened her words. "I guess for you I could make an exception. For a few nights."

"For *me*? You're the one afraid to be alone," Ravyn pointed out.

Her sister nodded. "I'm afraid for you to be alone, too. We don't know what that man—"

The candle sniffer interrupted. Ravyn hadn't heard her approach, but the woman was suddenly there, waving a hand toward the fifty different fragrances sold in the shop. "Are these the only scents you have?" She looked to be in her late forties, with reddish hair that showed streaks of gray. Her too-small yellow blouse gaped at the buttons. A silver choker encircled her fleshy neck.

Sorina turned a professional smile on her. "My sister

here makes them, and yes, those are all we carry. I'm sure if there's something specific you have in mind, she could create it for you."

The customer frowned, as if actually disappointed they were willing to accommodate her. "I don't know . . ." Her gaze swept over Ravyn. "She *makes* them?"

"Yes. And the jewelry, too."

"It's all a bit pricey for costume jewelry," the candle-sniffer remarked. "Or at least it *looks* like costume jewelry."

Ravyn tensed with irritation but didn't respond.

Sorina's mouth twisted down in a frown. "Oh, no. It's authentic. The jewels are real. My sister is a professional. She takes a great deal of pride in her work."

The two spoke as if Ravyn weren't standing there—which was just fine with her. Sorina handled the customer-service aspect of Gifts from the Heart, and Ravyn was the artist. Her people skills just weren't on the same level as her sister's. It was an irrefutable truth.

Ravyn glanced at the other customer, the man, and caught him staring at her. He was sort of scruffy, as she'd first thought, but not in a vagrant way. He was clean, just unkempt; his face showed a few days' growth of dark beard. Even from this distance, she could discern that his eyes were a startling blue, the mixture of shades like a cloudless sky at twilight.

His gaze locked on hers, and the conversation between Sorina and the woman faded into the background. Ravyn sensed a great sadness. Sadness and guilt. Although she didn't know the man's story, didn't know a thing about him, she felt a sudden kinship. She and this stranger were two souls searching for redemption. They were two wounded—

Her heartbeat accelerated, and her breath squeezed in her throat. She broke the stare, forcing her attention back to Sorina and the woman. What had just happened? She normally didn't get vibes so strong from simply looking at someone. What had caused the connection? She didn't know, and she didn't want to find out.

The woman broke eye contact first. Nick couldn't have. He *wouldn't* have. He hadn't wanted to. Something had sparked in him when he'd held her gaze. Something alive and real. Something that really mattered, for the first time in years.

Was this Ravyn Skyler, or was Ravyn the blonde speaking with the older woman? He'd gotten a vague description, and he believed the Skyler chick had dark hair. The blonde was a looker, though. She was definitely the killer's type. And with all the hair-coloring women did these days, either of the two could be the one Nick was looking for.

He couldn't take his eyes off the dark-haired woman, though. There was a sultry nonchalance in the way she moved, in the way she brushed a hank of hair back from her face. She wore black eyeliner that emphasized the green of her eyes. The wide, overlong sleeves of her silky blue shirt slid back on her forearms, revealing slender fingers laden with rings. Acid-washed jeans hugged long legs. Every move oozed pure sexual magnetism—like, Nick imagined, the magnetism of those sirens of myth who lured sailors to their doom.

"Can I help you?" she asked.

He hadn't even been aware she approached. Words froze inside him. He sucked in a breath and struggled for the ability to speak.

"Sir? Are you okay?" she asked in a voice that was a smoky blend of softness and sandpaper.

"Sorry. Yes. Just a little lightheaded for a second." Nick looked at the candle he held in his hand. How had that gotten there? He lifted it toward her. "Do you have this fragrance in the eighteen-ounce size?"

She stared at him for a moment. Not a friendly look. "I'll check."

As she turned and disappeared through a gauzy white curtain behind the counter, he suddenly wished he'd asked the blonde for the candle; he didn't want to let this beautiful creature out of his sight. He still didn't know if she was Ravyn Skyler, but he thought she was. He *hoped* she was. Then he'd have an excuse to be around her more.

God. What was wrong with him? He hadn't been attracted to a woman since Annie. Damn sure not like this! He wished he hadn't had those drinks this morning. Could she smell it on him? He reached into his shirt pocket, searching for a breath mint but coming up empty. Damn.

She returned quickly, but to him it seemed like hours. "I'm sorry. We don't have the eighteen-ounce size in Lavender Dream right now. I'll make some more later in the week, if you want to come back."

Lavender Dream? How manly. No wonder she'd given him an odd look.

He nodded. "I'll be back. Later in the week."

She returned his nod but didn't speak. Her eyes seemed veiled, as if they held deep secrets. Nick wanted nothing but to unlock those. And not just whatever information she had about the Tin Man. He wanted to know everything about her. Hell, he just wanted to keep listening to her voice. Wanted to watch her face as she spoke. Inhale her fragrance. She smelled faintly like the smoky outdoors, like a campfire in the winter. She was warm yet cool. She was utterly fascinating.

He blinked rapidly, as if coming out of a trance. Guilt slammed into him with the force of a tidal wave. In the five years since Annie's death he'd barely looked at another woman, and now he was lusting after a complete stranger? Muttering something in the way of a thank-you, he turned and groped for the front door. He stumbled outside of the shop, not able to breathe freely until he was standing in the fresh air.

That was when it occurred to him: *Ace job on the detective work, Lassiter. You're still not even sure if she was the one you came for.*

Chapter Nine

Nick drove slowly along the country road, his Mustang's headlights cutting through the layer of fog that had risen up around him. Gravel pinged the undercarriage of the car, sounding in the stillness of the evening like small-caliber bullets.

A teenage girl at a gas station in town had willingly given him directions to the cabin where the Tin Man had attacked Ravyn Skyler. Her wide brown eyes sparkling with excitement, the girl had all but offered to drive him. Apparently, a serial killer was exciting news in this area. There was nothing like the media to stir up interest.

He passed a field, was barely able to make out the silhouettes of cows meandering across the grass. Set back from the road was an old farmhouse that looked like something out of *The Texas Chainsaw Massacre*. Nick took a curve in the road, and as the teen had promised, a turnoff just past the bend led to the cabin.

The word *cabin* was actually generous; the building was more like a dilapidated shack. The logs were blackened in some places, faded in others. Huge chunks had rotted from the outer walls, and bullet holes indicated hunters used the structure for target practice. From the police reports Nick obtained, he'd learned that the killer had only enjoyed a short time here—at least, he'd only had a short time here with Ravyn. He'd only had time for his preliminary work: burning her with his knife.

Nick thought again about the woman he'd seen in the

shop. He'd since discovered—by crack detective work, which consisted of asking the woman who ran the café next door—that the dark-haired woman was indeed Ravyn Skyler. His reaction to her still baffled him. Nick chalked it up to too much booze and too long without a woman. It was a normal male reaction to long legs and fuck-me eyes. He definitely had to tread lightly there.

He turned off the engine and sat for a while, staring at the cabin. In his mind, Nick pictured a shadowed figure bending over Ravyn, pressing the red-hot steel of his knife against her pale flesh. There would be terror in those green eyes. She would have been helpless and innocent. At the mercy of a maniac.

His chest tightened, and Nick forced the image away. At least the girl had survived. When would the bastard strike again? Would the next victim be so lucky? There was no way to know.

Nick climbed out of his Mustang and walked toward the cabin, bending to slip under the yellow crime-scene tape. Trees shrouded the yard, still dressed in leaves that would start to fall in a few weeks. The killer would have had a measure of concealment here, but only through the spring and summer months and for part of the fall. This hadn't stopped him from killing year-round. The authorities weren't sure that he'd brought *all* of his victims here, but they suspected it. If he had, the Tin Man would need a new killing ground.

Nick tried the door, and it swung open. He stepped inside and saw why it wasn't secured. The only lock was one of those old-fashioned hooks, which had long since rusted. Dingy sheets covered the windows. The cabin smelled musty, as if some animal had made its home here not too long ago. The odor of burnt flesh lingered in the air.

In spite of the cool October breeze drifting through the

cracks in the walls, the cabin was warm. Underneath Nick's jacket, sweat trickled down his back and sides.

A hospital bed sat incongruously in the center of the main room. Straps hung from either side. Nick examined the ends, which looked as if they'd been cut clean through. In addition to the bed, there was a frayed orange sofa with yellowed stuffing poking from its threadbare upholstery.

Nick squatted in front of the fireplace. Ashes remained, but they had been sifted through recently. The CSI techs would have gone over everything. So, what was he doing here?

He thought back over Ravyn Skyler's account of that night. She hadn't been able to identify her assailant; she could only give the police vague details. He'd worn a beard, and she hadn't been able to make out his eye color because it was dark. The composite sketch in the newspaper had looked generic. A nondescript, bearded man. He could be anyone.

Nick stood, and his gaze roamed over the room once more. He noted the position of the bed, the window, the fireplace. He recalled her story. Something didn't quite fit. He wasn't sure what.

He crossed his arms and felt the bulge of the whiskey bottle in his jacket pocket. Pulling it out, he considered taking a drink. Just one. But unscrewing the lid, he hesitated and closed the bottle again. He'd driven here, and in spite of his lack of concern for rules in general, not drinking and driving was one he followed closely. Most of the time.

As he was putting the half pint back in his pocket, it slipped from his fingers. There was a brief moment of panic in which he anticipated the crash of broken glass, but it didn't come. He bent to pick up the bottle, relieved it was still intact. But before he could straighten, he noticed a

small, oblong, blue-gray object in the dust of the cabin
floor.

He picked it up and studied it. Some kind of medication? A capsule. Had the killer dropped it? Had the woman?
Neither? Did it belong to one of the many people who had
wandered through here over time? How had the CSI boys
missed it? Maybe he was just in the right spot at the right
time. Dumb, blind luck. If, that is, it wound up meaning
anything.

He peered closely at the writing. *Neoral* was printed in
red letters, and underneath, *100 mg.* Nick slipped it into
a baggie he'd brought with him, and placed that in
his pocket along with the bottle. Couldn't hurt to check
it out.

As he was about to leave, he heard a car pull up, followed by doors slamming. Shit. Whoever it was, he didn't
want them to find him here. But it was too late—he could
hear footsteps on the porch. He pulled his Beretta from its
holster.

The door opened, and two men walked in. The first was
Detective Carlos Mungia. The second was his partner,
Scott Harris.

It had been almost five years, but Harris hadn't changed
much. He was stocky, with narrow shoulders that didn't fit
his physique. His hair had thinned, and he'd tried that
goofy-ass comb-over thing. Craggy scars marked his face
and his nose had a hump where it had been broken. By
Nick.

Nick put his gun away and faced the two men.

Harris's eyes rounded, glittered with hatred. "Lassiter,"
he snarled. "What the fuck are you doing here?"

Nick didn't speak. He looked at Carlos, who gave no
hint of hostility, just exuded an air of annoyance. As if
Nick had just made his life a bit more problematic.

Nick headed to the door, cutting a wide swath around Harris. It wasn't wide enough. The cop's arm shot out and gripped his sleeve. "I asked you a question, fucker."

Nick reached out instinctively and grabbed Harris's wrist. A quick twist backward and the detective released his hold, yelping like an injured animal. "Keep your hands off me," Nick growled. His voice was low, but the danger was audible.

"Got any DUIs lately?" Harris glowered as he rubbed his wrist.

"Beat up any little girls lately?" Nick returned.

Detective Harris raised his fists, his pain forgotten as he lunged forward. Mungia grabbed him before he got to Nick and pulled him back. "Knock it off, Harris," he snapped. "Just let the guy leave."

Harris shook off his partner's hand, but he didn't make any more moves toward Nick. "Hell, he's probably drunk right now. I oughta haul his sorry ass in. Hear that, Lassiter? I oughta haul your ass in."

"Yeah, maybe you should. You wouldn't want to waste your efforts actually doing your *job*. You know, finding the maniac who's been chopping up women."

"Fuck you," Harris snarled. He lunged toward Nick once again, and this time Mungia was too slow. Nick sidestepped, not wanting to be arrested for assault, and Harris stumbled. The cop crashed right into the cabin door as it opened.

Chapter Ten

The detective's head cracked loudly on the wood, and he rose up like an enraged tiger. Before Harris could act on his rage, however, a newcomer stepped inside. He was an older man, probably in his early sixties. He wore a sheriff's uniform.

"What the heck's goin' on?" The man's gaze swept from Carlos Mungia to Nick and back to the panting Detective Harris, who glared and rubbed his hand across his forehead.

"Homicide, OCPD," Mungia told him, flashing his badge. "We're working the Tin Man case."

"All three of ya?" the sheriff asked.

"No," Harris spat, pointing a finger at Nick. "*He's* not. He's trespassing."

Nick stuck out a hand. "Nick Lassiter. I'm a private investigator. Just up here taking a look around."

"Sheriff John Whitehall." The sheriff shook Nick's hand as he introduced himself. His eyes narrowed. "Lassiter? From the city?"

Nick nodded.

"You the fella I read about in the paper a few years back? The one that risked his ass to save that junkie?"

A drug-crazed man had been holding his wife and child hostage. Nick was there with the hostage negotiators. They'd convinced the suspect to release his family, but he wouldn't come out. He said he was going to blow himself up. The wife told them her husband was strapped with explosives. Nick had gone inside and freed the man from the bomb, despite the guy waving a gun around and threatening to blow his head off. They'd both survived. Nick didn't think the guy remembered him with gratitude: he was currently doing a twenty-year stint in the federal penitentiary for kidnapping and aggravated assault.

"Yeah," Nick admitted.

"You also solved that series of rapes—the one where the guy broke into old ladies' houses, robbed 'em, beat 'em and raped 'em? He finally killed one of 'em. Then you nabbed him," the sheriff pressed.

"Yeah," Nick replied. "Hey, I was just heading out. Didn't mean to cause any trouble."

Harris glared at Nick. He didn't like the sheriff recounting Nick's successes. Nick didn't like it much himself. Most cops did the same shit as he'd done, and they did it every day. Nick had just happened to catch the media's attention. Mainly because of the way things had ended. The way his career had ended.

"You're also the one that wound up beatin' the tar out of your partner, right? Left the force not long after that, if I recall."

From the corner of his eye, Nick could see Harris. The detective's fists were clenched, and the air was suddenly thick with tension. "The media twists a lot of things around," he offered, in an attempt to deflect any further conflict.

"It didn't make the papers, but word around here is the sonofabitch beat up some twelve-year old girl. An interrogation gone bad in a case you and this guy was working. That true?"

A burst of air popped from Harris's chest as if he'd imploded. "That was a motherfuckin' lie!" he growled. "Cocksucker spread that shit about me, but it was a lie!"

Mungia grabbed his partner's arm, more forcibly this

time, and steered him toward the door. "Come on, Scott," he said. "We can come back. There's nothing left here we haven't gone over anyway."

Harris tried to shake him off, but Mungia didn't let go.

Whitehall's brows lifted in surprise. To Nick, it looked like feigned surprise. "Oh, geez, sorry 'bout that," the sheriff said. "Was you the fella?" He peered at Harris's scarred face. "That where you got them injuries?"

Harris didn't answer. He stood in front of Whitehall, breathing hard and glaring. Carlos still held him, but Nick noticed Harris wasn't making much of an effort to break free. A moment later, and without another word, the two detectives left. Nick had a feeling he'd run into them again.

Whitehall turned his penetrating gaze on Nick. "What's your story? Why're you here?"

Nick shrugged. "The husband of one of the killer's victims hired me to find the man who murdered his wife. I'm just checking out the crime scene."

The sheriff jerked his head toward the door. "If that bozo is on the case, can't say as I blame the husband." He shook his head and reached into his pocket. "I never knew what to think when I read about you doin' that fool thing with the druggie. Then all that other shit . . ." He pulled out a cigarette pack and held it toward Nick. "Want one?"

Nick nodded. "Thanks."

"Sure. Don't have a lighter, though. Sorry. Don't usually smoke 'em."

Nick pulled a lighter from his pocket and lit up. Whitehall put a different cigarette in the corner of his mouth but left it unlit. "As I was sayin', all that stuff I read about you . . . I figured you was either the dumbest goddamned cop around—or the best."

Nick took a pull from his cigarette and released the smoke. "Maybe a little of both," he admitted.

"I don't think you're dumb." Whitehall walked farther into the cabin and looked around, then turned back to Nick. "How long you been here?"

"Maybe twenty minutes. Probably five or ten before they got here. Why?"

"Whadda ya got?"

"Excuse me?"

"What's your theory?" The sheriff made a sweeping gesture around the room with his arm. "About what happened. About that night."

How much to tell? All of it was speculation, but Nick figured Whitehall was out to test him a little. Maybe to amuse himself. Whatever the man's reasons, Nick decided to play along.

"The guy heated the knife in the fireplace—the one he used to burn the girl. He tied her to that hospital bed. She was cut loose, I assume by those boys who found her. The hunters."

Whitehall nodded. "Yep. But that's almost all in the newspaper."

"The guy is about five eleven," Nick offered.

"How you figure?"

Nick motioned toward the window. "Those sheets aren't that old. They were likely hung by our man, in case someone wandered by and tried to peek inside. There's no chair for him to stand on. He probably wouldn't bother, anyway. He stood on the ground to hang the sheets, stretching a little. With the height of the nails and the angle at which they were driven in . . . I'd say he stood about five-eleven."

Whitehall pulled his cigarette from his mouth and flipped it back and forth between his fingers. "Go on."

"The girl is hiding something. She has to know a few more details about the killer than she revealed. She said she couldn't see very well, but it couldn't have been *that* dark in here." Nick pointed to the window. "The moon would have been on that side of the cabin. And it was almost full that night. As late as it was, it would have been far enough above the trees to provide some light through the droop at the top of the sheets."

He turned and pointed again. "Also, if our suspect heated the knife in the fireplace, he obviously had a fire going. The angle of the bed tells me the firelight would have illuminated him quite well, depending on which side he stood. And my guess is he'd want to face the door, keep an eye out for intruders. That side of the bed would definitely have been lit well enough that she could have seen *some* detail. Something about his height, weight, eyes . . ." Nick stopped. He hadn't strung that many words together in years.

"Is that all?" Whitehall asked.

"That's it." Nick didn't tell the sheriff about the pill. He wanted to check that out for himself. It was probably the only piece of information Whitehall didn't already have.

"That's what I thought. You ain't dumb. You could prob'ly find Jimmy Hoffa before those two dimwits could find their dicks." The sheriff took the cigarette he'd had in his mouth and slipped it back in the pack.

Nick looked at the smoke he held in his hand, wondering if it had suffered similar treatment. He stubbed it out on the floor. Picking up the butt, he stuffed it in his jeans pocket.

"Wonder why he calls himself Tin Man," Whitehall murmured.

Nick shrugged. "I wondered about that myself."

"Probably from the movie. You know, *The Wizard of Oz.*"

"What was the Tin Man's thing?" Nick asked. "I get them mixed up."

"You seen the movie?"

"A long time ago, when I was a kid."

Whitehall nodded. "The Tin Man was the one without a heart."

Like me, Nick thought. *Hollow inside.* "The guy's saying he's a heartless bastard. Makes sense."

"Maybe so, maybe so," Whitehall murmured. "Although most serial killers don't think of themselves that way. Maybe he's in the recycling business."

Nick raised his eyebrows. "Recycling?"

"You know. *Tin.*"

Nick gave a small smile. "I guess anything's possible."

The old sheriff put a hand on Nick's shoulder. "You need anything from me, let me know. The case belongs to the city, but I got my finger in the pie. Figured I'd better, if I want to see anything solved. Maybe us two together can get something done."

"Okay. Thanks," Nick said.

Unprompted, Whitehall offered up some information. "The SOB was a customer in the restaurant Miss Skyler ate in that night. Ran a check on credit-card receipts, but nothing came up that caught our fancy. No leads at all so far. You got as much on this guy as we do."

The sheriff sighed and walked to the door. Before he left, he turned back. "You're right about the girl, though, Lassiter. She's hiding something. I just can't figure out what—or why. But she's locked up tighter than Fort Knox." He tipped his hat back and scrunched his forehead. "What sticks in my craw is why she'd want to protect a psycho like this. I don't believe it's someone she knows. . . ." A chuckle rumbled from his chest, and the grizzled lawman shook his head. "If it is, I hope she takes him off her Christmas card list."

Chapter Eleven

"They've called a meeting of the elders," Sorina whispered to Ravyn as they made their way to the meadow where the weekly ritual would be held.

"From all the covens?" Ravyn asked in alarm, also keeping her voice low. She didn't want anyone to overhear.

There were twenty-some-odd covens scattered around the United States and Europe. Ravyn had met some of the other covens' witches, but the only elder she knew was Vanora, the elder of her own group. Whenever the elders called an unscheduled meeting, things were particularly bad. Had they discovered what she'd done? Surely not. Vanora would have called her in immediately.

Sorina shrugged. "Don't worry about it. I'm sure they'll just discuss the 'horrors of the outside world.'" She gnawed on her lower lip, her blue eyes clouded with worry. "Though maybe they'll implement more rules restricting our association with mortals."

Ravyn knew Sorina was concerned about effects to her engagement. Her loves of a normal life and Justin were much more important to her than her heritage or witchcraft. From the time they'd been children, Sorina had taken to the coven's teachings with a sort of nonchalance, as if being a witch was an afterthought. For Ravyn, being a witch was who she was, *everything* she was. Ravyn had never felt comfortable in the mortal world. She was out of place there, an imposter. While a child, living in the mortal world with her mother had caused her pain and anguish, and she'd learned early that she didn't belong. The coven was her haven, her only source of peace.

Sorina fit into the coven and the mortal world equally. In school she'd been popular and well liked. The other kids had tolerated Ravyn only because she was Sorina's sister. But being the sister of Sorina didn't always protect her. Once, when Ravyn was in the sixth grade and Sorina was in third, Ravyn had found an injured cat on the playground. She had knelt beside the animal, trying to help, and had placed her hands on it, willing it to heal. The cat had died anyway. Some of the kids came upon her and began screaming that she'd murdered the animal. She'd cried, and they'd made even more fun. She could feel herself losing control, wanting to hurt them . . . and Sorina had intervened just in time, calming both her and the other children. But from then on, anytime Sorina wasn't around, Ravyn's classmates taunted her.

She'd been chubby as a child, and after the cat incident, in addition to poking fun at her for her weight, they'd added *cat killer* to their insults.

There'd been one boy she thought was different: Brandon Tollers. He had black hair and blue eyes and looked just like John Stamos. Ravyn knew that he wasn't like the others, and that if she told him the truth, or at least part of it, he'd make the others stop. One day she'd found him sitting alone in the cafeteria. She'd slid in the seat across from him. Heart pounding, partly from looking into those blue eyes and partly from what she was about to do, she'd explained that she had powers, could do things other kids couldn't. She'd stopped short of using the word *witch*, but she'd attempted to explain what had really happened with the cat after making him promise he wouldn't tell the others her secret.

"You believe me?" she'd asked hopefully.

"Sure," Brandon had said, and Ravyn felt like a weight had been lifted. Things would be different now.

And they were. The kids tormented her even more, poking fun at her for thinking she was "magic." One day, she'd gone to her desk and found a pile of dead flies on top. "We want to see you bring them back from the dead!" one of the kids shouted. Brandon had told her secret. Had made things worse. His betrayal was almost the hardest thing about the whole mess. Now when she looked at him, instead of feeling that little lift in her heart, she felt as though someone were ripping at her insides. She should have known. Mortals were not to be trusted.

It took all of Ravyn's willpower to refrain from hurting him, hurting the others. The taunting and abuse carried through the rest of her school years. She was always the weirdo, the freak. As she got older, she could more easily resist the urge to retaliate, but the fact that she'd wanted to hurt the other children scared her. She knew how dangerous losing control of her emotions could be.

And now her loss of control had actually harmed another. It might even have been serious enough to force a meeting of the elders.

Unless they were meeting for some other reason. Perhaps they were convening to engineer a plan to stop the killer. Now that the violence of the outside world had touched one of their own, the elders were likely to become more active in aiding in the apprehension of the perpetrator. But if they were successful, Ravyn's role in what had happened would be revealed.

She and her sister crossed a bridge where the water on either side was clear and trickled melodiously over the smooth stones in the creek. The smell of woodland phlox, henbane and belladonna grew stronger the nearer they drew to the clearing, and as Ravyn took her place in the circle a cool gust of wind whipped the thin robe around her naked legs, making goose bumps shiver up along her flesh.

The night was moonless. The only light came from the fire in the center of the ritual circle and the candles flickering on the altar, miraculously unextinguished by the steady breeze. The reflection of those flames flickered across the faces of the gathered hooded figures.

Sorina stood across from Ravyn, on the other side of the altar. Elsbeth clasped Ravyn's right hand while Elsbeth's husband, Adalardo, held her left. Ravyn wondered if they could feel her misgivings through the simple touch of their hands. Were her palms damp? Did the trembling she felt inside travel through to her fingers?

Along with the pleasant tang of wood smoke from the fire, the air carried the scent of imminent rain. Here, however, in the copse behind the mammoth house of their high priestess Vanora, the coven was protected by the thick foliage of the overhanging trees.

Vanora knelt in front of the altar, her face shadowed by the hood of her robe. She held her athame by its ornate black handle, and she placed the ceremonial dagger's silver tip into a bowl of salt water. Her voice, deeply melodious and haunting, rose over the snap of the flames.

"I beseech thee, O Creature of Water, to cast out all impurities and uncleanliness of the world. Blessings be upon this Creature of Salt; let all malignity and hindrance be cast forth hence, and let all good enter herein. Wherefore so I bless thee, that thou mayest aid me. Guide us to halt the evil. Protect all innocent creatures. Make a shield against all wickedness and malevolence. Goodness and light shall we reap."

Ravyn reached down with the rest of the coven as they lifted their own athames from the ground. In turn, each of the witches placed the tip of his or her dagger in the bowl of salt water just as Vanora had. As one, they lifted the blades to the heavens.

In Ravyn's mind, she saw the face of the killer. She gripped her dagger in her hand . . . felt flesh give way as she thrust it into his heart. A hitching breath escaped her throat, and her head snapped up. The athame was symbolic, used only in rituals. Never was it to be used for any type of cutting, let alone to harm another being. She quickly looked around to see if the others had heard her gasp. Her face flushed with shame.

The others hadn't seemed to notice. In unison, they repeated the words to seal the ritual, their voices rising as one.

"Keeper of all that is holy and good. Thou hast power over evil. We do summon, stir and call you up to witness our rites and to guard the circle. We have faith in thee. The circle is cast . . . the power of good unleashed."

The ritual ended, they doused the fire and the candles. In silence the coven members next walked through the trees at the back of the property and into Vanora's three-story red Tudor.

On the many evenings when Vanora entertained, the house was alight with blazing colors and the sounds of laughter and clanging dishes. Tonight it was still and silent and dimly lit. Tables holding miniature lamps and burning candles were scattered throughout the house and inset near the large bay windows.

Ravyn went upstairs and changed into her blouse and jeans. The coven members—who, on the surface, were simply normal citizens of the surrounding communities, working and living in various jobs—arrived and left in street clothes but donned the robes for the rituals, then left them at Vanora's home.

When Ravyn walked out of the bedroom, her mother was in the hall. Sucking in a breath, she turned her head and attempted to walk past, but Gwendyl was not to be deterred. She rushed over, halting Ravyn's escape.

"Ravyn, darling." A smile lit her beautiful face, which was so much like Sorina's, if older. "How are you? I've been so worried about you." She reached out her arms, but Ravyn didn't go into them.

"I'm fine, Mother."

Gwendyl's arms dropped and her smile faded. She nodded. "Well, good. You're tough." She didn't mean it as a compliment, and Ravyn didn't take it that way. "I know you'll be fine."

They stood awkwardly in the muted light of the hall. Ravyn wondered why the two of them even pretended to care about one another. There was too much between them. Too much hurt, too much anger. Ravyn supposed that just as she herself did, her mother pretended for Sorina's benefit.

Ravyn barely remembered her father; he'd died when she was six. But she remembered his kindness, his stability, as opposed to her mother's neuroses. She remembered that he liked to do magic tricks for her and Sorina—albeit magic tricks somewhat more elaborate than those of most fathers.

One time, he'd taken Ravyn and Sorina to the movies. Ravyn had been sitting next to him, her eyes glued to the screen. Her father had leaned over and whispered, "Watch this." His hands pointed toward the front of the theater, and the movie screen began to twirl in clockwise circles, round and round, faster and faster. The other moviegoers had gasped, and their voices had risen in confused murmurs. Ravyn's father had held his sides, laughing so hard he'd spit popcorn out of his mouth. It was a memory Ravyn cherished, because it was one of the last she had of him. Her father had died a few months later.

Ravyn and Sorina's home life after that had been hell.

Her mother had never cared for her children, only about the current man in her life.

A door opened down the hallway, and Vanora came out of a bedroom and approached. "Ravyn, could I please speak with you for a moment?" she asked.

Ravyn's heartbeat stalled. While she was relieved by the excuse to escape her mother, she was gravely concerned about Vanora's wanting to see her. Now she would find out the reason for the meeting of the elders.

She nodded and made her way into Vanora's office, waiting while the coven's high priestess took a seat behind the large mahogany desk in the middle of the room. Ravyn took the seat across from her.

Vanora's face was ageless and unlined, although she was pushing seventy. Her fiery red hair was swept into an updo. Her lips were almost the same shade. Though her features were somewhat cold, she herself was not. Ravyn had been the recipient of the woman's warmth and kindness several times over the years.

"There was something amiss this evening," Vanora stated, her gaze shrewd and unwavering.

"Yes?"

"The circle was weak. You know we need everyone's full attention, their energy, for our work to be successful."

Ravyn nodded. For the first time, she hadn't been sure she wanted the ritual to be successful. "I'm aware of that."

"You were holding back tonight. Would you like to tell me why?"

Ravyn looked down at her hands where they rested on her lap. "I'm sorry."

"That's an apology, not an answer," Vanora replied.

Ravyn shrugged, still not looking at the elder. "I don't know."

"Yes, you do. I understand that you've been through a terrible ordeal, but we need your strength. We need it all the more. We need to help the authorities catch this man."

Cold apprehension slithered down Ravyn's spine. "I . . . I can't help them."

"You can. You don't want to," Vanora pointed out.

Ravyn's voice was a whisper. "I guess I'm afraid."

"Of course you're afraid—that's only natural. But facing your fear gives you power. In those fears, you shall find the strength to defeat your enemy."

"I'm sorry. I . . . I can't."

"You can, Ravyn. You must. The elders have asked that you appear in front of the council. They're disturbed about what may have happened while you were in the clutches of the killer. They . . . have their suspicions about how you escaped."

Ravyn's knees went weak, and for a moment she couldn't find her voice. "What? A council of elders? When? Where?"

"I've put them off for the moment. I assured them of your dedication. But they won't tolerate breaking the rules. You know that."

Ravyn nodded. "I know."

The coven members' power, their magic, came from the bond of their shared beliefs, from the rituals they performed and from observing the laws of the coven. These laws were strict and binding. With each transgression, a witch's powers became weaker. If they continued to stray from the teachings, the witch would become completely powerless. Not only would they risk a loss of their powers. If the elders got wind of a witch's disregard for the coven rules, a special council would be convened to determine if those violations were great enough to warrant banishment. Many times, when that happened, the ousted witch turned to black magic. That consequence—banishment with or without black magic—was abhorrent to Ravyn.

Vanora smiled, and the coldness melted from her features. It was as if an inner warmth radiated through her, softening her expression. "Don't despair, my dear. I have faith in you, and you must have faith in your coven. Now, go. Let us see if we can't help the authorities catch this monster."

Ravyn left Vanora's office feeling somewhat comforted by their talk. Vanora had been the coven high priestess for twenty years, and because of the strained relationship between Ravyn and Gwendyl, Vanora had been a mother figure to her. After the incident with the cat, Ravyn's mother had listened with only half her attention. When Ravyn had finished the account, her mother had said that perhaps she should lose weight and the kids would be nicer to her. Vanora, on the other hand, had kindly and calmly explained that children could be cruel but didn't know any better.

"I know it's difficult," she'd said, "but experiences like this will make you stronger. You must resist the urge to even the score. Instead, pray that your tormentors will learn the error of their ways, that they will discover peace and compassion within them."

Ravyn hadn't gone as far as to pray for the other children, but from then on she'd replayed Vanora's words in her head each time the other students were cruel. That had gotten her through the difficult years of adolescence. Then, as now, Vanora's words reassured Ravyn, giving her a measure of hope.

Ravyn felt guilty about her preoccupation with the Tin Man, anyway. Her sister was trying to plan the happiest day of her life, and even though Ravyn didn't like the idea of Sorina marrying a mortal, and though she damn sure didn't want Sorina to tell him about the coven, she knew that Justin truly made her sister happy. She needed to be available for Sorina in spirit as well as in body. For that reason, Ravyn made a vow to put the incident out of her mind. If the police caught the bastard, fine. If the coven's powers aided in his apprehension, fine. If he spoke to the authorities about what happened . . . well, that might not be so fine.

As much as she tried to convince herself to concentrate on her sister's happiness, the pall of evil hung heavy over her heart. She knew that things would never be the same. She would spend her days as the condemned had for hundreds of years before her: waiting for the noose to draw closed around her neck.

Chapter Twelve

Nick still lived in the gray-brick, single-story, three-bedroom home he'd shared with Annie. It was two bedrooms too large now that his wife was gone. He no longer hosted overnight guests, and he certainly wouldn't need the extra rooms for children. It was just him and Dog. Always would be.

He stared down at the newspaper clippings littering the surface of the coffee table. Nick hadn't clipped them himself. When he'd left the force, his partner at the time had given them to him. Keepsakes, he'd said. And Nick had kept them. The question was, *why* had he kept them? Their subject wasn't exactly something he wanted to remember.

Nick picked up the framed photo of Annie. She wasn't smiling in the picture. Her expression was pensive as she stared off into the distance. He didn't know what she was looking at, didn't remember who had taken it, but he'd always liked the picture, and she'd framed it for him. She'd always had a great smile, but there was something particular about her thoughtful expression in this photo that appealed to him. Her blonde hair was down around her shoulders the way he liked. She wasn't wearing a lot of makeup. The photo was simple and real—the way he remembered Annie. Simple and real . . . and gone forever.

He lay the photo on the table facedown and picked up his glass. Poured it full of whiskey. His gaze fell on the clippings again. Why had he taken on the Tin Man case?

Who was he kidding? The man in those articles was someone different, someone he could never be again. If he stayed on this case, he'd fail. Plus, he'd have to see the Skyler woman again. He wasn't sure why, but that thought made him supremely uncomfortable. He couldn't figure out why he'd had such a strong reaction to her, but didn't think he could blame it totally on booze. Or on his long stretch of celibacy.

Not wanting to examine his reactions further, he pushed all thoughts from his mind. Draining the glass, he poured another. Then, picking up the phone, he dialed Phil's number at the office. He got a recording that said the office was closed until Monday, as he'd known it would. It was easier to let someone down over voice mail than in person. He punched Phil's extension when the recording prompted, then left a message.

"Lassiter here. I'm afraid I'm going to have to withdraw from the case. The trail's cold, and I don't see it getting any warmer. The cops can do more than I can, so I don't feel right taking your money. I'll give you back what you've already paid me." Nick wasn't sure how he'd do that. He'd already spent most of it, but he'd figure out something. "Sorry, man. Good luck."

He thought he'd feel relief, but when he hung up all he felt was shame. Dog came over and lay on the floor beside his chair. Nick reached down and rubbed the animal's head, scratching the dog behind the ears the way he liked. At least he could make someone happy. Even if it was just a mutt.

"You need a treat, boy?"

Dog whimpered and wagged his tail.

"Yeah, me too," Nick said.

He went to the kitchen and came back with a couple of jerky treats. Dog wolfed them down while Nick twisted the cap off some Jack Daniel's. He'd decided to splurge on the good stuff tonight. After all, it wasn't every day he threw away his only source of income.

He flipped the television on. ESPN was showing highlights of Ken Griffey, Jr.'s return to the Seattle Mariners this past baseball season. Nick splashed more whiskey from the half-empty bottle into the glass and squinted at the television screen.

Junior swung the bat. He made contact, the crack like the shot of a pistol. Nick tipped the whiskey bottle directly to his mouth this time, not bothering with a glass. It wasn't as if he was sharing with anyone. He closed his eyes and savored the feel and taste of the liquor.

There was another crack, then another; in rapid succession they came, over and over. Why did Griffey keep swinging, when the ball was already sailing over the wall . . . ?

Something wet on Nick's hand made him jump. He opened his eyes. Morning sun streamed through the windows. Dog stood at the foot of the recliner, staring at him and wagging his tail. Nick looked at the television. The ESPN baseball show was over. A fishing program was on. The cracking sound still rang in Nick's ears, except it wasn't a bat. It was the front door. Someone wanted in, badly.

Nick set the bottle upright, mourning for a moment the loss of the Jack Daniel's that had spilled over his hand when he'd fallen asleep. He rose from the recliner and unsteadily made his way to the door. Phil Bodinsky stood there, his face scrunched up and dark like a thundercloud.

"I called in for my messages and heard yours. What the hell?" Phil pushed past without waiting for an invitation, and turned to confront Nick as Nick closed the door.

Nick scrubbed a hand over his whiskers, trying to erase the throbbing in the back of his head. He swallowed against the dryness in his mouth. God, he needed coffee. And a smoke. "How did you find out where I live?"

"I guess I'm a better detective than you are."

Nick let the shot roll off him. He'd heard worse. "Yeah, you are," he agreed. "So why the fuck are you here? You know as well as I do you're wasting your money."

Phil began to pace, and Nick looked away. His stomach was queasy enough without adding motion sickness.

"Speaking of money." Phil slammed a fist into his palm to emphasize his point. "I paid you well to do this job, and now you're pulling out on me?"

"I'll be right back." Nick turned to go into the kitchen. "Want some coffee?" he yelled over his shoulder into the living room. But Phil had followed, and stared as Nick fiddled with the coffeepot.

"What I want is some answers."

Nick filled the pot with water and measured four scoops into the filter, then leaned his palms on the countertop while he waited for the coffee to brew. He needed a jolt of caffeine, and he needed a big one. "I told you I'd give you a refund."

"I don't want a goddamned refund. I want this bastard stopped."

"If the police can't do it, why the hell do you think I can?" The smell of coffee filled the kitchen, making Nick feel marginally better. He took a mug from the dishwasher and before the pot finished brewing, filled his cup. Coffee dripped onto the burner, sizzling briefly before Nick returned the carafe. He rested one hip on the counter and gulped the hot liquid.

Phil began to pace. "The cops have hundreds of cases. This one's just a number to them," he ranted. "You have more time. Joe said you were good, a bulldog. Besides, of all people, I thought you'd understand."

"Why me?" Nick picked up a bottle of aspirin from the

counter and shook out three, swallowing them with his coffee.

For the first time since he arrived, Phil's voice was quiet, almost sounding sympathetic. "Joe told me about your wife. You know how it feels to lose someone you love."

Reaching into the pocket of his suit jacket, Phil pulled out a manila envelope. He withdrew a small stack of photos and shoved them under Nick's nose. The top picture was of a blonde woman. She sat on a porch swing, laughing. Her hair blew across her face, obscuring most of her features, but the joy in her eyes was evident.

"That's my wife Lindsey before that motherfucker took her from me. She was the sweetest, most beautiful woman in the world. We were going to have children. We were going to grow old together. Now I'll grow old alone." Phil's eyes misted, and he glared at Nick. "What would you do if your wife was brutally murdered? What would you do if the light of your world wound up looking like this?"

Phil slid the first photo away, revealing the one underneath. The same woman was there, except now she wasn't laughing. She was bloody and mutilated. She was naked and exposed, her pale flesh covered in burns and stab wounds.

Whiskey and coffee churned in Nick's stomach, threatening to make a dash for the floor. "Where the fuck did you get a crime-scene photo?" he asked. His voice was as shaky as Phil's hand holding the picture.

"Doesn't matter." Tears fell shamelessly down Phil's cheeks. "All that matters is that you stop him before he does this to another woman."

Nick stared at the photo, unable to take his eyes away. He didn't know if he could stop the sonofabitch. But he knew he couldn't say no to Phil. He knew that no matter what, this case was his. He had failed at too many things in his life and lost everything that mattered. If he ever wanted to look at himself in the mirror again, he had to do this and had to do it right.

He sighed and nodded slowly. Phil had accomplished his goal: Nick wouldn't stop until he or the Tin Man was finished.

Chapter Thirteen

"You ever think about popcorn and coffee?"

Nick looked at his tenant, Marvin the accountant, and wondered not for the first time what the hell the guy was talking about. "What *about* popcorn and coffee?" he asked, rubbing a hand over his face.

"Why do they both smell better than they taste?" Marvin grimaced as he took a sip from the mug.

"If you don't like coffee, then why are you drinking mine?"

Normally, Marvin's visits were only a mild annoyance. Today Nick had to restrain himself from pulling out his Beretta and pistol-whipping the guy's skinny ass. Nick had just been heading out to see the Skyler woman when Marvin popped in. He could have told him he was leaving and to just come back later, but he'd actually been relieved at the delay. Now he was beginning to rethink that.

Marvin shrugged. "I don't know, something to do?"

"*You* may not have anything to do, but I was just leaving," Nick pointed out.

The accountant's eyes widened, and his eyebrows disappeared into his bushy hair. "A case? The Tin Man, or a different one?"

"How the hell do you know about my Tin Man case?" Nick hadn't meant it to come out so sharply, but he was one wrongly chosen comment away from a psychotic episode.

Marvin's look of excitement changed to one of hurt. "I

hear things." He shrugged. "What, was it a big secret or something?"

Nick lit a cigarette. Marvin hated smoke. Nick hoped he'd hate it enough to get the hell out.

It didn't work.

"You know, I could help you." He sat forward in his chair, his pale brown eyes snapping with eagerness. "I could, like, go in and ask somebody questions or something. Nobody would ever guess I was a private eye by looking at me."

Marvin wore his usual worn-out Nikes and a cheap gray sports coat over a ratty Def Leppard T-shirt. Nick wanted to tell him that no one would even guess he was *employed*, but he'd hurt the guy's feelings enough for one day. "If I come up with anything I need your help with, I'll give you a yell."

Marvin's grin spread across his face, dimpling one pasty cheek and then the other. "Promise?" Apparently he hadn't heard the emphasis on *if*.

"Yeah, I promise."

"Thanks, man. I'll be right down the hall." Then Marvin left, waving smoke out of his face.

Nothing was left to keep Nick from leaving, too. Nothing except the dread of seeing *her* again. Ravyn Skyler. Even worse than the dread was the anticipation. That was what really had him worried.

The candle store smelled even better than it had the first time Nick was there. Before, the air had been heavy with some kind of berry scent. Today it smelled like cinnamon.

The blonde, who he'd learned was Ravyn's sister, Sorina, greeted him when he entered. "Hello, sir. What can I do for you?"

He couldn't stop his gaze from wandering around the

store. No sign of the sister, Ravyn. "I was in here last week. The other woman told me she could make an eighteen-ounce candle for me."

"Okay. Let's go over here and check. What scent?" asked the blonde.

Damn it, he needed to see the sister. Where the hell was she? "I don't . . . uh . . . let's see . . ." He pretended to think. He hadn't really forgotten. How the hell could he forget that he'd asked for Lavender Dream?

A movement from the corner of his eye made him turn. There she was—Ravyn Skyler. She wore a black T-shirt underneath a long-sleeved red blouse, which was buttoned halfway up, and black jeans. Her hair flowed loose around her shoulders. Damn. She was even more beautiful than he remembered.

"Ravyn, did you make an eighteen-ounce candle for this gentleman? He was in here last week and we didn't have that size. He can't recall the scent."

"Lavender Dream." Ravyn's reply was clipped. Not friendly. But all Nick could think was, *She remembers me!* "Yes. We have them."

Sorina Skyler walked over to the shelf of candles and reached up and chose one. "Here you go," she said.

What now? Nick had his damn candle; he'd lost his pretense. He needed to talk to Ravyn but didn't want to jump right into an interrogation. He didn't want her to know he was a PI. She'd been less than cooperative with the police so far, and he had no reason to believe she'd be any different with him.

"Excuse me," he said as Ravyn turned back toward the curtains through which she'd appeared. She stopped with her back to him, and he saw her shoulders stiffen.

After a moment, she faced him. She clasped her hands in front of her, rubbing the inside of her right palm with her left thumb. She looked at him for a long time. He shifted from one foot to the other, his hands slick on the glass jar he held to his chest.

"Yes?" Her eyes told him he was a nuisance, and that she was barely holding on to civility.

"You two own the store, right?" His gaze moved from one sister to the other.

"Yes, we do," Sorina answered. "Why?"

He hesitated with what he hoped was just the right touch of reluctance and embarrassment. "I have a problem, and I wondered if you might help me out. I wondered if you had any odd jobs around here I might do to earn some merchandise."

"Merchandise?" Ravyn snorted. "Want to stock up on Lavender Dream candles, do you?"

Nick gave her what he meant to be a charming grin. He had done a background check and knew the sisters had lost their father at a young age. It might be heartless, but he planned to play on their vulnerability in that area. This was for a good cause, so he was justified. Catching the Tin Man had to take precedence over the emotions of these women.

"Actually, I was hoping I could barter for some of your jewelry. For my daughter. You see, I'm divorced, and her mother has custody. She won't let me see my little girl, and every penny I make goes to attorney fees to fight for her. She's twelve and I haven't seen her in two years. I'm supposed to visit her soon, and I wanted to have a gift. Something really special. Like the jewelry you have here. I just know she'd love it."

Ravyn's eyes had lost a bit of their hardness, but she didn't comment. Sorina practically melted on the floor in front of Nick.

"Oh, you poor dear! How awful. Of course we can use

your help." The blonde walked over and placed a hand on his arm. "I'm so sorry. I know it must be very difficult for you."

Nick nodded. It was easy to let his eyes mist over for the imaginary daughter. All he had to do was remember the real child his dead wife had wanted, and how he hadn't taken the time to give her one.

He stole a look at Ravyn, but she wasn't looking at him. Instead, her venomous gaze was locked on her sister. Sorina either didn't notice or pretended not to.

"I really appreciate this." Nick addressed Ravyn as if she'd been the one to agree to his proposal.

Almost imperceptibly, she nodded. She shot her sister one more glare before disappearing into the back.

Nick went to the register to pay for his candle. Sorina gave him an impish grin. Her face alight with mischief, she was nearly as beautiful as her sister.

"I'm Sorina, by the way." She stuck her hand out, and he took it.

"Nick Lassiter. Nice to meet you. And thanks. I really appreciate this opportunity."

"My pleasure." Sorina's expression turned pensive. "My sister Ravyn is a little . . . antisocial at times. I get the feeling you kind of like her."

Nick gave a shy smile. "Are you trying to do a little matchmaking?"

Sorina shrugged. "She's so serious all the time. She seems so lonely, but she doesn't even know it. I just thought, you know . . . you seem *interested* in her. I mean, come on. Lavender Dream? Was that the first one you grabbed or something?"

"Yeah," he admitted. "Bet it impressed her."

Sorina laughed, a musical tinkling that echoed through the store. Nick wondered if Ravyn ever laughed like that. Probably not.

"You know, I'll be getting married soon. Ravyn could use help around here while I'm on my honeymoon. Who knows how well you two might hit it off?"

"Yeah?" Nick shrugged, knowing he wouldn't be around long enough for that to happen. He needed to find out what she knew about the killer and get the hell away. He didn't want any new entanglements. He couldn't afford them. "How do you know I'm not some psycho who might hurt her?"

Sorina stared at the curtain through which her sister had disappeared. "Believe me, you can't do any more than has been done already." Her gaze returned to him. "Besides, I can trust you. I *feel* it."

Yeah, right. Good instincts, Nick thought. *You sure can trust me. I've known you for only five minutes, and I've already deceived you.* "You must be an exceptional judge of character."

"I am," the blonde agreed. "But let me warn you, my sister is even more so. If you're not on the level with her . . . Well . . . let's just say you'll wish you had been."

Where had *that* come from? Ravyn's sister had gone from practically welcoming him to the family to threatening his health and happiness. He shook his head. "Don't worry. And thanks again. For the candle . . . and for everything."

"You're welcome. Why don't you come back Wednesday, and I'll show you what needs to be done?"

"Sounds great," Nick said.

She retrieved a blank sheet of paper from somewhere behind the counter and slid it in front of him. "Can you jot down some information for me to have on file? Name, address, phone number, emergency contact—things like that. You never know what might happen. I'd like to have it, just in case."

"Sure." Nick scribbled the info and handed the paper back to Sorina.

As he left with his candle, he wondered why his step felt a little lighter, and why he was experiencing a sense of eagerness. He also wondered why he was cursing the fact that Wednesday was still two days away.

Chapter Fourteen

Gingerly, painfully, Jay stepped out of the shower. The water was the worst part. He had to shower with his back to the spray the entire time to keep it from stinging his injuries. He was healing, coming along, but the pain . . .

He stood naked in front of the full-length mirror in the hallway. Sucking in a breath, he let his gaze drop to his groin. God. A film of sweat broke out across his body, despite his still being damp from the shower. He swallowed, fighting the urge to vomit. His penis was still there, but it was a shriveled red and black protuberance. Blisters had formed and burst, and now they oozed a milky yellow pus. The surrounding area, where his testicles had once been, looked just as bad, a mass of enflamed eruptions and charbroiled flesh.

The blisters made him think of that night: the agony, the stench. Funny, how the odor of burning flesh was so pleasurable until it was your own.

Marshall had been correct about Jay's prognosis. Jay could urinate, but sex . . . Well, even though he wasn't fully healed, he knew that would never happen again. The bitch had made sure of that.

Sexually, he'd been with only a few women other than the Chosen Ones, and they didn't really count. Not as sexual encounters. They were more. So much more. But sex *was* a big part of those encounters, he had to admit. The arousal. The satisfaction . . . He'd never ejaculated. No way had he been willing to take a chance on leaving his semen behind. But the acts had been satisfying nonetheless—maybe even more so, since he'd deprived himself of the ultimate release. But what about now? Was that pleasure gone forever? Had she taken that away from him?

She had. He was almost certain of it. Damn her! He slapped a hand against his thigh, and trembles shot through his body. She'd pay. Somehow, someday, she'd pay. She'd ruined his life.

Yet in spite of what she'd done, he couldn't stop wanting her. She wasn't only beautiful. There was something more. There was a facet of her attractiveness that called to him, some quality he couldn't quite define.

He tried to get an erection thinking about her breasts, about those tempting lips, that soft skin . . .

No good. He couldn't get hard. Indeed, she was beautiful, but she was also terrifying. Too terrifying.

He closed his eyes and forced himself to think of the others, the ones *before* Ravyn Skyler. Yes, these were also beautiful women. And unlike the bitch, they'd done everything right. The fear? He loved the fear. They'd begged him, promised they would do whatever he wanted. And when he'd toyed with them long enough, taken their last breaths from them . . . Oh, yes, it had been heavenly.

Both during and after, he'd always had a hard-on that was almost painful. Unfortunately, he'd had to wait until he returned home to take care of it. The waiting was difficult, and the swelling faded, but after he relived the scenes in his mind the erection always came back. And when he came, it was the most amazing thing—an orgasm that seemed to go on forever.

A tingle worked its way through Jay's belly and into his chest. His breathing became restricted. He wanted so badly to . . . No. Nothing. He couldn't get an erection. Not even a hint of one. Tears stung his eyes.

Big boys don't cry.

This time, the voice didn't make him flinch. His mother had been with him constantly since the night with Ravyn. As much as he'd always feared her, he now almost felt comforted by her presence. He knew she was happy about what had happened to him. She probably wished she'd done it herself.

"Go to hell, Mother."

Don't you ever speak to me like that! she shrieked in reply. *You know what I'll do, you smart-ass little cocksucker.*

In spite of his earlier bravado, Jay cringed. Yes, he knew very well what she would do. "I'm sorry, Mother," he whispered.

She didn't respond.

Good, he needed the peace, needed to think. What would he do about the woman? How could he make her pay, when he was afraid to go near her? Yet how could he live with himself if he didn't take revenge? And he had to find out how the hell she'd caused this, how the hell she'd maimed him for life. She'd been the only one to see his face and live. She alone could ID him and bring him down. But then, the composite in the newspaper looked nothing like him. The beard had disguised him, and there was no way anyone would connect him to that sketch.

He wrapped a towel around his waist and made his way to the recliner. Gently lowering himself into it, he flinched at the resultant explosion of pain. Picking up the bottle from the end table, he swallowed two of the pills and washed them down with a glass of water.

As he waited for the morphine to work, he wondered how his deformity would affect the future. His fantasy had always been to have his way with one of the women and take her to the brink of death, and then at the last moment save her. He'd ejaculate right there, at the moment of his greatest pleasure. What a power rush that would be! He'd never done it, because he knew it might mean getting caught, which was something he couldn't take, couldn't survive. To be at the mercy of people who wanted to punish him, to lock him up, to hurt him? But he'd always thought that maybe, someday, when he was ready to give everything up, this would be his final act.

Part of the thrill of the fantasy was the arousal he knew he'd feel. And then he wouldn't deprive himself of release. But now it was all ruined. By her.

If he was discovered, what the hell. He'd plead insanity—and he was pretty damned sure the plea would stick. He had to be insane to have done the shit he'd done. And if by some chance he *didn't* get caught? Well, maybe he'd try again. He knew what he needed now, knew what would make him feel better. As soon as he was able, he needed to get out of the house. He needed a hunt. It wouldn't be the same as it used to be, but it would be fun. Gratifying. He could find some joy in the chase, after all.

He absentmindedly fingered the scar on his chest as a thought occurred to him that almost made up for the injuries he'd suffered: he didn't have to give up his dream. Even though he wouldn't get the ultimate satisfaction he'd once imagined, he could fulfill all but the orgasm. And this way might be even better. Because when he made the fantasy a reality, the woman would be Ravyn Skyler.

Chapter Fifteen

Nick shaved and splashed on some Aramis cologne that had been a Christmas gift from his mother last year, then whistled as he walked toward Ravyn Skyler's shop and his first day working there.

It's a case. Keep that in mind, Lassiter, only a case.

How long would he have to work with her before he could broach the real reason for being there? And how did he expect to start the conversation, anyway? *Hey, how are you? Nice day, huh? By the way, tell me about the maniac that held you hostage and almost gutted you.*

Nope. That wouldn't work. And he wasn't sure what would. She was distant, cold. But he detected a warmth simmering underneath. He could sense it. He could also sense that if he ever unlocked the warmth, he might get burned.

When he walked in, he didn't see Sorina. Ravyn was there, however, and he gave her his best smile.

She didn't smile back. Her lips were set in a rigid line, the corners of her mouth slightly turned down. Her thick, dark hair was pulled away from her face, and she wore a shiny black blouse that lay softly against her breasts. Her nipples were clearly outlined.

It was cool in the shop, yet Nick felt a layer of perspiration break out on his skin. He raised his head and forced himself to look at her face. "Nice day." He gave her another smile, hoping it read more friendly than lecherous.

Her gaze was steady as she asked, "What do you really want?"

Nick's smile faded. "Pardon?"

"What are you up to? Why do you really want to work here?"

"I told you about my daughter. I'm just trying to find a way to get her some nice things." He shoved his hands in his pockets. "You know, the real question here is, What's your problem? Why do you dislike me so much?"

She stared at him for a moment before speaking. He noticed she did that a lot, as if carefully weighing each word. "I don't know you, so I can't very well dislike you."

Geez, if she didn't watch it, he'd be overcome by the warm fuzzies. He pulled his hands from his pockets and crossed his arms. "Your sister likes me," he pointed out.

Ravyn gave an unladylike snort. "My sister likes everyone." She made it sound as if Sorina's amiability were some kind of disease.

"Gee, thanks."

At that moment, Sorina came out through the curtains behind the register. Her smile burned away the icy wall Ravyn's attitude had erected, and she said, "Good morning. I'm so glad you're here!"

Nick shot a triumphant look at Ravyn. "Thanks. Me, too. I really appreciate this."

"Well, the place could use your help. There are a lot of repairs that need to be done, and we've just been ignoring them."

"Guess I'd better get started," Nick replied. He took her hand and gallantly placed a kiss upon it. "At your service, madam."

Sorina giggled. "Come on back. The first thing I'd like you to do is reinforce some shelving. I've noticed there are a few places where it sags a bit. We wouldn't want all that glass tumbling down on our heads!"

Nick followed her into the back, into a room where there were rows of shelves stocked with glass jars and boxes of various supplies. On the opposite side of the room was a small stove upon which sat a double boiler. Next to the stove was a table that held sheets of wax, a jar containing a multitude of wicks, and a small shelf where several bottles were lined up, each neatly labeled with the scent it held.

Sorina frowned. "I know it's a lot of work, but I guess I need you to empty one shelf at a time, reinforce it, reload it and then start on the next."

Yeah, that *was* a lot of work. But it would keep him around for a while. At least until he found an opening to ask about the Tin Man.

"Not a problem. I'll get started right away," he promised.

He worked for three hours and reinforced two sets of shelves. He hadn't seen either sister the whole time, and decided it was time to call it a day.

As he walked out front, he saw Ravyn pulling on a black leather coat. She didn't look at him, although he knew she was aware of his presence.

He called to Sorina, whom he couldn't see, "I'm taking off for the day. I'll be back in the morning."

"Great," her voice filtered back, and she appeared from around a corner. "We close in an hour, anyway. I'm just going to finish some things up. Then I'll be taking off, too."

Nick nodded and headed for the door. But the opportunity presenting itself was more than he could resist. Leaving at the same time as Ravyn? It was time to do a little real detective work.

He watched her pull out of the parking lot in a champagne-colored Sebring. Keeping a discreet distance, he followed. They drove south for fifteen minutes, toward Lake Thunderbird. Ravyn turned onto a gravel road where he knew he'd have a hard time staying with her and not being seen. He took a chance: he could monitor her route from quite a distance back, thanks to the cloud of dust her passing created.

She finally pulled into the drive of a house where he assumed she lived. Nick cruised by, shifting onto a dirt road just past her turnoff. There was a limited view of her home from where he sat. He just had to hope no other vehicles appeared. Not likely. The road didn't seem to lead to anywhere.

Ravyn's home was a log cabin with reddish trim, which backed up to the lake. Nestled in a cocoon of leafy trees, it was a haven of seclusion. It fit her. He could see someone with her penchant for privacy living out here. Not just living, but thriving.

He waited, watching her house, not even sure why. He needed to know where she lived and observe her a little, he supposed. But what exactly did he expect to learn?

He sat there until dark, not knowing what he anticipated but not really having anything else to do. When the lights burning inside the house went out, he started the car. He pulled forward, making a U-turn in the road. But just before he drove away, he glanced in his rearview mirror and saw a figure heading out Ravyn's back door—a female wearing some kind of flowing black gown.

What the hell?

Nick circled back and pulled his car as far off the road as possible, into the tree line. He climbed out and keeping alongside the underbrush, made his way down the fence that divided her property from the dirt road. Damp leaves slapped against his face, and the smell of moist earth mingled with the scent of lake water. He could feel mud clinging to his shoes but didn't care. He had to see what she was up to.

He spotted her at the edge of the lake, and he squatted

down behind the fence to watch. She lifted her arms, and her gown blew against her body. He could see the outline of her breasts tight against the fabric. He thought back to seeing her nipples earlier, and he sucked in a breath. God, she was beautiful. Strange, but beautiful.

His body reacted. Taking a deep breath, he tried to make his erection fade, but he couldn't help it. Ravyn Skyler was an enigma, pushing him away yet unconsciously drawing him closer. He thought there'd been something in her eyes when she looked at him. A reluctant desire. Although it had been a while since he had seen, or looked for, that type of reaction in women, he was fairly certain he'd detected it in Ravyn.

Lightning flashed for a brief moment, surrounding the exact spot where she stood. He blinked and shook his head, knowing he had to have imagined what he'd just seen. There wasn't a cloud in the sky! The rain they'd had yesterday had been followed by sunshine all day today, so it couldn't have been lightning. But he'd seen *something*. What the hell was happening here?

If Ravyn noticed the lightning, it apparently hadn't fazed her. Unmoving, she stood at the edge of the water, a light breeze lifting her gown around her legs. What was she doing? And how long was Nick going to remain crouched down in this uncomfortable position watching her?

He knew the answer to that one: until she went inside and he could no longer see her.

Chapter Sixteen

Late the next morning, aching and stiff from his lengthy surveillance of Ravyn Skyler, Nick crawled out of bed, swallowed some coffee and showered. Then he went to see the hunters who'd found Ravyn after the attack.

The boys lived out in the country on an acreage, in a manufactured home that was surprisingly large and nicely furnished. Sixteen-year-old Carl sat on the edge of the living-room sofa, his hands nervously clutching his bony knees. His brother Cameron, two years older and a tad more courageous, slouched beside him, the only sign of his discomfort a rhythmic tapping of his camouflage boots.

The parents were out. Nick was glad about that. Whatever he could get from these boys would be easier without the adults sitting in.

"So, tell me exactly what happened." Nick sat in the chair next to the sofa, leaning slightly toward the boys in a conspiratorial pose.

"We already told the cops," Cameron spoke up.

"I know. But I'm not a cop. I'm a private investigator working my own case, and I'd like to hear your story."

Carl's eyes slid toward his brother, then back to Nick. "We was . . . hiking." He swallowed. "Hiking in the woods, and we heard a commotion, so we went running."

"Hiking?" Nick's brows rose, and skepticism colored his tone.

Carl's gaze roamed again, this time leaping all over the

room until finally landing on the floor in front of him. He said nothing.

"Look." Nick sighed, making sure to keep his voice level, calm, trustworthy. "I don't care about the poaching."

The heads of both boys snapped up like the lids on two Tic Tac boxes.

"I know you were hunting out of season, and I promise that I don't give a damn. I just want to know what happened with the girl."

Cameron slid to the edge of the sofa and began speaking rapidly, as if once he'd decided to come clean, he was anxious to get it all over and done with. "Yeah, we was hunting. We heard this awful screaming. We went running, and just as we got close to the cabin, we heard the sound of a car driving off. We went inside real slow, 'cause we was scared."

Carl took the story from there, his apprehension gone as he was overcome by the remembered excitement of the experience. "The girl was tied to the bed. She was in pain, we could tell, but calm as pond water. We untied her and dialed nine-one-one on my cell phone. The cops talked to us, and we told 'em what happened. They let us go, and that was it. We never saw the man what did that to her."

"How quickly would you say you arrived at the cabin after you heard the screaming?" Nick asked.

Cameron's eyebrows drew together. "We was only a little ways off. I'd say we got there about three to five minutes after we heard 'im scream."

"Wait. *Him?*"

The brothers nodded in unison. "Yeah. Him. That's what was really fuck—" Cameron stopped in midcurse and looked at Nick from under the brim of his University of Oklahoma cap. "Messed up about the deal. We run to the cabin and go in. There's this girl, no dude around. But it was a *man's* scream. Never did figure that one out."

Nick couldn't figure that out either. Why the hell would the murdering psycho scream and run, and Ravyn Skyler not utter a sound?

The morning Nick Lassiter was due to arrive for his third day of work, Ravyn tried once more to talk some sense into her sister. She didn't like Nick's being there. Not one bit. A stranger hanging around too much was not a good idea. They'd been over it daily since he'd been hired, but Sorina wouldn't budge.

"Poor guy, he loves his daughter so much. I feel sorry for him, and we could use the help," Sorina reasoned, the same as she had the mornings previous.

"We've gotten along fine so far without him."

Sorina shrugged. "You never know. Sometimes it's a good idea to need someone."

Ravyn harrumphed. "Sometimes being needy just makes you pathetic." When pain flashed across her sister's face, Ravyn regretted the words immediately.

Sorina lifted her chin. "Sometimes being cold makes you lonely and bitter."

Ravyn sighed. "I'm sorry, Sorina, I didn't mean it."

Her sister nodded. "I know. It's okay. And you know? Nick seems like a pretty good guy." She grinned. "And he's *hot*. I could tell he likes you. I thought maybe you two would hit it off, if you gave him a chance. I don't like seeing you so lonely."

Ravyn knew Sorina was only trying to help, but she didn't *need* the help. She didn't want it. "There's a difference between being alone and being lonely. I'm fine, Sorina. Really."

The bell above the door dinged, and Sorina looked over

Ravyn's shoulder, a smile lighting her face. Ravyn turned and her body tensed with irritation.

Nick.

She clenched her fists at her sides, burying them in the folds of her blouse. She resisted the urge to disappear into the back. She wouldn't run from him. No way would she let him see the effect he had on her.

"Morning, ladies."

"Good morning, Nick." Sorina practically gushed, but Ravyn only nodded.

"Want me to start on those shelves again?"

"Actually, I'll be working back there today, so you need to find something out front to do," Ravyn spoke up.

Sorina the Traitor shook her head. "Not much out here to do. He can work on those shelves while you're pouring candles. I'm sure it won't be too much of a distraction."

Ravyn tried to choke back resentment as she nodded. "Fine." She turned and marched through the curtain, determined to ignore the interloper for the entire day.

It wasn't easy. As much as she hated to admit the truth, Sorina was right—Nick was hot. He wore a white T-shirt tucked into well-worn Levi's that hugged his rear end. He smelled good, too. Once in a while, as he walked near her to place a box on the floor, his woodsy, masculine scent would drift over. The scruffy cheeks were gone, and she kind of missed them. There was something rugged and sexy about the way that dark stubble emphasized the blue of his eyes. But none of that was important. It was nothing to her. She once again went about the business of ignoring him.

She did a pretty good job for the next hour as she poured candles and carefully set the wicks. That is, she managed until he spoke.

"You have any pets?"

Ravyn shook her head and didn't turn around.

"I have a dog," he offered, even though she hadn't asked. "He just showed up one day last year, so I kept him."

Sighing, she swiveled in her chair. There was nothing to do at the moment other than wait for the candles to set, and she couldn't very well keep her back to him while doing absolutely nothing.

When he didn't comment further, she lifted her eyebrows. "You've started this riveting conversation. I assume there's more?"

He clutched his chest and staggered back as if wounded. "Riveting, huh? Ouch. I was just trying to start a little dialogue—you know, get to know one another. I guess that's asking too much."

Ravyn crossed her arms and leaned back in her chair, purposely keeping her gaze above chest level so she wouldn't see the way the tool belt slanted across his lean hips. "What do you want to know about me? I make candles and jewelry. I have one sister and a mother. I live alone. No pets. I like long walks in the rain and old music . . . you know, Otis Redding, the Platters, Elvis Presley. Anything else?"

He gave a satisfied smile. "See? Was that so hard? My turn. I work construction, and I have two sisters and two parents. One dog, a golden retriever named Dog. I don't like long walks *anywhere*, and I'm not crazy about oldies. Not crazy about Elvis's music, although the later stuff was pretty good. I like his movies, though."

"Are we done?"

He let out a low whistle. "Man, chatting with you is more work than repairing these shelves."

"Then maybe you shouldn't try so hard."

"Wanna hear a joke?"

Ravyn blew out a breath and said, "If I listen to your

joke, will you let me get back to work? In silence this time?"

"Sure."

When she gave a slight nod, he put his hammer down and leaned a hip against a shelf. He rubbed his hands together and smiled.

"Okay, here goes. There's this little boy sitting on a park bench with a dog lying at his feet. A man walks up and sits down next to him and says, 'Hello, son, does your dog bite?' The little boy says, 'Nope.' The man reaches down to pet the dog. The animal promptly growls and takes a chunk out of the guy's hand. 'Geez!' he shouts, holding his injury. 'I thought you said your dog didn't bite!' 'He doesn't,' the boy says. 'That's not my dog.'"

Ravyn laughed in spite of herself.

Nick smiled. "You have a nice laugh," he told her. "You'd think it'd sound rusty, since you never use it."

"Very funny," she muttered.

Still grinning, Nick straightened and said, "Well, guess I'll let you get back to work."

Ravyn nodded, but she stared at him just a moment longer. She noticed that even when he was joking, there was sadness lurking in his eyes. Was it because of his daughter? Suddenly she wanted to lay her hand over his heart, feel it beating beneath her palm until she knew what put such sorrow there. But just as quickly, the urge was gone and she turned away.

She tried to concentrate on her task, but she was aware of Nick working behind her. Aware of his movements, of his breathing. He didn't try to make conversation again, but she couldn't have been any more aware of him if he'd played a drum solo in the middle of her workbench.

The bell jingled out front. Using it as an excuse, Ravyn went out to help Sorina with the customer. Dealing with people was something she normally avoided like a root canal, but this time it would be a welcome distraction. Things were starting to feel a little too easy with Nick, a little too enjoyable.

She was irritated when Nick followed, but she forced a smile as she stepped out of the back. The smile died on her lips when she saw the man standing just inside the door of the shop. A man she'd thought—hoped—she'd never see again.

Chapter Seventeen

Ravyn couldn't breathe. It was as if the newcomer's very presence had sucked all the air from the room. "What are you doing here?" she demanded, her throat aching with the effort it took for her to say those few words. From the corner of her eye she saw Nick flick a glance at her. He was probably deciding she was rude to everyone.

"Come on, baby, you're not happy to see me?" His voice was as smooth as fine whiskey. His hair was a wild mass of gold that would almost have looked like an angel's halo, if she hadn't known he was the Devil himself. He wore a tight black muscle shirt and jeans. A tattoo of a python wrapped his arm from elbow to wrist.

Sorina stood behind the counter, her normally kind face tight with anger. Sorina didn't hate anyone, but if she ever decided to try, Kayne would be at the top of her list.

"What do you want?" Ravyn's lungs felt restricted. It was all she could do to speak.

Kayne moved closer, bringing with him the musky scent she remembered so well. Instinctively, Ravyn stepped back.

"I heard what happened," he said, his voice filled with false concern. "I heard what that madman did to you. You were nearly murdered by a vicious serial killer. I was so worried, so horrified. Are you okay?"

Everyone was silent. Ravyn sucked in a breath. The last thing she wanted was for Nick to know such a personal detail about her. The last thing she wanted was to have to deal with some random asshole's morbid curiosity.

"I'm fine," she gritted out between clenched teeth. She took Kayne by the hand and pulled him into the back room, dropping her hold as soon as they were out of sight. But she knew it was too late. Nick had already heard. *Damn.*

With the curtain closed behind them, she and Kayne were hidden from view but still within earshot, so she kept her voice low. "You can drop the concerned act," she spat. "You don't give a damn about me or anyone else. I told you I never wanted to see you again."

"That was a while back, baby. I thought you'd miss me as much as I miss you. Besides, I told you, I was worried."

He reached out a hand, but she slapped it away. "That's a lie. I don't know what you're up to, but it's not concern that brought you here. And how dare you say something so private in front of a complete stranger? How did you find out what happened, anyway?"

Kayne looked down at his hands, spread them out as if the answer could be found between his splayed fingers. When he raised his eyes to meet her gaze, they glowed. It was a whirlpool of power that could suck her in, if she wasn't careful.

His entire face seemed to transform into something different, something evil. "Life has changed since I last saw you," he said. Even his voice was different. Although he still spoke quietly, there was a booming presence behind the words. "You wouldn't believe what I can do now, what power unleashing the spirits has given me."

A chill raced up Ravyn's spine. The energy emanating from Kayne was so strong, it was almost palpable. She wanted to step back farther. At the same time, she was mesmerized by his words, by his presence. "What do you mean?"

"I found myself in a town called Wyldewood. Ever heard of it?" When she shook her head, he continued. "I just wandered in, and in no time at all, I owned it. Everyone does my bidding. Everyone there lives to please me."

"You can't mess with free will. You *know* that," she chided. But her voice was no more than a whisper, and there was no conviction behind her words.

"Oh, but I can. I've learned the secret."

"But that will weaken you. You know that using your powers for forbidden goals will make you weaker until eventually you completely deteriorate."

Slowly Kayne shook his head, and the action was like that of a snake charmer. "I'm learning to overcome that. You can do it, too. I'll show you. We'll rule together. I can absorb the soul of another, and I will be replenished. Transcendent."

She'd read something of this in the book of black magic he'd given her. She'd been curious, yet at the same time afraid to learn more.

In spite of her misgivings, she asked, "What happens to that person?"

Kayne shrugged. "They are also reborn . . . so to speak. They lose their old soul, their old personality. And yes, there's the possibility of death. I haven't attempted it yet, so I'm not certain." His gaze gripped hers as he continued to speak in that hypnotic tone. "It's not too late to join me. You and I together would make a hell of a team. There's nothing we couldn't do. Nothing we *won't* do. I can help you with your problem."

Somehow she found her voice, but when she spoke it didn't sound at all like her. "What problem?"

"Him. The bastard who dared touch you. Dared threaten you. Together we can make him suffer as no human on earth has ever suffered."

Her brain told Ravyn to tell Kayne no, to make him go away so this strange feeling would leave too. But his words drew her like the pull of the earth on the moon. *Make him suffer?* *Yes.* She parted her lips, her head already nodding in agreement, the words forming in her throat, words accepting his offer and—

"Is everything okay?"

Ravyn and Kayne turned as one, swiveling toward the speaker. Nick had come into the back room. What was he doing here? He had no right to pry in affairs that had nothing to do with him!

"Everything's fine," Ravyn heard herself say. But with the interruption, reality returned. Her skin suddenly felt greasy, as if she'd come in contact with something vile. Kayne.

She glanced back at her old lover. His eyes blazed with fury. Cords of muscle in his neck stood out, emphasizing a small tattoo of a dagger just below his Adam's apple.

Kayne turned on Nick, his voice still low pitched but thrumming with rage. "Who the hell are you, and what do you think you're doing, walking in on us?"

"Sorina was worried about Ravyn. Asked me to come back here and check. You have a problem with that, pal?"

Nick was a few inches shorter than Kayne. His shoulders were wide and his arms muscular, but Kayne's physique was that of a warrior of old. Ravyn could imagine Kayne in battle gear, bare chested beneath a breastplate, golden skin pressed hotly against cool metal. . . . And of course there was the dark-forces thing Kayne had going on. She couldn't forget that. No, Nick didn't stand a chance against him.

He didn't seem aware of that fact. He stepped closer.

Kayne's eyes simmered, his face contorted with fury, and the air in the room dropped a few degrees. Couldn't Nick feel that? Didn't he know things weren't quite normal? Ravyn didn't see a hint of fear or hesitation. Part of her was tempted to let the two men go head-to-head. She didn't really care which one was the victor. They could shred one another to pieces as far as she was concerned.

But she couldn't allow that; Sorina would be furious with her. At least, that's what she told herself while lifting a hand to intercede between the two men.

"Okay. Stop it. He was just leaving, weren't you, Kayne?" The look she gave her ex-lover was a challenging one. She knew that if he called her on it, she would lose, but she took the chance regardless.

"Yes," he said, surprising her. He cast a scorching look at Nick and reached out for her hand. A chill that was part excitement, part revulsion raced through Ravyn, causing her skin to tingle from her fingers to her breasts. "But I'll be back."

She waited breathlessly for him to place his lips on her hand. Those lips that had trailed across her most intimate parts, that had spouted words of everlasting love and desire. All lies.

He didn't kiss her. Instead, he gently released her hand. For a moment it hung suspended between them. Then she let it fall to her side.

Kayne disappeared through the curtains. Ravyn and Nick stood silent, the air between them heavy with tension. The quiet was broken by the sound of the front door, and Ravyn released a breath. Kayne was gone.

She turned to Nick. "Sorina sent you back here? She normally likes to handle the role of protector herself."

"She said she wasn't sure what she'd do if she came back here and confronted your pal." He shoved his hands in his pockets. "Old boyfriend?"

Old boyfriend. Somewhat tame sounding, considering her and Kayne's history. She'd been eighteen when they met, so young, so impressionable. He'd had a commanding presence—and he was a witch, not a fickle mortal like her mother's boyfriends. He'd showered her with affection, with praise, making her feel as if she was the only thing in his life that mattered . . . which was something she'd never had, growing up. Everything had seemed perfect, the whole till-death-do-us-part scenario. Although, in the end, it had been the dark forces that had parted them, not death. When Kayne had wanted her to join him in his new and disturbing quest, she'd been devastated, pleading with him not to let the darkness take control, to stay with her. When she'd given him an ultimatum to shun the dark side or lose her love, she felt as though he'd crushed her heart in his powerful fists, for he hadn't chosen her. And he'd been banished by the coven.

"None of your business," she told Nick, hoping none of what she was feeling came through in her tone. "Please, just leave me alone."

"You know, I was just trying to help," Nick explained. "Your sister thought you were in trouble and needed rescuing. Maybe instead I interrupted your little love tryst. Is that why you're pissed?"

Ravyn released a breath and shook her head. "I'm not pissed. I'm just annoyed . . . about everything."

"So, is what he said true? About the serial killer? About what happened?"

"That's also none of your business."

"Look, maybe I could help you. Sometimes it helps to talk about things."

She stared at him. What was *with* this guy? What would it take to get him to leave her alone? Well, she knew how to make him leave her alone, but she'd done enough damage with her powers lately. "I don't want to talk about anything. Not with you. What I'd really like is for you to please leave. I think you're through for the day."

Nick sighed, shaking his head. "I'm going. I'm sorry. Really. About what I've done and about whatever happened to you. If you ever want to talk, let me know. I'll see you tomorrow, okay?"

She didn't reply. She simply stared, waiting for him to leave so she could give in to the mass of tremors surging through her body. Tremors of fear and anger.

Chapter Eighteen

Jay stood in front of the café next door to Gifts from the Heart. A few customers were scattered among the wrought-iron tables and chairs on the patio, but most had opted to dine indoors. The unseasonably warm temperatures the area had enjoyed for the past few days had fled, bringing a cool wind and a light misting drizzle.

Jay was glad about the rain for two reasons. One, it meant fewer people on the streets. Two, it gave him an excuse to carry the umbrella he used to hide his features. Just in case she spotted him.

A breeze carried the smell of food from the café, for a moment overpowering the scent of rain in the air. Soon both smells were gone, and all he could detect was burned flesh. The odor wouldn't go away; it was with him all the time now.

A woman holding a little girl's hand walked toward him. Her eyes flicked to Jay, then away. She hurried past, tugging on her daughter's hand. Jay's fingers gripped his umbrella in white-knuckled rage. Had the woman been frightened of him? He was a *surgeon*, for God's sake! A healer. Why would the bitch be afraid of him?

He suddenly realized his face was heated, scrunched up, and in spite of the cool day he was drenched in sweat. He then became aware of his other hand, which was hovering in front of his crotch, aching to touch himself yet afraid of the pain it would bring.

He dropped his hand and let his gaze slide to the

ground. He couldn't draw attention to himself. He needed to keep a low profile. He'd taken a leave of absence from the hospital, claiming exhaustion. There was nothing yet to raise a red flag. Of course, all this depended on whether Marshall could keep his damn mouth shut. If he couldn't, Jay would have to take care of him, too—but he didn't really want to. He'd never killed a man before, wasn't sure there would be much thrill in it. Of course, when you were talking about Marshall Weindot, the "man" thing was definitely in question. But Jay didn't want to do his dirty deeds too close to home. Sort of like the maxim that an animal shouldn't shit where it eats and sleeps.

A dark-haired man left the store. Jay had seen him before. Was it Ravyn Skyler's boyfriend? They didn't act very intimate with one another. But, of course, how could one become intimate with a she-devil? So far, the only person he'd seen her with on a regular basis was the blonde woman. Her sister, Sorina.

He looked up at the clouds, wondering if the rain would ever stop. His reconnaissance mission over for the day, he limped toward where his car was parked several blocks down the street.

His injury was less painful than before, almost manageable with the pain medication. He was very close to ready for a hunt. The only thing left to do was home in on the prey.

Nick sat in his office, sucking on an Altoid, pretending that was what he wanted instead of a drink and a smoke. He swallowed. How could his mouth be so dry with the mint on his tongue? He'd been eating mints continuously to keep from wanting a drink. They seemed to make him want a drink more.

In spite of the breeze coming through the half-open window, his office felt warm and oppressive. Outside, a mower roared, and the smell of freshly cut grass wafted in. Both the noise and the smell annoyed him, and he wondered if they were worth putting up with. Trying to ignore them, he stared at his computer screen.

He was researching each of the Tin Man's victims. Nothing had snagged his attention so far, although one vic did have a VPO out on an old boyfriend. Victim protection orders were pretty common stuff, but it might be worth checking out at some point. Nick jotted down both the victim's and the boyfriend's names. He looked up the guy's address and wrote that down, too, also entering the information in the computer on the spreadsheet he'd created.

He'd spoken to the employees who'd been working at Caribbean Nights the evening of Ravyn's attack. None of them saw anything unusual. They remembered the three women celebrating something, but hadn't noticed a bearded man watching them. They'd seen Ravyn's car still in the parking lot after closing, but said that wasn't unusual. Lots of times customers met one another at the restaurant and went home together, returning later to pick up the extra car. By the time the police came to check it out, they'd already heard about what had happened. None of them could give any further information.

Nick shifted in his chair, his skin tingling, itching, burning with his need for a drink. The feeling would pass; he just had to ignore it. He forced his mind back to the case.

Questions kept pounding at him. Why had Ravyn survived, when the others hadn't? Why had those boys heard a man scream instead of a woman? What had been going on with Ravyn's strange sojourn out by the lake the night he followed her? And what was it about the woman that made him want her even more than he did whiskey?

The office door opened and Marvin popped his head around it. "Hey, you busy?"

Nick huffed a breath out and clenched his jaw. "A little. What's up?"

"Just heading out and thought I'd stop by." Without an invitation, Marvin came into the office and sat in his usual spot across from Nick's desk. He wore a new Led Zepplin T-shirt. Nick guessed it was new because the clear plastic strip with the letter M for medium printed on it was still stuck to the front.

"Need any help with the case yet?" Marvin asked.

Nick sighed, his irritation increasing as the mower noise outside seemed to grow louder. "Not really."

Marvin pushed his lower lip out, reminding Nick of a child who's been told he can't have any candy. "There's not *anything* I can do?"

"Okay, fine. Maybe there is." Nick didn't know why he said it, other than that he was tired of the other man asking. "Here are the names of the Tin Man's victims." Nick tore off the piece of paper and shoved it across the desk at Marvin. "I'll send you the link for a Web site where you can search for information about them. Jot down anything you see that raises a flag. Anything that might link the victims or make them a target. You understand?"

Marvin's face beamed like xenon headlights. He picked up the sheet of paper and held it almost reverently. "Sure, I can do that. I watch a lot of those forensic investigation shows. I know exactly what kind of data you're looking for."

Right. You couldn't even find the sticker on your T-shirt. But Nick didn't say that. He said, "Great. Let me know what you learn. Take your time—I want you to be thorough and not miss anything. How about you just give me a report by the end of next week?"

Marvin nodded ecstatically. "Sure thing, dude." He left the office, all but skipping, his head bent over the sheet of paper.

Nick leaned back in his chair and closed his eyes, feeling as if he'd accomplished enough for the day. He'd learned there was nothing new to know about the victims, and also he hoped he'd gotten Marvin off his back for a week.

He felt bad for the guy. In the course of their acquaintance, through conversations that Nick hadn't initiated, he'd reluctantly learned that Marvin had had a rough childhood: a dad who came in and out of his life, a mother who took out her frustrations with the dad on Marvin and his sister. No friends to speak of. His only friend growing up, other than his sister, had been a love of numbers. He had an uncanny knack for them and was an excellent accountant. Unfortunately, his appearance deterred many clients, and Marvin's business was about as successful as his personal life. When Nick had advertised office space for rent, Marvin had been the only one who'd answered the ad. Guess it was apropos. Two misfits brought together by fate.

Yeah, Nick felt bad for him, but Jesus, it wasn't as if he didn't have plenty problems of his own.

Chapter Nineteen

Ravyn opened the door to find her sister, whose arms were weighted down by plastic grocery bags. Taking a few to lighten her load, Ravyn stepped aside and let Sorina in, then followed her to the kitchen.

"Are you trying to gain weight before the wedding?" she grunted as she heaved the bags onto the counter.

"This is my last night to let loose. After this, I'm going on a prewedding diet. Swearing off junk food. But tonight I live it up."

Ravyn pulled tortilla chips, bean dip, candy bars and assorted other snacks from the bags. "Good grief! You're planning to OD on junk food!"

Sorina grinned. "I brought stuff for margaritas, too."

"Now you're talking. Grab the blender and I'll cut the limes."

Fifteen minutes later, the two sisters were seated on the sofa, holding icy margaritas and munching on Ruffles and French onion dip.

Ravyn grabbed the remote and began flipping through the movie channels. "Scary or sappy?" she asked.

"Sappy," Sorina responded. "Oooh, yeah, there we go. *The Notebook*." She grinned. "We'll see if you can keep from crying."

"You *want* me to cry?" Ravyn shook her head, surprised. "What for?"

"You never do. It would be good for you."

"Yeah, right."

"Seriously, you really need to learn. It's scary the way you keep all your emotions bottled up."

Ravyn sipped her margarita and shook her head. "There's nothing bottled up. I have nothing to cry about. Don't see the good it would do, either."

"Trust me, it's cathartic." Sorina worried her bottom lip with her teeth, then warned, "What I'm about to tell you might make you want to cry."

Ravyn blinked. "What's that?"

Sorina took in a breath, held it, then let it out slowly. "I'm going to tell Justin the truth."

"What?"

"I want to tell Justin about us. I just don't think I can marry him without telling him. He'll figure it out eventually, or at least see something that will make him wonder, you know?"

"You *can't*." Ravyn's voice was sharp.

"Ravyn, you don't understand. I can't keep something like this from him."

Ravyn set her glass on the coffee table and rubbed the condensation from her hands onto the thighs of her jeans. "You don't know if you can trust him. Not *really*. You don't know how he'll react."

"I do know," her sister argued. "I love him. That's all I need to know."

Ravyn gave a derisive laugh. "Right."

"Every man isn't like Kayne, you know," Sorina said. There was a hint of tears in her voice.

"No, not like *him*, maybe," Ravyn agreed. "But it's not worth the risk. A mortal? For God's sake, Sorina!"

"Not all mortals are bad. Justin is proof of that. And then there's Nick."

Ravyn rolled her eyes. Nick? That guy was really starting to get under her skin. She definitely didn't trust him. One look at those tempestuous blue eyes and she just knew he was trouble. A tingle skipped over her flesh, and she shifted in her seat.

"Didn't the past teach you anything? Didn't Mother's total betrayal of you, her total lack of concern for her child, that she allowed that man to—"

"Don't." Sorina's voice was tight.

"Don't what? Don't speak the truth? Don't remind you of what can happen when you get too close to a mortal?"

Sorina's face scrunched up, and Ravyn knew her sister was going to cry. She took Sorina's trembling hands in her own.

"I'm sorry. Really, I am. Let's not talk about it anymore. Just promise me you'll think about it more before you tell Justin the truth. Think about what it could mean. Think about the consequences. All of them."

Sorina sniffled and wiped her hand across her nose. Nodding, she squeezed Ravyn's fingers. "Okay." She was silent for a moment, then turned her watery gaze to Ravyn. "I want to ask you something, and I want to know the truth. Are you really okay? I mean, after what happened?"

"I'm fine." Ravyn turned in the other direction and picked up her glass, taking a long gulp.

Sorina placed a hand on her arm, and Ravyn turned back to face her. Sorina's eyes, normally so trusting, were full of suspicion. "What are you hiding?"

Ravyn pulled away and stood. "Nothing. You want another drink?"

Sorina shook her head. "No, I want you to tell me the truth. Something's going on. You know you can trust me. Talk to me."

Yes, Ravyn knew she could trust her sister. And she didn't feel right about keeping the truth from her. So . . . maybe it was time to come clean.

Not looking at Sorina, she began to pace. "I lied to you about not using my magic."

"What?"

"I used it to escape. I burned him."

"Burned him?" Sorina repeated.

"I . . . set his genitals on fire."

A gasp escaped Sorina's lips. "Oh, Ravyn! You didn't tell me! I didn't . . ."

"I knew it was wrong. It was just . . . out of my control. I was so angry, so outraged . . ."

Sorina stood and stopped Ravyn's pacing with a hand on her shoulder. Looking into her sister's eyes, she smiled. "You weren't wrong. You had to get away. That man is evil. I know we aren't supposed to harm another, but when it comes to life or death . . . sometimes we have no choice."

Ravyn shrugged. "Maybe."

Sorina hugged her. "It'll be okay. You did the right thing."

Ravyn sighed, feeling unreasonably aggravated with her sister for letting her off the hook so easily. She loved her with all her heart, but sometimes she was annoyed by Sorina's sunny outlook, her unfailing faith in mankind, her forgiveness, her perfection. No wonder their mother loved Sorina better.

"Let's cast a protection spell," Sorina suggested.

"That's not necessary."

"Please? Just to make me feel better."

Ravyn sighed. "Okay, fine."

Together, they cleared off Ravyn's oval coffee table to use it as a makeshift altar. Ravyn gathered the necessary items. She placed sandalwood incense in a censer and positioned it in the center, along with a round mirror. Around the perimeter, they placed nine white pillar candles.

Sorina nodded toward Ravyn, indicating she should begin. One by one, Ravyn lit the candles, repeating each time, "Light of the Goddess protect us."

Once all the candles were glowing, Ravyn picked up

the mirror, and, making sure the flames were reflected in its surface, she chanted, "Great Goddess of the Lunar Light, secure us all this night. With this mirror to reflect the flames, your eternal protection burns bright."

She began to circle the table, keeping the flame of the candles reflected in the mirror. Sorina followed her lead, silently circling behind her. They had made six turns when the air in the room changed, charged with an electrical surge of energy. An aura of peace settled over Ravyn, and she was glad she'd let Sorina talk her into casting the spell.

"Now, the brick dust," Sorina said.

Brick dust was used to keep away evil. Ravyn and Sorina sprinkled it around all the doors and windows. Anyone who meant harm would not be able to pass the thresholds now.

"Feel better?" Ravyn asked.

Sorina nodded, and they doused the candles. "Now we can watch the movie."

"Wanna make a wager?" Ravyn asked.

Sorina's eyebrows lifted. "What kind?"

"I bet I can watch this movie without crying, and I bet you can't."

Sorina shook her head and laughed. "Only a dupe would take that bet. You're a freakin' robot."

Ravyn punched her lightly on the shoulder, then jerked a thumb toward the kitchen. "Shut up and go make me another margarita."

Sorina laughed and headed toward the kitchen. At the doorway, she stopped and looked back at Ravyn. "I love you," she said.

Smiling, Ravyn replied, "Back at you, sis."

Ravyn tried to open her eyes but couldn't. She wasn't sure if she was dreaming or awake. She was aware of Sorina's soft snores next to her in the king-size bed, but she couldn't see her.

A whisper traveled through the darkness. The words were indecipherable.

"What are you saying?" Ravyn mumbled softly, half incoherent. "Who are you?"

The voice became clear, although it still spoke in a whisper.

I'm your soul, your everything.

With those words came recognition. Kayne. Fear raced through Ravyn, and she knew she should wake up, but couldn't. A touch shivered over her breasts, lightly grazing her belly and moving down to her thighs.

She shook her head. *Please stop.*

You don't want me to. You've missed this as much as I have.

Yes . . . no! A lump came to her throat. She squeezed her legs together but felt them being gently pried apart. She shook her head back and forth on the pillow, unable to resist the pull, even though there was no true force exerted. *What are you doing to me?*

Loving you. Having you. As I always should have. As I will forever.

The sensation was stronger now: a hand on the inside of her thighs, stroking, hovering just below the crotch of her panties. Hot moisture trickled between her legs. Her nipples tightened. She still couldn't open her eyes.

A moan left her throat, and she thrashed her head from side to side. *No, no, no.* She raked her hand downward, pushing at an invisible force. The sensation left as abruptly as it had come.

You'll come to me. In time, you'll see that you need me.

No, I don't need you.

Not now, but you will.

Ravyn's eyes flew open. Her breath came in heavy

pants, and where moments ago she'd been engulfed in warmth, now she was freezing, her teeth chattering violently in the frigid air of the room.

A dream. Only a dream. But it had seemed so real. She squeezed her eyes closed, trying to shake off the lethargic feeling of being somewhere between sleep and wakefulness. She looked over to Sorina's side of the bed, hoping she hadn't woken her sister. But the bed was empty.

A flutter of panic tickled her heart. Where was she?

"Sorina?" Ravyn called out.

No answer.

She tried to pull the covers off but couldn't. Her arms were weak. It was as if her mind was awake but her body was still in a deep slumber. She couldn't keep her eyes open.

"Sorina," she whispered just before she fell asleep once more. The faint scent of musk surrounded her as she slipped back into oblivion.

Chapter Twenty

She was different from her sister. They were both beautiful, but this girl's beauty was softer. Like a sunlit meadow of delicate flowers. Ravyn's beauty was that of a wild creature like a panther: untamed, feral.

Jay couldn't believe how easy it had been, how easily he'd taken her. But the voice had instructed him, and here she was. All his.

He hated losing the cabin, didn't like bringing his victims to his home, but it was probably safer this way. Finding alternate locations was a bit too risky. The only way they would discover evidence here is if the authorities searched his basement. And if things got to that point, he was screwed anyway.

The girl's eyes fluttered. The sedative was wearing off, so he would need to give her Valium. The voice had told him she couldn't hurt him as long as he kept narcotics in her system. That's where he'd made the mistake with Ravyn: he'd let the drugs wear off. He wanted this one awake but under the influence.

The voice—not his mother's this time, for this voice was masculine, mesmerizing—was guiding him. He didn't recognize the speaker, but he knew he could trust the voice. It had told him everything he needed to know. But this would be the true test. This would prove everything.

The woman in his bed opened her eyes and looked up at him, and Jay's heart pounded, partly from fear and partly with excitement. He studied those blue irises for any change that would warn him of pending danger . . . but he saw nothing except confusion.

Her brow creased, and her words came out in a hoarse whisper. "Who are you?"

Jay smiled. "Who do you think I am?"

The girl swallowed, closed her eyes. Tears squeezed from between her lids, "Please don't kill me," she said.

"If you know who I am, you know that's a futile request." He injected the Valium into her vein as he spoke. "Are you afraid?"

She nodded. "Please, I know you don't want do to this. You're in pain, or you wouldn't want to hurt others. Someone's been very cruel to you."

Jay gave a harsh laugh. Counseling from a soon-to-be victim? This was a first. "What the hell do you know? You would be wise to worry about yourself, not me."

"I *am* worried. Oh, God. They'll be devastated. Ravyn . . . Mother . . . Justin." The girl's words slurred. "We're getting married."

"There's going to be a very long postponement," he whispered, leaning so close that he could see the pores in her smooth cheeks.

"Where are we? I was at Ravyn's, I heard Arthur outside. . . ." Her eyes flew up to meet his. "Is he here? Have you done something to my cat?"

He hadn't seen a cat. The voice had told him Sorina would be outside Ravyn's home, and she had been. Had the voice also placed her cat there to lure her?

The *how* didn't matter. Not really. Sorina was here. And she was his.

The voice was giving him power, control. He knew the voice was on his side. There was no end to what he could do. He could even make his ultimate fantasy a reality. . . . But not now, not with this one. That fantasy would take some planning. And it required a particular someone to share it with.

Jay stepped back and while Sorina watched, pressed the trigger on a blowtorch and held the blade to the flame.

Fresh tears filled Sorina's eyes, spilling over and soaking her hair as she lay on her back. She *was* afraid. Beautifully afraid. Eyes blazing with terror, yet muddled from the Valium, she whispered, "Please."

Jay's groin tingled. *Yes.*

He hesitated when he saw something else in her eyes. Sympathy? She felt *sorry* for him? What the hell was wrong with her? Didn't she know what was going to happen? Didn't she realize what he was capable of? He was sure she did, and yet she still felt sorry for him.

He shook off the twinge of remorse that wriggled like a worm inside his gut. He held the knife in front of her face and leaned toward her, and he celebrated the moment her sympathy turned into despair.

On Monday morning, Nick's cell phone rang just after Dorothy doused the witch with a bucket of water. He paused the movie and picked up.

"I told you I'd keep you in the loop," Sheriff Whitehall said. "It's not in the papers yet, but it will be soon."

"What will be in the papers?"

"They found another vic."

Nick closed his eyes. He hadn't found the bastard in time, and now another girl was dead. He swallowed and looked back at the screen. Judy Garland's features were frozen in a look of horrified confusion. Much the way he felt right now. "Shit," was all he could manage.

"Yep, my thoughts exactly. A homeless guy found her down in Bricktown last night. Looks like she was killed sometime between Saturday night and Sunday morning."

Bricktown was a restored warehouse district in downtown Oklahoma City that was now a tourist attraction. It boasted several shops and restaurants, a movie theater and a Triple-A baseball stadium. However, some of the nearby areas were derelict and dangerous. Nick wasn't surprised that location had been the chosen place to dump a body.

"Does the OCPD know who she is?"

"They didn't, so they faxed me a photo hoping I might. Which was the damndest thing of all. I recognized her. And that really threw me for a loop."

"Yes?" Nick prompted. *Get on with it, old man.*

"You know the Skyler woman?"

Nick doubled over in his recliner as if he'd taken a punch to the gut. "The—? Oh, God." Spots swam in his vision, and he squeezed his eyes closed. "Jesus," he choked out past the lump in his throat. A roar started in his ears as if they were pressed to the inside of the world's largest seashell. "Jesus," he said again, the word leaving him in a *whoosh* of air.

The roar was so loud, he almost didn't hear Whitehall's next words. When they finally penetrated his panicked brain, he gasped in a mixture of relief and revulsion.

". . . her sister. Beautiful girl, too. They're heading over to get the mom so she can ID the body."

"Sister?" Nick repeated dumbly. As if a black curtain lifted, his vision cleared and he started to breathe again.

"Yeah. Sorina Skyler. I met her the night I went out on the call about her sis. Sorry sonofabitch. What do you make of him going after the sister? Can't be coincidence."

Sorina. Nick felt guilty at his relief that it wasn't Ravyn, and at the same time nauseated. Sorina was a good person. Kind, compassionate, beautiful. Innocent.

Motherfucker.

"Are you sure it's her?" Nick asked.

"Pretty sure. We'll know more after the mother takes a

look. Sorry-ass thing to ask a momma to do, though, you know?"

"Yeah. I know. Listen, thanks for the info. I gotta go," Nick grunted.

"Sure. I'll give you a yell if anything else comes up."

Nick dialed Ravyn's shop, wondering if she knew about her sister yet. When she answered, he couldn't detect anything in her voice. He wanted to ask if Sorina was there, hoping Whitehall had made a mistake. But if Whitehall hadn't, asking about her dead sister would be too cruel.

"Are you there alone?" Nick asked instead.

A brief pause. "Yes. Sorina was supposed to be here, but she's not, and I haven't been able to reach her."

A sick feeling wound through Nick's chest. "Hang tight. I'm coming over."

"Why? What's going on?" There was a trace of apprehension in her voice.

Nick raced to his car as he spoke, the cell phone stuck to his ear. "I'll explain when I get there."

Heart laden with sadness, he drove to her shop. He dreaded giving Ravyn the news, but he'd rather it came from him than a stranger or the television. At least, he thought he'd rather it came from him.

She was still alone when he arrived. She stood with her hands clasped, rubbing the inside of her right palm with her left thumb, a nervous tic he'd seen more than once. She looked at him calmly, but a tiny twitching at the corner of her mouth betrayed her anxiety.

He took her hands in his, and she tensed but didn't pull away. "I'm afraid I have some bad news," he said.

Something changed in her face. It was subtle but unmistakable. A white line formed around her lips. The amber flecks in her eyes seemed to melt away until there was nothing but the shimmer of emeralds.

"It's Sorina," Nick continued. "They found a woman's body, and they think it's her."

Ravyn stared at him for a moment, then spoke. That smoky voice was strained and cold. "Think?"

"They need someone to ID the body. Your mother should be on her way there now."

Ravyn turned away, nodding, as if she were in a trance. "Sorina spent the night with me Saturday night. When I woke, she was gone. I tried to reach her all day yesterday and again this morning. I called and stopped by her apartment, but she wasn't there. Her fiancé is out of town, so I couldn't ask him. I knew something was wrong." She shed no tears, just tightened her lips; the white around her mouth and the look in her eyes were her only reactions. Was she in shock? Did the truth need to be confirmed before she could grieve? It would hit her sooner or later, most likely sooner, and when it did, she'd be a wreck.

"I'll drive you to the station," Nick suggested. "I have some friends there, and maybe they can make this a little easier on you."

She opened her mouth, and he thought she was going to protest, but after a moment she looked at the ground and nodded.

Chapter Twenty-one

Ravyn was silent during the drive, and Nick didn't try to talk to her. The hysterics hadn't started yet. They would probably happen when she knew for sure the dead girl was her sister.

He felt a tightening in his throat and wondered if he might cry before she did. He hadn't known Sorina extremely well, but he'd liked her. A lot. She was warm and friendly, one of those people he immediately respected. One of those people the world couldn't afford to lose. Like Annie.

When they arrived at the police station, Nick led Ravyn inside and spoke to the woman at the window.

Betty smiled, her plump face lighting with pleasure. "Hey, Nick, how are you?"

"I've been better. I need to see . . ." He stopped when he saw Betty look over his shoulder and grimace.

He turned. Jacqueline stood behind him, awkwardly shifting from one foot to the other. He hadn't seen her since he'd turned in his badge. Hadn't spoken to her since the night Annie died. He couldn't. The guilt wouldn't let him.

She looked good—but then she'd always been a beautiful woman. She was tan, with large brown eyes and an athlete's trim body. Her short auburn hair framed her face, bobbed at the line of her jaw.

Ravyn looked from her to Nick but didn't speak.

Finally Jacqueline said, "Hello, Nick."

He gave her a nod. "Jacqueline."

"What are you doing here?"

"I'm here to see Carlos." Carlos and Scott were the lead detectives on the case, and he damn sure didn't want to talk to Harris.

"Follow me back," Jacqueline said.

Nick and Ravyn followed as the woman slid her badge through an electronic reader and opened the door, holding it with her foot so they could pass through. She walked the pair back to Carlos's desk, and the detective looked up when they approached.

"I'll leave you with him," Jacqueline said. "Take care of yourself, Nick."

"You, too. Thanks," he replied. He didn't watch as she walked away, but he breathed easier when she was gone.

Carlos stood and shook Nick's hand. "What brings you here?" he asked.

"The girl they found in Bricktown. Has the mother ID'd the body yet?"

Carlos didn't speak for a few moments, probably wondering how Nick already knew about the crime, but he didn't ask. "They can't find the mother." His eyes went to Ravyn, and Nick saw that the detective recognized her. He and Harris had interviewed her, no doubt.

"This is Ravyn, the sister."

Carlos nodded, then addressed Ravyn. "Would you mind taking a look? See if it's your sister?"

Nick placed a comforting hand on her arm. "Are you up to it?" he asked. "You don't have to."

For a split second he saw a crumpling of her features, and knew she was about to lose it. But as quickly as it came, the expression was gone, and he wondered if he'd imagined it.

She lifted her eyes. "Where is she?"

Carlos drove Nick and Ravyn to the morgue. Nothing

was said during the trip. Ravyn sat with her hands clasped in her lap, staring out the passenger window.

Nick spread Carmex under his nose as they pulled into the parking lot, and he offered some to Ravyn. When she shook her head, he shrugged and followed her and Carlos inside.

Nick hadn't been here for years, but even using the lip balm, the olfactory assault was the same as he remembered: the sour stench of decay, a smell like rotting produce left out in the sun too long. Even though the smell of antiseptic was strong, it couldn't mask the other underlying odors. He clamped his lips together and tried to breathe as little of the putrid air as possible.

Nick and Carlos stood a few steps back as the ME pulled out a metal drawer. A sheet covered the victim from the neck down. Her grayish skin was so pale that it almost made her blond hair look black. There were no visible marks on her face, but Nick could only imagine what the flesh beneath the sheet must look like.

Ravyn stared, dry-eyed and expressionless, for what seemed like several minutes.

Sighing, Carlos leaned toward Nick and whispered, "So, it's not her?"

His throat tight with unshed tears, Nick stared in amazement at Ravyn's stoic demeanor. "No," he whispered when he could speak around the stone in his chest. "It's her."

Carlos's eyebrows drew together. He glanced at Ravyn. "Miss . . . is this your sister?"

She stood silently for a few more moments. Then, nodding, she stepped back and walked past them out of the room.

Ravyn sat alone in her darkened living room. She hadn't turned on a light since Sorina's death. Hadn't left the house. Hadn't cleaned up the remnants of their sleepover. Watered-down margaritas still sat on the coffee table amid a bag of Doritos and a bowl of bean dip.

They'd cast a protection spell. It had worked—inside the house. But Sorina had gone outside and left herself vulnerable. The evil couldn't pass the brick dust, but it could entice Sorina outside. Or at least, from every indication, including the police investigation, that's what appeared to have happened. Sorina, for some reason, had left the house in the middle of the night.

Ravyn remembered how she'd felt the death chill right after the Tin Man first attacked her. She'd known something more would happen, yet she hadn't done anything about it. She hadn't gone and done her duty, hadn't helped the police. If she'd done more to assist the authorities in capturing him . . .

A raw ache tore at her chest, traveled up her throat and stopped there. She hadn't shed a tear. Hadn't cried since she was a child. Would she feel better if she did? She thought not. Tears wouldn't bring Sorina back.

A knock sounded on her front door. She thought about ignoring it, but it could be the authorities. They might have found out something about the killer. They'd interviewed her after she'd identified Sorina's body, but she could tell they were again disappointed in her answers. Still, there was nothing more she could offer.

She opened the door. Justin stood there, a large box in his arms, his eyes bloodshot and tear filled. He was good-looking, although his buzz cut, tattoos and large-gauge ear piercings weren't her thing.

"I thought you might want some of her stuff," he said, his voice raw and strained.

"Come in." She led him inside. As he set the box down and opened it, she said, "You don't need to." Reaching out a hand to stop him she added, "I'll go through it later."

He nodded. "If there's anything else you want that's not here, let me know."

"Thanks." She noticed a black garment at the top of the box. She reached out and picked it up. It was a witch costume, and she smiled at the memory. When they were in junior high, Sorina had dressed as a witch for Halloween. Ravyn had been nervous and humiliated, but Sorina thought it was hilarious. Ravyn had always envied her sister's gusto for life and her nonchalant attitude. Everything had been easy for Sorina. Everything except surviving to her twenty-eighth birthday.

Underneath the witch costume was a photo of Justin, Sorina and Ravyn. Justin pulled it from the box and let out a sob, dropping to his knees. Ravyn stood awkwardly, then reached out a hand and placed it on top of his head, not saying anything. Not knowing what to say.

After a moment, he stood. "I'm sorry. This is just so hard. I feel so guilty. I was gone when it happened. If I had been in town . . ."

"It wouldn't have made a difference."

He nodded and wiped at his eyes. "I better go. Your mother is out in the car."

Ravyn was taken aback. "Is she? Why?"

"She has Arthur. Since you're allergic, she didn't want to come in. She didn't want to bring him inside, and she didn't want to leave him alone in the car."

But Ravyn had meant to ask why the hell was her mother here, period, not why hadn't she come in. "Why does she have Arthur?"

"I travel too much, so she's taking him."

"No, she's not," Ravyn said.

"What?"

Ravyn didn't answer. Instead, she swept out the door and to Justin's car.

Her mother looked at her through the window, then

opened the door and stepped out with the cat in her arms. "Ravyn, darling, how are you? I didn't want to bring the cat in, but I so wanted to see you." Gwendyl's face was mottled and covered with tears. For once, her makeup was streaked and haphazardly applied.

"Give me the cat."

"What, dear? You don't need to be near him with your allergies. I'll take care of him."

"You couldn't take care of your daughters, you can't take care of yourself, so how the hell are you going to take care of the cat?" Her mother's face blanched, and fresh tears leapt to her eyes. Ravyn was unmoved. She reached out, palms up. "Give me the cat."

Gwendyl's gaze dropped to the scar on Ravyn's palm. The cat squirmed in her arms, and she eased her hold. Raising her head to meet Ravyn's eyes, her face pale, she silently handed over the cat.

Ravyn turned to go back into the house when her mother spoke. "You were never satisfied. Nothing I did was ever enough."

Haltingly, Ravyn turned back. "Nothing you did? Good God, you put every man that came into your life before us. And the only one you stuck with for any length of time was the sonofabitch that raped my sister."

Justin gasped, and Gwendyl cut her eyes at him. She turned back to Ravyn. "That's not true. Don't say that."

"You know it *is* true, Mother. You knew it, and you let it go on. I wanted to leave so many times. I wanted to get away from you, but I couldn't leave my baby sister behind. Now she's gone. The only reason I had to ever look at you again is gone. Get out of my sight and don't ever come back."

"Please," Justin interrupted tearfully. "Please don't fight. Sorina wouldn't want this."

The two Skylers looked at him but didn't respond. He

shook his head and climbed into his car, slamming the door and blaring a rock station on the radio.

"I'm your mother," Gwendyl growled at Ravyn. "I love you, and I did the best I could."

"You mean, like the time you burned my hand when I was eight years old, just so I'd remember not to do magic in front of your husband? Just so he wouldn't know you were a witch?"

Gwendyl shook her head. "That's not true. I did it to protect you, to protect our secret for all of us. You were such a wayward child, always up to something, always practicing magic. I just wanted to show you what could happen. I didn't mean to hurt you." Her lower lip trembled and she reached out a hand. "I love you, Ravyn. You're all I have now."

Ravyn shifted her sister's cat in her arms, comforted by the feel of his warm body, knowing that Sorina would have wanted her to care for him. She stared at her mother, then shook her head. "You should have thought about that a long time ago. It's too late for us."

Chapter Twenty-two

Ravyn stared toward the front of the funeral home. She watched her mother's performance through a blur of grief, feeling oddly removed from the events around her. Justin took the mike after her mother left the podium, but he couldn't form a coherent sentence, so deep were the sobs strangling his throat.

Sorina's ashes would be scattered in a ritual, but for now they sat in an urn at the front of the room. Gwendyl and Justin had asked Ravyn to say a few words, but she'd refused. The only things she needed to say were to Sorina. There was no need to address this group of people, some of whom were complete strangers to her.

After the service was over, Ravyn turned to leave and caught sight of a small figure slipping outside the door. There was something familiar about it, and . . . Wait, she knew! It was her crazy neighbor. What the hell was *she* doing here? The time had come for a confrontation.

Ravyn headed toward the door, ignoring the sympathetic murmurs of those who recognized her as Sorina's sister. She noticed Nick at the back of the room and gave him a quick nod before opening the door and stepping outside. The sight that greeted her made her halt in her tracks. A horde of reporters and cameramen filled the lawn.

A woman with stark red lips and pale blonde hair slicked back in a tight ponytail stuck a microphone in her face. "How does it feel to survive an attack by the

Tin Man, only to have him murder your sister?" the reporter asked. Her voice carried over all the rest of the hubbub.

Ravyn stared, and the reporter's gaze flickered uncertainly. Then the mask was back in place. "Miss Skyler, how does one recover from such a tragedy? Your survivor's guilt must be overwhelming."

Ravyn clenched her hands at her sides, wanting to slap the woman across her perfect features. Taking a deep breath, she ignored the reporter and stepped off the porch.

She tried to push her way through the crowd, but the media hounds closed in, blocking her way, shoving cameras and microphones into her face. She gritted her teeth and halted. Indiscernibly, she flicked her fingers toward the mob. A series of pops sounded, and murmurs rose from the cameramen as they gaped at the smoke wafting from their cameras.

The blonde reporter squealed and dropped her microphone. "The damn thing shocked me!" she shrieked.

Ravyn ignored them all and followed the retreating figure of the old woman. She was just on the edge of the grounds when Ravyn caught up. Reaching a hand out, Ravyn grabbed the woman by the shoulder and whirled her around. She wore a gray coat over a navy dress, and black lace-up oxford shoes. Pale green eyes in a timeworn face peered at Ravyn from beneath a shock of white hair.

"Who are you?" Ravyn demanded.

The woman shook her head. "Just someone who cared about your sister." Her voice was surprisingly strong, considering her appearance.

"How did you know my sister? Why have you been watching me? I know you live near my home. I've seen you sneaking around. Who are you?"

The woman sighed. She gazed into Ravyn's eyes, and her expression softened as her shoulders slumped. "Can we go somewhere and talk?"

There were benches several feet away, between the funeral home and the road. Ravyn motioned toward the benches, and the stranger followed her.

When they were seated, the woman reached out and took Ravyn's hand. Her own was dry and wrinkled but warm. She squeezed Ravyn's fingers gently, and Ravyn looked at her in surprise but didn't pull free.

"Who are you?" Ravyn asked again.

Tears filled the woman's green eyes. "I'm your grandmother. Your father's mother."

Ravyn wasn't sure she'd heard correctly. When the words sank in, she knew they weren't true. They couldn't be true. "What? That's impossible." She jerked her hand from the woman's grasp.

"Because you were told I'm dead?"

Ravyn narrowed her gaze. "I remember you—I mean, her—from when I was very small. But she went away, and Mother said she died."

The woman clasped her hands in her lap and shook her head. "No, child. I didn't die." She gazed toward where the mourners and reporters were slowly exiting the parking lot. "Though sometimes I wish I had."

"Why would she lie to us?" Ravyn asked. But even as she said the words, she knew they were ridiculous. Her mother would lie about anything.

"Let me start from the beginning." The woman leaned back on the bench and slumped as if suddenly exhausted. "Your father was dying, and I loved him more than life itself. I was desperate to save him, so I made a grave mistake. I turned to the dark arts."

Ravyn gasped. "You? You're a . . ."

She nodded. "Like your Kayne, I was driven from the coven. Unlike him, I did it for my son. I wanted to save him."

Ravyn ignored the fact that the woman knew about her personal life, knew about Kayne. She was a witch, and she'd been practically stalking her, so she probably knew pretty much everything. "You didn't have to practice black magic to save him. We have the ability, although it's at tremendous personal cost."

"Right. But in doing so, we lose our place in the coven and a part of ourselves; we're weakened. I didn't want that. I wasn't sure what kind of shape he'd be in, even if I saved his life. I knew he'd need me." She gave Ravyn an apologetic look. "I knew he couldn't count on your mother."

"But you didn't save him. Father died."

"What did your mother tell you about how your father died?"

"Just that he was ill."

"He had brain damage from a beating. Some men at a bar jumped him and nearly beat him to death because they thought he was in a cult, after they saw him do magic."

"He was performing magic in public? At a bar?"

"I'm afraid so. He was reckless and had a drinking problem. The combination was very dangerous." The old woman looked at Ravyn as if hesitant to say the next words, and she spoke slowly. "Your mother loved you very much but was afraid you would be like him. That the same thing would happen to you. She lived in fear. You were so smart, so powerful."

"Is that why she burned my hand with a candle?" Ravyn gave a harsh laugh. "How thoughtful."

"I know you thought she did it to protect herself, but it was actually to protect you."

"Huh." Ravyn snorted. "Don't you think that was a bit extreme?"

Her grandmother nodded. "Your mother can be unstable, and yes, she went about punishing you in the wrong way. But never doubt that she loved you girls very much."

"Oh? You really believe that? Do you know what happened to Sorina?" Ravyn felt the threat of tears clogging her chest, but she swallowed them back. "What she let *that man* do to my sister?"

The woman gave a quick nod. "What happened to Sorina was inexcusable. Your mother couldn't accept that her husband was hurting her daughter, so she ignored it. Eventually she gained the strength to do what was right. Eventually she divorced him."

"Eventually, she divorced them all. Even the good ones." Ravyn shook her head, disgusted. "Why are you defending her?"

"I'm not. I just want you to have the whole picture. I want you to know the entire truth about your family and your past. Your mother and I have never gotten along. I hated her for taking you girls away from me. I haven't been able to be with you since you were six and Sorina was three. But I've always been nearby. Always watching you. I wanted to protect you both. And now this . . ." Her voice trailed away, and tears trickled down along the creases in her face.

"What happened to my father? If you began practicing black magic to save him, why isn't he here?"

The old woman dabbed at her tears and shook her head. "I healed him. He was fine. But . . ."

"But what? What happened?"

"He couldn't stand what it had done to me. He couldn't stand what I'd become, that I'd reverted to black magic, and he couldn't live with your mother's betrayal."

"Betrayal?"

"Even while he lay dying . . . she took other lovers. She wouldn't settle for a man who couldn't give her all the things she desired, so she found others to take his place." The old woman swiped at a fresh wave of tears, snuggling more deeply into her worn gray coat. "Once he was in his right mind and saw what was happening, he took his life."

Ravyn's hand flew to her mouth. Her father had killed himself? Her grandmother had turned to the dark arts and risked her own well-being to save her son and then lost it all, anyway?

"Was it worth it?" she asked.

"What?"

"Would you do it again? To save your son?"

The old woman looked into Ravyn's eyes and slowly nodded. "I would do it a thousand times to save someone I love. To save him . . . to save you. I would have done it to save Sorina, if I could have."

Ravyn looked away. Her grandmother must know that she could have saved Sorina and hadn't. That if she'd found the Tin Man right after he attacked her, he never would have had a chance to claim another victim, she'd never have lost her precious sister. Her grandmother knew her failure.

Ravyn stood. "I need to get back." The conversation with this woman was a bit more than she'd been prepared for. She felt drained and incredibly sad. "Good-bye."

But as Ravyn turned to go, her grandmother's voice stopped her. "You did all you could. It wasn't your fault. But now it's up to you to find him. You must find and destroy him. Trust Nick."

Ravyn stopped and turned, wanting to ask the woman what she meant, wanting to ask what she knew about the man who'd been helping out at the store. But she couldn't. For some reason, Ravyn was afraid of the answers. Afraid to know more than she'd learned already. Without responding, she quickly walked back to the parking lot of the funeral home.

Chapter Twenty-three

When she arrived at her car, Nick was standing next to it. He looked somber and handsome in a charcoal gray sport jacket, black shirt and black silk tie. His blue eyes offered sympathy, and for a moment she wanted to take what he offered. It was strange, considering she'd only known him for a few weeks, but he seemed familiar, solid—as though if she rested in his arms, if she let him shut out the world, all the bad would go away.

She blinked, giving herself a mental shake. Where had that last thought come from? Had to be the grief and strain of the past few days.

More sharply than was necessary, she said, "What are you doing?"

"Waiting for you. We need to talk."

Ravyn shook her head and walked over to open the driver's side door. "I'm a little drained. I've had enough for one day. It will have to wait."

He reached out and placed a hand on her arm to stop her. Ravyn's eyes flew to his, and she pulled away.

"It can't wait," he said softly. "There's something I have to tell you."

She sighed. "So, tell me."

He looked around. "Can we go somewhere to talk?"

Ravyn shook her head wearily. Why did everyone want a heart-to-heart today? "Whatever you have to say, we can talk right here. I'm ready to go home, so make it quick."

"Okay. I lied to you."

Ravyn shrugged. "So? Everyone lies. I barely know you. Why should it matter?"

"What if I told you my lie contributed to your sister's death?"

A hard and sharp pain ripped through her stomach. For a moment she couldn't speak. Swallowing, she shrugged and tried to keep her voice steady as she replied, looking straight into his eyes. "Then I'd say that you and I have something in common."

Surprise flickered in his gaze. "What are you talking about?"

Ravyn looked away, watched the breeze pick up the fallen leaves on the sidewalk and carry them a few feet before dropping them again. She felt similar, as if she were being carried along in a breeze with no purpose, an insignificant part of nature that wouldn't be noticed if she disappeared forever.

She jerked on the door handle and turned back to Nick. "I tell you what. I won't ask you to confess your sins, and you don't ask me to confess mine. Deal?"

"Jesus." Nick shook his head. "And I thought I was a cold sonofabitch. Your sister's dead. Don't you even care?"

Clenching her teeth, she growled, "Of course I care. But what good would it do to get all worked up and bare my soul?"

She started to climb inside her car, but he grabbed her arm. "Because that's part of what makes us human."

Ravyn looked at his hand, then up at his face. She pulled away and slipped inside her car. "Good-bye, Nick."

"Ravyn, wait. I have to tell you this. Please."

She bit her lip and looked up at him, leaving the door open. "What?"

"I'm a private detective." His eyes searched hers, but she didn't react. "I was hired by the husband of one of the Tin Man's victims to find the killer. That's why I came to your store. I wanted to get close to you to find out what you knew about him. I didn't need a job. I don't even have a daughter. . . ."

Ravyn turned to stare out the windshield. She processed this information and felt mild surprise, but not betrayal. Not really. What did it matter? She barely knew him, and she was accustomed to subterfuge. She'd done it herself.

"Is that it?" she asked.

"Good God, if I'd told you the truth, if I'd talked to you and your sister, she may not have—"

"It wouldn't have made a difference. Now, I really do need to go." Ravyn tugged on the armrest, and Nick stepped back, hands in his pockets. As soon as she'd slammed the door, she drove away. She didn't look back.

It was early evening, and the sky was dark with the threat of rain. Each morning and afternoon since the funeral three days ago, Nick had both called Ravyn and driven by her shop, only to find it was still shut. In spite of the tight control she seemed to have on her emotions, or maybe because of it, he was worried.

He drove out to her lake house, wondering how she'd react when he showed up uninvited. He'd have to explain how he knew where she lived, but that wasn't a big concern. She couldn't think any less of him than she already did.

He knocked on the door and waited. No answer. Her car was in the driveway. What if she'd done something to herself? What if . . . ?

He knew he shouldn't, but it wasn't like she was his greatest fan anyway. If he did this and she hated him . . . well, things would pretty much be the same. He stepped back, prepared to kick the door in. Then he stopped. Stepping forward, he tried the knob. Unlocked.

Nice, Lassiter, almost broke down an open door.

He let himself in and found the house in darkness. "Ravyn?" he called out. No response.

She had to be home, but the silence said otherwise. Fear kicked up his heart rate, and he moved quickly through the darkened room. He had no idea where a light switch might be.

"Shit," he muttered when his shin came in contact with a hard surface. A table. He stopped and looked around. His eyes had just begun to adjust, and he could make out shapes of the furniture. But no Ravyn.

He headed toward a set of stairs that led up to a loft. That was when he heard it: muffled crying. It couldn't be Ravyn, could it?

He stopped and turned toward the sound, followed it into the kitchen.

There she was. Although it was also dark in this room, the illumination from the LEDs on the stove and microwave gave enough light for him to see. Ravyn sat on the floor in the corner, her knees drawn up, a large white cat cradled in her arms. She wore a forest green Eskimo Joe's sweatshirt over frayed blue jeans, and her feet were bare. Her hair was pulled back in a ponytail and looked dull and lifeless, as if it hadn't been washed in days. Her eyes streamed and her nose was red. Her face was devoid of makeup, and she looked softer, more vulnerable without the heavy black eyeliner she normally wore.

She sneezed and then hiccupped. Nick wasn't sure if she was crying or having an allergy attack. Baffled, he went over and dropped onto the floor beside her.

She turned to him, not showing any surprise at his sudden appearance in her kitchen. "I can't do it. I can't even take care of her cat!" The words ended on a sob.

"What?"

She looked down at the animal and shook her head.

"Arthur is Sorina's cat. She loved him, but I'm allergic to cats, and I can't take care of him. She was always doing for others. The one time she needs me . . ." Another sob wrenched her body. She swiped a sleeve across her nose, and that one action seemed so fragile, so childlike, it rocked Nick to the core.

"Hey, it's okay." He slipped the cat out of Ravyn's grip and held it in one arm while he put the other arm around her shoulders.

She covered her face in her hands but didn't pull away. "I haven't cried since I was eight years old."

Her shoulders shook beneath his arm, and his breath caught. Small, keening wails of grief poured forth, punctuated by snuffles as she tried to catch her breath. He wanted to pull her against him, hold her tightly to his chest until she was all cried out. But he knew touching her at all was pushing it. So, he listened, keeping his touch comforting but impersonal. All the while his insides churned with sympathy, with an ache to ease her suffering, to absorb her pain.

She turned her face to him, and in the dimness he could see the swollen eyes, the red nose, the blotchy complexion. And still she was beautiful.

"Sorina said I needed to learn how to cry." Ravyn looked away and her voice dropped to a whisper. "She just didn't tell me how to stop."

Nick put the cat down and pulled her tighter into his embrace, to hell with the consequences. "Just let it out, baby. Just cry until you can't cry any more."

She let her head fall onto his shoulder. Her bones felt delicate, frail, beneath the thick material of her sweatshirt as her shoulders vibrated with sobs. The in and out of her breaths was soft and warm against his neck. He thought he'd be content to hold her like this for eternity.

Much sooner than he wished, she lifted her head and

pulled away. The spot where she'd rested against him felt oddly cool and bereft.

She rubbed a hand over her nose and sneezed once more. "What am I going to do? I can't take care of him. Justin travels all the time, so he can't. And my mother . . ." She gave a laugh that sounded more like a sob. "She can barely care for herself."

"I tell you what. My parents live out in the country, and my mother loves animals. What if I take Arthur to her? He'll be there anytime you want to check up on him."

She turned her face to stare at him, and he saw a softness in her features he'd never seen before. "You'd do that?"

He stared down at her tear-ravaged face, the shimmering green eyes, the tiny quiver in her lower lip, and thought, *I'd die for you.* But Nick didn't say the words aloud. Just thinking them scared the hell out of him.

"Yeah. Sure." He stood and pulled Ravyn to her feet. He found a switch on the wall behind them and flipped on a light. She squinted and blinked at the brightness, and he wondered how long she'd been in the dark.

He opened the refrigerator and found a bottle of water. Twisting the lid off, he handed it to her. As she drank, he asked, "Have you eaten anything?"

Her brow creased. "Today?"

He sighed. "When was the last time you ate?"

She gave a little shrug. "I don't remember."

Nick went to the sink and washed his hands. He searched through the cabinets and fridge until he found soup and the makings of a grilled cheese sandwich. "Wash your hands and sit."

She did as he instructed, and when the food was done he put it in front of her. "Eat, and I'll take the cat to my parents'. They live about half an hour from here, so it will take me a little while, but I'll be back. Then we'll talk."

She nodded but didn't make an effort to eat.

"I can either wait here until you finish or go ahead and get him out of here so you can start to feel better. Promise me that if I leave, you'll eat."

"Okay." She picked up the spoon and began eating the soup. She took a bite of the sandwich.

"Will you be all right until I get back?"

She nodded and between bites said, "How long does it feel like this? I've never lost anyone. Well, not since my dad, and I was so young. How long does it hurt?"

Nick sighed. "It never completely goes away, but it gets better each day. You'll have moments when you think you're okay. Then something comes along to sucker punch you, and you never know what it will be. A song, a forgotten item tucked away somewhere, a place you've been together . . ."

"You're talking about your wife."

Nick's throat was tight as he nodded. "How did you know?"

Ravyn shrugged, and her gaze flicked away for a moment. "You said you didn't really have a daughter, but I could tell you were once married. And . . . you seem so sad all the time. Did she die?"

Nick nodded. Ravyn didn't ask how, and he didn't say. Instead, he changed the subject. "By the way, I guess you're wondering how I knew where you lived?"

"I assume it's because you've followed me here at one time or another."

Nick lifted his brow, surprised that she'd said it so matter-of-factly.

Ravyn shrugged. "You wouldn't be much of a PI if you hadn't." She managed a small grin, and Nick smiled back.

Nick was reluctant to leave her alone. After all, Sorina had been taken from Ravyn's house. But he knew if the Tin Man wanted her, he could get to her anytime. The only way to avoid that was for Nick to be with her 24-7, and he couldn't see Ravyn going for that. Plus, Sorina had gone outside, alone, in the middle of the night. Had made herself easy pickings for the madman. "I'll see you in a little while," he promised. "Eat. And lock up tight."

Chapter Twenty-four

Ravyn's sneezing attack eased, and she showered, scrubbing her hair and letting the warm water cascade over her body. Her skin tingled as feeling returned, and it was then that she realized she'd been walking around in a daze, numb and zombielike since the day she'd seen Sorina lying lifeless in the morgue. Her heart squeezed with the pain of missing her sister, the grief a gaping hole in her soul.

Hot tears stung her eyes, but she pressed the pads of her thumbs against her closed lids and stopped them from falling. "Sorina," she moaned into the steam. "I'm so sorry."

Her anguish over her sister was compounded not only by her guilt, but by the insane wrongness of it all. Murder was an even bigger atrocity in the covens' world than in the secular world. If Sorina had died accidentally, by fate or by the natural order of things, that would be difficult enough. But her sister had been stolen by someone who had purposely, maliciously, taken her away and made her suffer. It was more than Ravyn could bear.

Stepping out of the shower, she toweled off her body and hair. Not bothering with makeup, she dressed in jeans and a black, long-sleeved pullover.

She vacuumed and dusted while waiting for Nick, getting rid of all traces of Arthur. Poor thing. He missed Sorina, too. She wanted to care for him but couldn't. She'd have to visit him as much as possible. It was the least she could do.

Nick was gone an hour and a half, and when he returned Ravyn was dismayed to find herself glad to see him. The lights were on this time, and she led him to the living room, where they both took a seat on the sofa.

"I want to find him," Nick began. "I wish I'd done it in time to save Sorina, but I didn't." His eyes became hard. "I have to get him before he kills someone else. I *will* get him."

"I should have done more," Ravyn murmured. "But I . . ." She trailed off and shook her head.

"You're holding something back." Nick's voice held curiosity, but she didn't detect accusation.

"No. I just . . . Maybe I could have told them more. But those cops who interviewed me . . ." She shuddered. "That *one*. He had mean eyes." She didn't tell Nick what she'd felt when she shook Detective Harris's hand, because she knew he wouldn't believe her. "I just knew I couldn't trust him."

"Scott Harris," Nick said.

"Yes. How did you know?"

"I know he and Carlos are on the case. I once worked with Harris. Let's just say I know him well."

Ravyn nodded, hardly processing his words. "I didn't think they would find him, anyway. And I thought he would stop after . . ." She had been about to tell Nick what she'd done. How could she have explained that? "After I got away, I figured he'd stop because he'd be afraid I'd identify him." She gave a short laugh, but it tore at her throat and almost turned into tears. But she wouldn't cry again. No way would she cry again.

"Then he murdered my sister. While I lay sleeping, unaware, she was . . ." She shuddered and looked at Nick, sure her torment must show in her eyes. "How do you think that makes me feel?"

Nick sighed. "Guilt does you no good. You have to do

the best you can to move forward. We need to stop this maniac. That's all we can do."

"We?"

"I need your help. You saw him. I want you to get with a sketch artist and give him all the details you can recall."

"I already did. With those detectives," she reminded him.

"I want a picture for *us* to use. Maybe without the beard. It could have been a disguise, or he could have shaved since then. We can use the new sketch and the one from the paper."

"No," Ravyn said after a moment.

Nick looked shocked. "You won't help me?"

"Yes. I mean, no. I mean, I'll help you. But not just by talking to a sketch artist. I want to help with the investigation. Every step of the way."

Nick shook his head. "I'm sorry. I work alone. You have no idea what's involved. I need all the information you can give me, but that's where your part ends. There's really not any more you can do."

"There *is* more I can do," she vowed. She had to tell him, at least part of the truth. Otherwise, there was no way he'd let her help. "I have a gift. A psychic gift."

He laughed. "A what?"

"I get . . . impressions. I know you don't believe me, but I can prove it."

He sat back and folded his arms across his chest, giving her a smug grin. "Is that right?"

She wanted to wipe the smirk off his face. Her fingers itched to do just that. But she would only show him her psychic powers, not any other.

She stood and moved in front of Nick. "Stand up."

He shrugged and stood, the look on his face saying he was humoring her. She took his arms, pulling them away from his body. She placed a hand over his chest while she looked up into his eyes. The blue in them darkened, and beneath her palm she felt his heart speed up. He swallowed loudly but didn't speak.

"Your wife died"—Ravyn closed her eyes as images swept through her brain—"of cancer. She's been gone for quite a few years. Maybe four . . . no, five."

He stiffened and his heart beat even faster. She felt something then, and her eyes flew open. Looking up at him, she saw him blink. He stared at her as if she held the key to his destruction. His eyes were bright with unshed tears that made the blue in them look like the sea just before a storm.

Her voice was barely above a whisper as she said, "It wasn't your fault. She would have died anyway. It wouldn't have mattered if you'd been there."

He gripped her hand and pulled it away from his chest. "What the hell are you doing? How do you know . . . ?"

His fingers were hurting hers, but she didn't pull away. "I told you how. Let me help you. I have to help you."

He shook his head but looked like he wanted to shake *her*. Finally, he sighed and released her hand. Pulling out his wallet, he retrieved a business card that he dropped onto the coffee table. "Be at my office Monday morning. I'll have a sketch artist there, and we'll get started."

Ravyn sighed and nodded.

Nick stared at her a moment longer, then left without another word.

That night, Ravyn took Sorina's ashes and drove to Vanora's. Once again she stood in a circle with the other coven members in the woods at the back of the property. Her mother was there, but Ravyn ignored her.

This time, Ravyn wore a thick robe that almost kept the wind from biting into her flesh—almost, but not quite. The coven members were somber as Ravyn offered her sis-

ter's ashes to nature, and they all watched them float away
on the wind. The only sound was that of Gwendyl weeping, but Ravyn saw Vanora wiping away tears.

Holding hands once again with Elsbeth and Adalardo,
Ravyn stared into the candles flickering on the altar in
the center of the ritual circle. The low murmur of voices
rose around her as individual prayers were offered up for
Sorina's soul.

Ravyn's heart palpitated with grief, loneliness deep and
dull inside her chest, but she couldn't cry. She'd given all
the tears she had. Mesmerized by the lull of the voices and
the flicker of the candlelight, she let her eyes drift shut.

Then she saw *them*. Images came and went in the darkness of her mind's eye: Sorina in her white gown. Outside
Ravyn's house. She was calling for Arthur. There was a
man walking boldly up behind—

No! Ravyn screamed in her brain, but the image didn't
change. Sorina's head snapped back as the man's hand
covered her mouth and pulled her flush against his chest.
A white cloth fluttered from between his fingertips and
her sister's lips. Sorina went limp—

Ravyn's eyes snapped open and sobs tore at her chest.
But they didn't escape. Dully, she stared at the flames
of the candles, her mind screaming with the images of
her sister. And not just images, she knew, but a replay of her
sister's final moments.

Chapter Twenty-five

Ravyn looked out over the water from her perch on the large flat rock and watched a pontoon boat glide by. She thought about Sorina, about the man who'd killed her sister.

She heard a noise and turned to see Nick approaching. She watched him until he stood directly in front of her, noting he wore his standard attire of Levi's and T-shirt, this time a blue one. She also noted, reluctantly, that he looked good.

She put a hand over her eyes to shade them and looked up at him.

"Hello," he said. "How are you?"

"I'm okay." She shrugged.

His gaze took in her outfit—jean shorts and a red tank top. "Warm day for almost the end of October. Especially after as cold as it's been the past few weeks."

"Yes," she agreed. "Wasn't it Will Rogers who said if you don't like the weather in Oklahoma, just wait a minute, it'll change?"

Nick smiled. "Something like that." The smile faded and he said, "Look, I came by to apologize."

"Apologize for what?"

"The way I acted after you shared your . . . intuition. I was just a little . . ." He shrugged and looked away as if searching for the right word. He turned back to her. "I guess I was caught a little off guard."

"I understand. No problem." She scooted to make room for him. "Want to sit?"

Nick dropped down next to her. "It's nice out here."

"Yeah. I come out here when I want to think. It soothes me." A canopy of trees flanked one side of the rock, making Ravyn feel secluded, secure.

"I can see why." He fell silent, and at that moment a boat sped by on the water, the roar of the motor making speech impossible. When the noise receded, Nick looked up at her. "I'd like to ask you some questions before we get started on the case. Things I've wondered about."

Her heart sped up a few beats, and a knot settled at the base of her throat. She drew a deep breath, smelling a hint of rain in the air and the scent of someone grilling meat. "What questions?"

"I talked to the boys who found you. They said a scream brought them to the cabin."

Ravyn nodded. So far, nothing threatening. But before he spoke again, it hit her: she hadn't screamed. She knew what he was going to say next.

"They said it was a man. They heard a *man* screaming, not a woman." He peered at her, his expression curious.

Ravyn shifted on the rock, tugging at the hem of her cutoffs, even though they were a modest length. She felt exposed, vulnerable. She swallowed, her mind searching for an explanation Nick would buy. She had nothing.

"I have no idea why they'd say that. My voice was hoarse from the drugs, the gag . . . Maybe they thought my scream sounded like a man's."

His eyes moved from her out to the water, then back. "Maybe that's it," he said. But he didn't sound convinced.

"Anything else?" she asked, hoping like hell there wasn't.

There was.

"I just can't get past the fact that he let you go. Did anything else happen that you haven't told the police about? I mean, dislodging the gag, screaming. Doesn't sound like enough to scare off our man. That would just excite him, make him want to finish you off more quickly."

Ravyn lifted the hair off her neck, blaming the muggy day for the layer of perspiration on her skin. But she knew it was more than that. Nick's questions were making her nervous because he was on the right track. How much would he pry out of her?

"I can't say for sure. I don't know exactly why I was spared. I wondered about it myself. Maybe he heard the boys crashing through the trees, and that scared him." She broke off, suddenly tired of the questions and suspicion, tired of not being able to be truthful. "Look, I've told you everything I can. I agreed to meet with a sketch artist and help you find him. I don't know what else you want me to say."

Nick stood. His eyes were sad. "That's it. Just wanted to clear up a few things. And apologize," he added as an afterthought. "I'll see you in my office tomorrow morning, right?"

Ravyn nodded, a trickle of apprehension running across her skin. This was going to be difficult. He made her want to confess everything, but she knew that was impossible. How could she work with Nick and find the monster without his discovering what she really was?

She didn't know, but after what had happened to Sorina, she had to take the chance.

Nick's office was in a grayish building badly in need of a paint job. Weeds grew in what looked like it should have been a flower garden beneath a window next to the entrance.

Ravyn opened the door and stepped into a receptionist area with a desk that held a phone and a computer. No

photos, papers or pens—there was nothing else of secre-
tarial use. She guessed Nick didn't employ a receptionist.
The room smelled faintly of stale cigarette smoke and fresh
coffee.

A hallway led off the lobby, but when she stepped to
the opening she saw two closed doors. She had no idea
which room belonged to Nick.

"Hello?" she called.

The door on the right opened, and Nick stepped out.
"Come on in." He stood to the side and let her walk past.

His office was almost as barren as the front room, with
a few baseball photos on the wall, a phone and a computer
on the battered desk along with an empty ashtray.

He pointed at a black chair with cracks in the vinyl.
"Have a seat."

She did, and he propped a hip on the edge of his desk
and crossed his arms. "The sketch artist will be here in a
few minutes. He's a buddy of mine from the police force.
He's doing this in a nonofficial capacity. In the meantime,
we need a game plan."

"I need to visit the crime scene. The place where he
held me."

Nick raked a hand through his hair, then gripped the
edges of the desk on either side of him. "I'm still not sure
this is a good idea."

"I am. We have to stop him."

Before Nick could reply, the door opened and a thin,
frizzy-haired man stepped in. "Oops, sorry. Didn't mean to
interrupt." His almost-opaque brown eyes clung to Ravyn
as he added to Nick, "I just wondered if you've checked out
this VPO."

Nick sighed. "No, Marvin. I'll take care of it soon,
though."

"I could check it out for you. Maybe go talk to the guy."

"No. Don't do that. I'll handle it." Nick scowled, his agitation clear from his tone of voice and posture.

"Can I go with you when you talk to him?"

"We'll see," Nick replied. "Right now, I'm in the middle of something else."

The guy acted as if he wanted to say more, and lingered at the door. Finally, he nodded. "Okay, cool. Just let me know what you need me to do next." His eyes slid back to Ravyn. "Sorry to interrupt, miss."

"It's okay," she responded, but she didn't introduce herself. Nick hadn't introduced them, and she didn't want this guy to know who she was, just in case he'd heard what happened.

Not long after Marvin left, there was a knock on the door, and a man entered who looked to be in his early thirties. He wore round glasses with frames the same shade as his reddish hair.

Nick straightened from the desk. "Jeff." He stuck out a hand, and the younger man took it. "This is Ravyn Skyler. Ravyn, Jeff Goddard."

The man gave her a sympathetic look before offering a brief handshake. "Nice to meet you. Should we begin?"

Ravyn nodded. Nick stood in the corner while the sketch artist took a seat at his desk.

Gently, Jeff said, "First of all, tell me about that night. Tell me exactly what happened."

Ravyn's eyes flew to Nick. "I thought I was just going to describe what he looks like."

Nick nodded. "You will. But first he needs the whole picture of that night. Details come out as you talk about the event." He walked over and knelt beside her chair. "I'll be right here. Just tell him everything you remember."

"Okay," she said quietly. Nick's warm fingers closed over hers, and she began to speak. She didn't look at Jeff. Instead, she stared down to where Nick's hand rested on hers.

"Good," Jeff said, after she'd been talking for nearly half an hour. "Now, describe his features."

Ravyn took a deep breath. "Brown hair, neatly combed to the side. His eyes . . . I couldn't see their color, but they were . . . hard, slitted." She shivered. "He was average looking, not handsome, not ugly."

Jeff's fingers worked busily over the sketch pad as she gave more details. Without looking up, he asked, "The nose? Pug? Large? Crooked? Straight?"

"Straight. Sort of long."

After a few more seconds of activity, Jeff flipped the sketch pad over so Ravyn could see what he'd drawn. Her heart hammered in her rib cage, and she sucked in a breath. The sketch was her kidnapper. Minus the beard, but him. More of a likeness than the one the artist at the station had drawn. Jeff had even captured the eyes.

Ravyn wanted to look away but couldn't. She felt Nick's fingers tighten on hers, so she slowly nodded. "That's him."

Jeff tore the paper off the pad and handed it to Nick. Nick rose and walked with him to the door. Ravyn was barely aware of the artist leaving, but she could hear the muted voices of the men as they said good-bye.

Nick returned to her side, not speaking. She looked up at him, seeing the promise in his eyes. They would find this man. Together, they would stop him. Even if it was too late for her sister.

Chapter Twenty-six

The next morning, Nick answered a knock and found Ravyn at his door a few minutes ahead of schedule. Her skin was so pale it was almost translucent, and a faint tinge of blue beneath her eyes bore witness to the toll the past few days had taken.

Nick invited her in, and she followed him into the living room. Ravyn walked immediately to the coffee table and bent over, picking up a photo of Annie. "She was beautiful."

Nick nodded, swallowing a lump in his throat. "Yeah."

Ravyn looked at a wedding photo still on the table and then raised her gaze. "You've lost weight."

He shrugged. "That was ten years ago. The past five, I haven't taken very good care of myself."

She placed the picture carefully back down on the table. "Smoking and drinking."

He nodded. "Yes. But I haven't had a drink or a cigarette in several days. I need to stay sharp. Can't make any mistakes until this bastard's caught. After that . . ."

"After that?" she prompted.

"I plan to go on a marathon binge."

"You know that drinking doesn't cure the pain. It only numbs it for a little while," she remarked.

Nick shrugged. "Yeah, well, that's okay. Being numb for a little while is better than feeling all the time."

She stared at him for a long moment but didn't reply.

"I'll get my jacket and we'll head out," Nick said.

As they stepped into the yard, Dog came bounding around the side of the house. When he was no more than six feet away from Ravyn, he came to a halt. He stared at her, backing up a few steps, growling low in his throat. His hackles rose, and his ears pricked, then lay back as the growl turned into a whimper.

"What the hell?" Nick muttered. "Dog, what's wrong with you?" He turned to Ravyn. "Sorry. I've never seen him react that way to anyone."

She shook her head. "It's okay. Maybe he detects Arthur's scent on me."

Nick didn't remind her that it had been several days since he'd taken Arthur to his mother's. Or that the dog hadn't reacted that way when Nick came home after handling the cat. "Maybe so," he agreed, but as he opened the door of his Mustang and let Ravyn slide in, apprehension trickled along his spine.

Why the hell had the dog reacted like that? And what was it about this woman that wasn't quite right? Could it be her psychic abilities? Is that what the animal had reacted to? Just another in a long list of unanswered questions. But for now they had a much more important one to answer: where the hell was the murdering bastard called the Tin Man, and did he have another innocent young woman in his clutches at this very moment?

They pulled up in front of the murderer's cabin less than an hour after they left Nick's house. Ravyn sat in the car, staring out the passenger window, not moving.

"Are you okay?" Nick asked.

She nodded but didn't look at him. After a moment, she opened the door and stepped out.

The trees surrounding the cabin had lost most of their leaves, but they still cast parts of the building's interior in shadow. Nick stood just inside the door and watched as

Ravyn walked around. She stopped in front of the cabin's fireplace and reached out a hand as if to touch it, but didn't. Her arm dropped to her side.

She turned to where the bed still sat at the center of the room. The police had finished processing the scene and had taken everything they needed for testing, but they'd left the mattress and frame behind. Whoever the owners were, they hadn't bothered returning and cleaning up.

Ravyn stood by the bed for a moment and slowly reached out a hand, just as she had with the fireplace. "Hospital," she said in a low voice.

Nick nodded. "Yes. It's a hospital bed. That's where he held you?"

She turned to him and he saw terror in her eyes. "No. I mean, I see a hospital. I don't know why, but we have to go there. It's a very strong vision." Her tone was that of a person in a trance, yet she visibly trembled. "We have to go there now."

The hair on the back of Nick's neck stood on end, and he spoke in the same low tone Ravyn was using. "What hospital?"

"Grace Specialty Care."

Grace Specialty was one of those modern architectural structures with columns of glass and black triangular shapes set into its design. As they went through the revolving doors, Ravyn stopped abruptly, almost causing Nick to run into her.

Mosaic burgundy and teal carpet matched the wallpaper, and a rose-colored crescent desk sat in the center of the lobby with a sign above it reading INFORMATION in teal letters. A woman with short, dark hair and large, round glasses sat at the desk, looking down and flipping the pages of a magazine.

"What now?" Nick asked, but Ravyn didn't answer.

Slowly she moved forward past the information desk to the bank of elevators. He followed her inside, not speaking as she punched the button for the fourth floor.

When Nick stepped off the elevator with her, it hit him: that same dizzy, sick feeling he'd had the last time he was in a hospital. With Annie. The smell of antiseptic and the other hospital smell he was never quite able to identify assailed his nostrils, and he tried not to breathe it in. He closed his eyes and rested a hand on the wall to steady himself.

The floor hubbub only made it worse. Nurses' shoes squeaked along the shiny tile, and in the main waiting room was a family with two small children running around a coffee table, squealing, competing with the television that was blaring a news show. The noise seemed to ebb and swell in time with Nick's rising nausea.

Ravyn seemed unaware. She stood with her back to him, peering down the hallway. But when she turned toward Nick after a few moments, she asked, "What's wrong?"

Nick shook his head. "I'm not feeling well. Hospitals do this to me. What are we doing here, anyway?"

"I'm not sure. I . . ." She put her hand on his shoulder. "Do you need to go outside?"

He nodded, and they stepped back onto the elevator.

Once outside the front doors of the building, he was able to breathe again. She helped him to a bench, where he placed his elbows on his knees and rested his face in his hands, feeling weak and foolish. He needed a drink. All that talk about giving it up was bunk. Already he craved the strong, soothing taste of whiskey. He didn't know how he'd survive without it.

"Stay right here. I'll be back." Ravyn held out a hand. "Give me the sketches."

"Why?"

"I need to ask a few questions. Something brought me here. Maybe someone inside will recognize our man."

Fighting nausea, Nick handed her the folded composites from his jacket pocket. He tried not to think of his shame at his weakness as Ravyn disappeared through the hospital doors, reminded himself that this might simply be a lark. He leaned back against the bench and took deep, full breaths of the crisp October air.

She was back in half an hour, just about the time his nausea abated. She shook her head. "Nothing. No one knew him. With or without the beard." She turned back to look at the hospital doors. "I don't understand. The compulsion was so strong. Something here . . ."

Nick stood, ready to leave. "Maybe it'll come to you later," he said. But he didn't believe it. He couldn't deny she had some kind of weird ability, but the psychic voodoo bullshit was a bit much.

He stuck his hand in his jacket pocket and pulled out his keys. When he did, a baggie fell to the ground. Inside was the capsule he'd found at the cabin the first time he went. "Ah, hell. Forgot about that."

"What is it?"

"I'm not sure," he admitted. A thought occurred to him. "There's a pharmacy inside, right? On the ground floor?"

Ravyn nodded.

"Come on."

They went back inside, and this time Nick didn't feel any sickening sensations. The pharmacy sat in the lobby area, far away from the rooms where people went to die.

A pretty young woman with copper-colored hair smiled from behind the high counter. "Can I help you?"

Nick handed her the baggie. "Can you tell me what this is? What it's prescribed for?"

She studied the pill through the plastic. "I'll be right back."

She stepped behind a row of shelves, and Nick heard her voice, along with the deep rumble of a man. In a few moments, she reappeared.

"This is Neoral. It's a form of cyclosporine. The most common use is in treatment after a kidney, liver or heart transplant to prevent tissue rejection. It's also used to treat the symptoms of rheumatoid arthritis or psoriasis." She handed the pill back to Nick, who took it and thanked her.

"Where did it come from?" Ravyn asked as they stepped outside once more.

"I believe it came from the killer." It wasn't a huge lead, but it was something. They could deduce that he had arthritis, psoriasis, or someone else's organs.

Chapter Twenty-seven

About six feet beyond the hospital doors, Ravyn felt an inexplicable pull and looked down at the ground. A child's baseball cap lay on the sidewalk, and she knelt to pick it up. As soon as she touched the brim, a tremor of electricity moved through her body. She gripped the hat so tightly in her hands that she nearly crushed the bill.

Not the boy's father, she heard—no, *felt.* Images flashed, slamming into her consciousness. She squeezed her eyes closed and let them come.

The hospital lobby—she could see it as clearly as she had a few moments ago, when she'd been inside. A man striding past the information desk, carrying a small boy. She couldn't so much see the man as she could sense him. But she could see the child in heart-pounding clarity. He was maybe four or five years old. His round cheeks were mottled and wet with tears. His pudgy hands shoved against the man's shoulders, his upper body straining to push himself away. An Atlanta Braves ball cap sat askew on his thick blond hair.

"I want my mommy!" The boy's wails were punctuated by breathless gasps as he struggled.

"Mommy's at work, son. We're going to pick her up now." The man cast a long-suffering look at the receptionist, and she responded with an empathetic smile. The cap lost its precarious perch just after the pair exited the hospital.

"Not his father," Ravyn choked out, her voice strangled, her throat raw.

"What?"

Nick had spoken, but his words barely cut through the vision that had her firmly in its grip. The last of the images assailing Ravyn was a black, extended-cab Tacoma truck with tinted windows exiting the parking lot. Her gaze snapped to Nick. "Let's go."

"Where? What the hell—?"

She wasn't listening. She rushed toward his Mustang, not bothering to see if Nick followed.

Two patrol cars pulled into the parking lot. Had someone called about a kidnapping? If she went to them, explained what she'd seen, they either wouldn't believe her or would keep her here too long, asking questions, further prolonging the time the boy was in danger. She couldn't take that risk.

Nick caught up to her and took hold of her arm, turning her to face him. His gaze locked onto hers, trapping her with that inscrutable blue intensity. "What's going on?" he demanded.

She felt fear in the back of her throat but spoke past it. "I can't explain. Please, if I take the time, it will break my connection. Please, just trust me. A child's in trouble."

Confusion, then skepticism, flickered across his features. "Look, this is . . ." He stopped. Perhaps something in her expression convinced him. He shook his head and gave an exasperated sigh. His grip on her arm loosened, and his hand slid down to so he could grasp her fingers. "Come on," he ground out between gritted teeth. Then, tugging on her hand, he led her to his car.

Sorry motherfucker. Jay slammed a fist into his thigh. He'd been watching them—watching her and had seen *him*. Too many times. And now he'd seen them together at the hospital. *His* hospital. Not the one where he worked, but his just the same. He watched from inside his car as the asshole opened the door for Ravyn, then climbed in on the driver's side.

The Mustang exited the parking lot, but Jay remained where he was. No need to follow them. He'd already checked around, and he knew who the man was. Knew what he was up to, too. It was Nick Lassiter, PI. Helping a damsel in distress.

The sonofabitch had come closer than the stupid-ass cops ever would, and he couldn't have that. Lassiter was good—or he had been at one time. Yes, Jay had found out everything he could about Superhero Lassiter. The pig had sported an impressive record while on the force. Of course, he'd turned to shit since then, so why did Lassiter think he could bring him down? He was the Tin Man. He was invincible.

But something had to be done. Lassiter was getting too close. He was also spending way too much time with Ravyn. Anyone who knew a damn thing about any of this should know that Ravyn belonged to *him*.

Still, the thought of bringing Lassiter down made Jay nervous. Not only had he never killed a man, he'd never even had a physical confrontation with one.

Nervous, my ass, you little fairy. You're afraid. You're the same little chicken-shit mouse you always were.

Jay sucked in a quick breath and clamped his hands over his ears. "Go away!" he shouted, his eyes tightly closed as he rocked back and forth.

He was so busy shutting out his mother's voice that he almost missed the other: the voice he'd grown to count on. The voice that would bring him all his greatest desires, bring him power and glory.

You don't have to get close in order to kill him, it suggested.

"I don't?" Haleck's words squeaked out of him as if he were the mouse his mother accused him of being.

You can do a lot of damage and be nowhere close to your victim, my friend.

Jay took the voice's meaning. He sat up straight and gripped the steering wheel of his car, excitement and apprehension battling inside him. "Explosives? I don't know anything about explosives."

I'll help you.

Jay smiled and wiped away his tears. "Yes, you will," he realized in a whisper. "Yes, you will."

Ravyn's method of giving him directions was kind of creeping Nick out. She sat in the passenger seat, eyes squeezed shut, hands clasped in her lap, knuckles white with the effort. She would say things like "Turn right at the next stop sign." And "You need to speed up a little, or we'll get caught by a train." Just seconds after the Mustang crossed a set of railroad tracks, the arms lowered for the approaching train.

Not long after that, she said, "Slow down, there's a cop a few miles up the road."

When they cruised past the patrol car, going a few miles under the speed limit, Nick said, "When are you going to—?"

She held up her left hand like a traffic cop, effectively silencing his words.

She directed him to a middle-class neighborhood and instructed him to stop in front of a brick house with white siding. A black, extended-cab truck was parked in the driveway. Before Nick could shut off the ignition, Ravyn was jerking the door open and bolting from the car.

He didn't know why they were here or what she was getting him into, but he must have trusted her, because he followed, catching up just before she reached the door. He expected her to knock, but instead she twisted the knob. Locked.

"Do you really think you should—?" Nick began.

She shushed him again, and he wondered if he was going to be able to complete even one sentence today. He opened his mouth to try once more but stopped when he heard crying coming from inside the house. A child.

She vigorously jiggled the knob. Even though Nick was certain it had been locked, now the door swung open. Not knowing what else to do, he followed her inside.

The deserted living room was neat and clean—not a sign of anything amiss. But the cries of a child could be heard, growing louder until a man holding a squirming and crying little boy beneath one arm approached from a hallway off the side.

"What the hell are you doing?" the man demanded. He was in his early thirties, with short, well-groomed hair and a neatly trimmed mustache.

"Release the child," Ravyn said.

"Who are you? What do you think you're doing in my home? Get out now, before I call the police."

"Ravyn," Nick whispered. "I don't know what you're doing, but—"

"I said, release the child," Ravyn demanded, her gaze on the man, not acknowledging Nick. "We both know you're not going to call the police."

The man's confident expression wavered. He reached behind him with his right hand, retrieved a .38 from his waistband. He swung it around and held it against the boy's head. Nick tensed, knowing he didn't have time to pull his own weapon without further endangering the child.

Ravyn remained calm. "I wouldn't do that if I were you. You should drop the gun and release the boy."

The man laughed, his eyes now wild with fear or insanity. Or both. "I'll waste him, I promise. Get the fuck—"

A blue flash lit the room, and Nick felt a jolt of electric-

164 ALICIA DEAN

ity. Shock held him immobile, suspended for a moment in disbelief, his mind trying to assimilate what was happening. Before he could, the kidnapper emitted a pain-filled, feminine shriek. He released his gun, which clattered to the floor, and the hand that had held it bent outward at an unnatural angle.

The man let the child slide to the ground and dropped to his knees, cradling his hand. His face was contorted in pain, and he gave a keening, high-pitched wail. "What did you do to me?" he screeched.

Ravyn ignored him, moving instead to pick up the child.

Nick grabbed the man's gun, feeling a surreal wonder, still not sure what had taken place.

"Call the police," Ravyn instructed him. She kept cooing and stroking the child's head until his sobs subsided.

Nick could barely contain himself while the police questioned him and Ravyn. Although he was anxious to ask Ravyn a few questions of his own, it took hours before the police were satisfied and let them leave.

As it turned out, the mother had been visiting a friend at the hospital. She'd left her son in the waiting area "for only a minute" while she'd gone to the ladies' room. When she returned, he'd vanished. The man who had taken him was Victor Worburton, a registered sex offender who'd served time for sexual battery with injury of a child under twelve. He'd been released from prison six months earlier.

When the police were finally finished with Nick and Ravyn, and they were driving back in his Mustang, Nick finally got the chance to speak. He said, using as much restraint as he could, "What the hell was that?"

Ravyn took a moment to answer. She'd been subdued, almost lethargic, since the rescue. "What was what?"

Nick's grip tightened on the steering wheel. "Don't play with me, Ravyn. What happened back there?"

She shrugged. "I had one of my visions. I followed it, and you know the rest. That man was going to molest and maybe kill that boy. We helped rescue him, the pervert's going to prison, end of story."

"Okay, I got all that," Nick ground out between clenched teeth. "But what did you do? How did that asshole's hand suddenly break? And what was with the lightning or whatever happened back there in that house? Tell me what's going on!"

"I don't know what you're talking about," she replied. "Somehow he injured his hand. Maybe he has weak bones. What's that disease, that brittle-bone disease? Osteo imper-something-or-other. Maybe he has that."

"Bullshit."

She ignored him and continued. "And I didn't see lightning, but there was some kind of electrical current. Maybe faulty wiring? I was going to ask you the same thing. I don't know much about that electrical stuff. I figured, being a man, maybe you would."

She was good, he'd give her that. She almost had him convinced that she'd used nothing but a little psychic precognition. Almost, but not quite.

Chapter Twenty-eight

Two days after the hospital visit and rescue of the child, they were no closer to the Tin Man than they'd been when they started. Nick had been trying to get his hands on a list of local organ recipients, but those were highly confidential. Besides, the villain's transplant could be heart, kidney or liver and could have taken place years ago. And in another state. It would be like looking for a golf ball in the Amazon rainforest. Going by the man's self-imposed moniker of Tin Man, Nick guessed he could probably eliminate the kidney and liver transplants, but that only narrowed the search by a little. And it still didn't give him access to any records. And of course he didn't know for sure that the pill belonged to the killer.

The only thing he'd accomplished was spending more time with Ravyn—and increasing his desire to see her more each day. In spite of being convinced that she was holding something back, that she wasn't exactly what she seemed, he couldn't stop his growing feelings for her. He found himself thinking about Ravyn a lot. Thinking about Annie less each day. To be honest, more and more he had trouble recalling the way his wife's voice had sounded, her fragrance . . .

He shook his head. *You owe her more than this.* "I'm sorry, Annie," he whispered into the empty room.

The doorbell rang and Dog trotted over, but the beast stopped just short of the door and backed away, whining.

"Crazy mutt," Nick murmured.

He swung the door open and Ravyn stood there. He didn't like the way his heart did a little tumble at seeing her so unexpectedly. And when he invited her in, he didn't like that the house seemed a tad less lonely. He found the realization exciting on one hand, but irritating as hell on the other.

Dog snarled at her, growling low in his throat. Ravyn squatted down and put out her hand. "It's okay, boy. Come here." Her voice was gentle, coaxing.

Slowly the animal walked closer, head down. Ravyn reached out and lightly scratched his neck, murmuring soothingly about what a good boy he was. Dog came even closer and let her stroke the fur on his back while she slid a hand down and scratched his belly. He wagged his tail and gave a whimper, much as Nick figured he himself would if she touched him like that.

Suddenly, Ravyn's hands stilled and she closed her eyes. Her breathing slowed, and he saw a shiver pass through her body. "He's a hero," she said.

"What?"

"His owners didn't know, didn't realize." Her eyes were still closed. Nick and Dog fell completely silent as she spoke, held unnaturally still. "He saved the baby, but they thought he was trying to harm her. The toddler was going out to the road. He stopped her, knocking her down in the yard just as a car passed. The parents came out and saw him standing over her. . . . They thought he was attacking her. They got rid of him. The man wanted to have him put down, but the woman said no, they'd dump him in the country."

She'd been speaking as if in a trance. Now Ravyn opened her eyes and stood, gave an embarrassed laugh.

"Wow," Nick said.

"Sorry. It all just came to me. I didn't think about it, I just . . . spoke."

Nick squatted and rubbed Dog's head. "You're a hero, boy." He was more convinced of Ravyn's abilities than ever, though he didn't know why. Her assessment just seemed . . . right. He truly believed Dog's story.

He looked back up at her. "Anyway, what's up? I doubt if you stopped by to have a vision about my dog."

"No, I didn't," she agreed. "We need to do something."

"Such as?"

Throwing her hands in the air, Ravyn stalked into the living room. Nick followed. Her leather coat flapped around her long legs as she paced the small area. "I don't know. Something. You're the investigator. What's next?"

Nick slumped onto his sofa. Leaning forward, he rested his elbows on his knees and shook his head. "I have no freakin' clue. I'm out of ideas."

Ravyn tossed a handful of her thick hair over her shoulder and crossed her arms, stopping on the opposite side of the coffee table. "Think," she cajoled. "There has to be something."

He scrubbed his hands over his face. When he lifted his head, his gaze fell on the surface of the table. He froze. "Where is it?"

"Where is what?"

"The photo."

She looked down to where only one photo, the one of Annie, rested on the table. "Your wedding photo?"

He nodded. "It's not here."

"You didn't move it?"

He clenched his jaw and spoke in a clipped tone. "If I had moved it, would I be asking where it is?"

"Sorry." She sighed and uncrossed her arms. "No, you wouldn't. Sorry."

He stood and shook his head, realizing he was being irrational. "No, *I'm* sorry. I'm a little on edge, but I shouldn't take it out on you." Looking around the room, Nick searched for the photo, realizing he must have moved it. But he didn't find the picture. Instead, he saw a thick coat of dust on Annie's knickknacks.

What, he wondered, did Ravyn think of a widower living among lace doilies, with a sewing machine nestled in the corner of a room covered in pink and mint green wallpaper? He didn't tell her he'd kept things just as Annie had left them. That all these years he'd foolishly hoped she'd come back.

His gaze returned to Ravyn, and their eyes locked for a moment before she looked away. Stuffing her hands in her coat pockets, she cleared her throat uncomfortably. "You must have loved her very much."

"I did," he replied. A smothering blanket of depression fell over him, and he struggled to break free, struggled to breathe.

Silence hung heavy in the room before Ravyn spoke. "The missing picture is just one more thing for you to feel guilty about, right? Like the woman at the police station?"

He honestly wasn't surprised that she mentioned Jacqueline. Ravyn had clearly sensed something there, and she was right. But how could he tell her about Jacqueline? How could he tell Ravyn that he'd been with her as his wife lay dying? Nothing had happened. But if he hadn't gotten the call from the hospital, he couldn't swear that it wouldn't have. He'd been drinking, and lonely, and Jacqueline was a very difficult woman to say no to. He wasn't sure he would have said it many more times.

He'd gotten there too late. Annie's parents were there, though they hadn't been when she died. She'd died alone. All because he was with another woman, seeking solace.

He closed his eyes, crushed by the memories, crushed by guilt.

He didn't even realize she'd moved, but suddenly Ravyn was there. She touched his cheek, and it was then that he became aware of his tears. Embarrassed, he stepped back and turned away. Scrubbing a hand over his face, he said, "Maybe you should go."

She put her hand on his arm. "Come with me."

"What?" He laughed shakily. "Come where? It's late."

"Please. Trust me. We'll take my car."

He had no idea why, but he nodded. He pulled his jacket off the hook by the front door and followed her through the dark yard to her car.

They drove to her house and she led him inside. He waited while she went up the loft stairs. Was he supposed to follow? Was she offering a little sexual healing? Even though he knew that wasn't the answer, he had to admit he liked the idea.

But, no. That wasn't Ravyn Skyler's style. He had no idea what she was up to, but he knew it wasn't a quick roll in the hay.

She came down the stairs wearing a black gown similar to the one she'd worn when he followed her that one night. Although it was long and completely covered her body, the satiny, nearly sheer material shimmered against her flesh as she walked toward him, and he felt his male response, immediate and intense.

He swallowed, and it made a dry clicking noise in his throat. He didn't know what to do next, but he couldn't speak, almost couldn't breathe as he anticipated her next move.

She took him by the hand without a word and led him toward the back door. It was then that he noticed the candles she held in her left hand. What the hell?

Without speaking, they walked across the damp grass to where a row of trees divided her yard from the water. Ravyn stopped by a low tree stump and placed the silver pillar candles on top, pulling a candle lighter from a hollowed-out place in the stump. He knew she'd never get the candles lit with the breeze coming off the water, but they caught as soon as she touched the flame to their wicks.

They stood next to the flickering candles, and she turned to face him, placing a hand over his heart. "Close your eyes," she whispered. They were the first words she'd spoken since they left his house, and he did as she instructed. "Turn your face to the sky." He did, and felt the light of the moon shining down on his closed eyelids in the darkness.

She began to speak softly, and his entire body relaxed. His mind seemed to drift away, as if he was in some kind of trance. Her words floated down on him like a soothing rain. "It wasn't your fault. You must let go."

He shook his head and started to protest, but Ravyn placed a finger over his lips. "Shhh, let it go," she commanded. "Annie knows how much you loved her. You've lived with the guilt long enough. Let it go."

Eyes still closed, he felt tears squeeze against the lids. If Ravyn knew where he'd been, what he'd almost done . . .

His breath caught in his chest at her next whispered words. "You would have done no wrong. You were seeking comfort and that is all. Annie knows this, and so should you."

An awareness moved through the night and over Nick. He could feel Annie's soul, her gentleness and her love. He stood silent, letting the sensation seep through him, wanting to feel close to Annie once more.

He could sense Ravyn standing next to him, but she didn't speak. The only sound was her soft breath, the wind rustling through the trees and the lapping of the water. He didn't know how long they stood there—it could have been seconds, could have been hours—but an odd serenity filled him. He heard another voice, feminine but not Ravyn's, whisper, *Let it go.*

He sucked in a breath. *Annie?*

His guilt expanded. It tore at him until he thought he couldn't stand it another second. And then, just as suddenly, it left—cleanly, as if a surgeon had lifted it out with a scalpel. His heart was finally, beautifully, at peace. His soul felt light and airy, as if it might have floated out of him and up to the heavens.

He wasn't sure how long he stood there, but he was suddenly once more aware of Ravyn's touch on his chest. It had been there the entire time.

He opened his eyes and stared down at her, wanting to speak, but wonder kept him from doing so. Instead, he took her face in his hands and ran his thumbs over the velvet softness of her cheeks. A sigh whispered from her lips, soft and warm on the flesh of his fingers.

All thoughts of Annie fled as he drank in the beauty of the woman before him. Her eyes had turned a dark emerald in the moonlight. A breeze tickled over his skin and lifted her hair, sweeping it over his hands. Her gaze searched his, and he rubbed a thumb over her bottom lip. He wanted to kiss her and knew she wanted it, too.

He dipped his head, but just before his lips touched hers, he saw a brief flash in her eyes, just the tiniest flicker of wariness. Soon it was gone, vanished as quickly as it had come. But it was enough. He couldn't do this, not during such a perfect moment, not when he finally felt close to

Ravyn. He wouldn't spoil things. Wouldn't shatter her trust.

He groaned and leaned his forehead against hers, his eyes tightly closed. Softly he said, "Thank you," then released her and stepped back, quickly, before he changed his mind.

Chapter Twenty-nine

Promising to stay on the sofa, Nick convinced Ravyn to let him spend the night. It was late, and he didn't want her driving home alone after dropping him off.

She tried to ignore the currents running between them as she spread a sheet and blanket over the couch. Out by the lake, she'd thought he was going to kiss her, but at the last moment he'd pulled away. She was relieved—and a small part of her was disappointed. She'd only wanted to help him with his grief, with his guilt. She'd never intended to get so involved. Not with a mortal. She'd certainly never intended to feel what she'd felt as his hands cupped her face.

Call it a moment of insanity, but she'd wanted him to kiss her, wanted to know what it would be like to taste his lips on hers and feel him against her body. And that kind of thinking was not only crazy, it was dangerous. Getting close to a mortal would spell certain disaster. Especially getting close to a mortal who was an ex-cop. Yes, that would definitely be crazy.

She straightened and smiled. "Hope it's comfortable enough for you."

"I'm sure it will be," he replied.

She started past him, and he reached out and took her arm. "Ravyn."

She stopped, looking down at his hand, then back up at his face. "Yes?" she said, pulling free from his grasp and taking a step backward.

"I just wanted to say . . ." He sighed and shook his head. "That was amazing. I really appreciate what you did."

She nodded. "You've already thanked me, Nick. It's late. Good night." And without looking back, she hurried to the steps and climbed up to her loft.

She slipped into bed, wishing for the first time that her bedroom was closed off from the rest of the house. Out in the open like this, with mere stairs separating her from Nick, she felt too close to him. As if they were sharing a room. So much so, she could hear him tossing on the sofa. Tortured by his nearness, she lay in the dark listening to his movements, until finally all she heard was his steady breathing and knew he'd fallen asleep.

She shifted in bed, watching the play of moonlight on the ceiling and thinking about Sorina. And about Nick. Even though she'd lost her sister and felt more alone than ever, somehow, when Nick was around, the loneliness was a little less severe. Her eyes drifted shut, and she frowned in the semidarkness. Nick was definitely going to be trouble.

Ravyn . . . , came a voice.

What? Who are you? her mind asked. But she knew. Somewhere, deep inside, she knew.

I'm coming for you. You know that, don't you?

Please leave me alone. Please?

A brush across her nipple made her gasp. *You don't really want that, do you?*

She felt a tightening in her lower belly, and she sighed as a light stroke parted her thighs. She tensed, wanting him to touch her there. She wanted to feel his hands all over her, wanted the kiss she'd been deprived of earlier. Wanted the kiss that Nick had failed to—No! Nick was a mortal.

Do you want me to stop? the voice asked softly.

Ravyn shook her head on her pillow, giving in to the

sensation. *Mmmmm. No, I don't want you to stop. Please don't stop, Nick.*

The air seemed to charge with electricity. A white light streaked across her closed eyelids, and a booming clap of thunder shook the room. Her eyes flew open, and Ravyn crashed out of bed, the covers clasped tightly to her chest. She stared wildly around, waiting for the pounding of her heart to subside.

On shaking legs, she made her way to the railing and looked out over the downstairs. Nick somehow still slept peacefully on the sofa. He hadn't seen the light. Hadn't heard the thunder. It was only for her. And she knew why.

Kayne.

The next morning, after Ravyn dropped him off at home, Nick watched her drive away, wondering how he'd spent the night with a woman like that and hadn't laid a finger on her. His body still ached from unfulfilled desire, but his heart felt lighter than it had since Annie's death. Nick didn't know how she'd done it, but somehow Ravyn had fixed something deep inside that he hadn't even known was damaged.

He showered and dressed, driving to the address of the boyfriend with the protection order. This wasn't a vital lead, but it was something. It was also something Nick could do without Ravyn's all-too-disturbing presence to screw with his libido.

The house was in south Oklahoma City, a neighborhood that had been decent once upon a time but over the years had fallen into disrepair and crime. Donald Moses's home was a white frame with a lawn that needed a good mow. Assorted junk was piled haphazardly on the small porch.

Nick knocked, and after several seconds, the door opened. The man who answered was bleary eyed and shirtless, with a tattoo of a lizard on his narrow chest and another Nick couldn't identify circling his upper right arm.

"Yeah?" he asked, squinting at Nick through the screen door. He scratched at his forearm, and his right shoulder jerked up and down, both the itching and involuntary movements indicators of methamphetamine use.

"Donald Moses?"

"Who are you?"

"I'm Nick Lassiter, a private detective. I wondered if I could ask you a few questions about Juanita Collins."

Moses dropped his gaze, and when he raised his bloodshot eyes again, a sheen of tears glistened there. His voice had an added hoarseness. "What questions? I don't know anything about what happened to her."

"She had a VPO out on you. Must have been a reason for that."

Moses nodded, and Nick saw shame in his eyes. "We fought a lot. I hit her a few times." The eyes turned hard. "But I didn't fucking kill her. You need to get the hell off my property."

The sudden switch to anger threw Nick off for a moment, and he could see how the VPO had come about. "Just a few more questions. Where were you on the night of April tenth?"

"None of your goddamned business."

Moses started to close the door, but Nick held up a hand and the man paused. "If you'll just answer my question it would clear some things up. Otherwise, I'll have to go to the cops."

"They've already been here, and I'll tell you the same thing I told them. I was in jail, man, and I was there a week before and three days after. So go fuck yourself."

Moses slammed the door. Nick didn't knock again. If the guy had been in jail, that would be pretty easy to confirm. And it would prove this was just what Nick had thought it was: a dead lead.

He left, stopping by the OCPD to check out Moses's story. Betty ran the check. Just as the man had claimed, he'd been incarcerated before, during and after Juanita's murder. If he hadn't killed her, the one victim Nick knew he was acquainted with, he hadn't done the others.

Ravyn went to Nick's office to talk to him about their next move, and to find out if he'd located the missing photo. It was probably nothing at all, but that detail had begun to bother her. In this crazy, unexplainable mess, anything could be significant.

The guy she'd met on her previous visit was there, though Nick was not.

"Hey," the guy said. He smiled, his crooked teeth showing briefly between chapped lips. "You and Nick are working together on the case, right?"

"Yes," she admitted.

"Yeah, I'm working with him, too. I was just going to check something out. That VPO I mentioned before? Gonna go talk to the boyfriend. Something fishy, if you ask me."

Ravyn wasn't sure if this plan was approved by Nick, but she thought it was a good idea, especially if something new had come to light. Nick wasn't around at the moment, and she wanted to do something. "I'll go with you," she suggested.

"Hmmm, not sure if a lovely lady like you should tag along on a dangerous mission like this." The guy crossed bony arms over his T-shirt, momentarily covering its "I'm not as think as you drunk I am" slogan.

Ravyn gave him a smile that was more sarcasm than sweetness. "I can take care of myself. Don't you worry your pretty little head about me."

The man's eyes rounded and he grinned. "I guess you can. Let's go. We'll take my car."

As Nick pulled into the parking lot, his mind ran over what he'd learned about the other vics. Nothing, really. There was no link that he could see. Juanita's VPO was the closest fact he had to anything suspicious, and that had turned out to be a nothing. No surprise there: VPO offenders usually didn't turn to serial killing.

Nick was almost to the front door when it struck him that Ravyn's car was in the parking lot and Marvin's was not. What was she doing here, and where the hell was he? He had a bad feeling, and so he hurried his step.

The front door was locked, which probably meant neither of the two was around. Which probably meant they were together. The bad feeling grew, settled in the pit of his stomach and shot fingers of dread up his spine.

Inside the building, Nick found his brilliant deduction confirmed. No one was there. But what the hell were they doing together?

He went into his office, and his gaze fell on the computer. Suddenly knowing where Marvin and Ravyn had gone, he found his knees weak with fear. The Tin Man's list of victims, along with Moses's address, was currently displayed on screen. Nick hadn't clicked out of the file before he left.

Chapter Thirty

Donald Moses's house was in a neighborhood of similarly designed homes, some well cared for, some not. The yard next door held two children's bicycles and was neatly mowed, a carefully cultivated flower garden blooming beneath the window. Moses's was a disgrace.

Ravyn stood beside Marvin on the porch, trying not to brush against a tattered red chair surrounded by empty beer cans and car parts. Marvin rang the doorbell.

A man opened the door who looked as though they'd just woken him, even though it was well past lunchtime. He wore cutoffs and no shirt, proudly displaying several tattoos on his torso. His brownish-blond hair was long and dirty, and through the screen door Ravyn could smell both body odor and alcohol.

"Who the fuck are you?" the guy growled.

"W-we're investigators," Marvin replied. "We w-wondered if we could please ask you . . ." He tapered off and looked at Ravyn helplessly.

"Juanita Collins had a VPO out on you," she said. "We'd like to ask you a few questions about that."

The man's face reddened, and he flung the screen door open, banging it into Marvin, who stumbled back, nearly falling off the porch.

"The fuck you will," Moses roared. "I'm goddamned sick and tired of this shit!"

"Take it easy!" Ravyn put her hands up in a placating gesture, but Moses ignored her and whirled on Marvin.

Before she knew what was happening, the man had Marvin by the shirtfront and was slamming his fist into Marvin's face. Marvin tried to cover, but Ravyn knew from the blood that at least a few solid blows had landed.

"Hey!" Ravyn shouted. She grabbed Moses's arm, and he released Marvin and turned to her. Marvin slumped to his knees on the porch, cradling his bloody face.

Demented eyes raked over Ravyn, gleaming with violence and lust. Moses grabbed her hair and twisted it around his hand, using it to pull her closer.

"Let me go," she snarled.

"Not till we have some fun," he replied. He brushed the ends of her hair over his lips and slipped several strands into his mouth, wetting them with saliva.

Behind him, Ravyn saw Marvin struggling to his feet. "Leave her alone," he gurgled, still covering his mouth and nose with his fingers.

Moses's other hand rose to grip Ravyn's throat. She reached up and clawed at his wrists, but he was strong, and her efforts had no effect. Without turning, Moses said to Marvin, "I'll snap her neck if you get up, little man."

Marvin stilled, looking guiltily from Ravyn to Moses. She tried to tell him with her eyes that it was okay.

Moses released her throat long enough to grab the neck of the blue tank top she wore under her white gauzy overshirt. Pulling it away from her body so he could see her breasts, he murmured, "Nice." His fetid, hot breath caressed her cheek. "I like tits."

His grip on Ravyn's hair brought tears to her eyes, but she tried not to let him know he was hurting her. "It's probably kind of exciting," she suggested, "to see them on someone other than your sister."

His rheumy eyes crackled with anger. Then the reaction was gone, and he threw his head back and laughed. "You think you're pretty smart, huh?" He released her shirt and gripped her neck again, this time with more pressure. Ravyn began to feel as if she were drowning, asphyxiating, swinging from a hangman's rope.

"Let . . . go . . . of . . . me," she choked out.

"Not before me and you have some fun. Might even let Q-tip here watch—if he's a good boy."

Ravyn's voice was a low warning. "If you don't let go, you'll be sorry."

"Yeah? Why do ya think that?" Moses had begun alternately squeezing and caressing her neck, and she felt close to passing out. Or worse.

"Because I can do things to you that you won't like," she promised.

Moses laughed, sending a gust of sour breath into her face. "Oh, you'll do things to me, all right. But I promise, I'll like 'em."

"Don't think so. What I'll do to you is worse than crashing from meth. Worse even than going to your mailbox and discovering your welfare check isn't there."

He blinked as if in disbelief, then his grip on her hair and throat tightened. "You smart-ass bitch," he ground out, shoving her against the side of the house.

"Hey!" Marvin protested weakly, but neither Moses nor Ravyn acknowledged him.

Moses pressed a thumb into Ravyn's windpipe. Releasing her hair, he dug his fingers painfully into the flesh of her right breast.

A wave of tremors went through Ravyn. Her fingers tingled, heat moving from her toes up through her body and into her hairline. She closed her eyes, fighting the rage, searching her mind for another way to end this. But the skin on her face continued to tighten and burn.

Her eyes snapped open, and she stared into Donald Moses's face.

He gasped. "What the fuck . . . ?"

* * *

Nick's worst fears were confirmed when he screeched to a stop in front of Donald Moses's house. Marvin was on his knees on the porch, looking up at Ravyn and Moses as if praying to them. Moses had Ravyn backed against the wall. But as Nick watched, he released her and stumbled back. Had he heard Nick arrive?

"Hey!" Nick shouted, pulling his Beretta and racing up onto the porch.

Ravyn closed her eyes, and Nick could see her chest rising and falling with deep breaths. Moses turned a wild-eyed gaze to him, his expression twisted with fear. He fumbled for the screen door and waved a hand wildly, as if shooing a swarm of bees.

"Get away!" His voice was reedy, weak. "All of you just get away and leave me alone."

Ravyn's eyes were open now, and she looked at Moses for a moment before going over to help Marvin to his feet. The screen door shut, and in half a second the wooden door did the same.

"Are you okay?" Ravyn asked Marvin softly, ignoring Nick altogether.

"Yeah, other than being a puss, I'm fine."

"He took you by surprise." She soothed his fears as the two of them stepped off the porch.

Marvin looked up at Nick as they passed, but he didn't speak. Nick figured the look in his eyes was too much of a warning not to make an attempt at dumb explanations.

"What the fuck are you two doing here?" he demanded, stepping off the porch behind them.

"Following up on a lead," Ravyn replied.

Nick glanced at Marvin. "Even though I told you not to? Even though you could have gotten both of yourselves killed?"

Marvin shrugged and nodded.

"He needs to be seen to," Ravyn cut in, as if Marvin's bloody nose was an important issue.

"He's got a goddamned bloody nose," Nick snapped. "Which is a lot less than he'll have when I get through with him."

"I'm sorry," Marvin said. "I shouldn't have come here, and I shouldn't have brought Ravyn."

"I'm a big girl," Ravyn insisted. "I came because I wanted to."

"Well, both of you are fucking out of your mind," Nick grunted.

"We were trying to follow up on a lead that *you* chose to ignore," Ravyn snapped.

By now they had moved to the street and were standing in front of Marvin's car, which was parked in front of Nick's. "Do you have any tissue or napkins in there?" Ravyn asked.

Marvin nodded and bent inside, retrieving a small stack of yellow fast-food napkins and pressing them to his nose.

"I checked this lead out already," Nick said. "Not that I have to report to you. This asshole was in jail when his girlfriend was killed."

"You knew that?" Ravyn asked. "You should have told us."

"How was I supposed to know you'd go all Nancy Drew and Hardy Boys on me?"

"We were supposed to be working together."

Nick sighed, hanging on to his temper by a very thin string. "You need to get home and clean yourself up," he told Marvin. "I'll deal with you later."

"My car is at your office," Ravyn said. "I rode with him."

"No kidding?" Nick used thick sarcasm, hoping to hold his anger at bay.

Marvin slid inside his beat-up Toyota and drove away,

still holding the wad of now-reddish napkins against his face.

"Get in," Nick told Ravyn, not looking at her. "I'll take you to your car."

She got in, and they drove to his office in silence. There was a lot Nick wanted to say, but everything ended with him taking over where Moses left off and wringing her fool neck.

They climbed out of his car, and Nick followed her to hers. "That was an idiotic, foolish, dangerous stunt," he began as she reached it.

She turned to him and glared, lifting her chin in defiance. "I was handling it just fine."

"Really? Were you?" Nick reached out and trailed his fingers over the angry red marks on her throat. "Was this part of a devious ploy to give him carpal tunnel syndrome?"

She pulled back, and her eyes snapped with golden sparks. Her lips pressed together so tightly that small lines appeared at the corners of her mouth. "As I said," she managed, still clenching her jaw, "we're supposed to be working together on this. You shut me out."

Nick stepped closer, not touching her but close enough that she backed against her car. Close enough to feel the heat coming from her body. Her breasts rose and fell with her breathing as she stared at him.

"You're not my partner," he said. "Not you, not Marvin. Marvin is a pain in my ass who happens to rent office space from me, and you . . . you're . . ." Nick trailed off, his breath catching in his throat at the look in her lovely emerald eyes.

"I'm what?" Her voice was soft, entreating.

He released his breath, growling at her. "You are the most frustrating, enigmatic, enticing female I've ever met."

"Is that a good thing or a bad thing?"

The air between their bodies zinged, a current of electricity compelling him to close the space and press against her soft curves. Without thinking, without giving himself time to hesitate, as he had before, he stepped closer and bent his head, touching her lips with his. She tasted of mint and woman, of smoky campfires and moonlight. She tasted like heaven.

She moaned, and her hands came up and linked behind his neck, her body pressing against his. Nick gasped, the feel of her soft curves against his hard planes so unexpected, so excruciatingly pleasurable, that he knew he'd never get his fill, could never get close enough.

Heat raced through his blood, pounding along his nerve endings, making him weak with need. He reached down and slipped his hand beneath both shirts she wore, feeling the silky flesh of her back. He ran his fingers along her lower spine, pressing her even closer to him. Her round, soft breasts pushed into his chest, and all he wanted was to feel skin against skin, to slip his body inside hers and release the tension she'd created since the very first moment he laid eyes on her. His erection pulsated, and for a moment he had the horrifying feeling he was going to come in his pants like an untried teenager.

It took his passion-dazed brain a moment to realize that her hands had moved from around his neck and were pushing against his shoulders. She wrenched her mouth from his and stared up at him. Nick saw the same dazed yearning in her eyes that he felt through his entire body.

"Oh, God," he murmured, ashamed at his loss of control and what had almost happened right here in broad daylight. "I'm sorry."

She shook her head. "Not your fault." Her voice was breathless and strained.

Aware that her body was still tormentingly close to his,

Nick stepped back. He raked a hand through his hair and took a long pull of oxygen into his lungs, wishing it were laced with nicotine. "You can't work with me anymore," he said quietly, not looking at her as he turned away to put even more distance between them.

"What?" She grabbed his arm and he turned to face her. "You want me to stop because we kissed? That's ridiculous. We'll just keep a professional distance from now on."

Gently, Nick pried her grip from his bicep. "It's not because we kissed," he replied. *Though there's no way in hell I can be around you and keep my distance.* "It's because you nearly got yourself killed. I never should have involved you in the first place."

She shook her head. "I'm not quitting now. You need me, and I *have* to do this."

Nick wondered what she thought she'd accomplish. "Finding him won't bring your sister back," he reminded her. *And going looking for someone who clearly wants to hurt you seems foolhardy.*

"I know that," she said, her voice thick with emotion. "But it will keep him from hurting anyone else. I'm doing this with or without you. If you don't want to work together, fine." She crossed her arms and lifted her chin. "But I swear to you, I won't stop looking. I'll do it on my own."

Nick rubbed a hand wearily over his face. He believed her. And after what he'd seen today, he couldn't take the chance of her going off alone. "Fine. But from now on, you don't do anything without me there. Understood?"

"Understood," she agreed.

He sighed. "Now go home and stay there until I figure out our next move." When her eyes narrowed suspiciously he added, "I'll let you know before I do anything. I promise."

Apparently satisfied, she turned and got into her car.

Nick watched Ravyn drive away, waiting for his erection to subside and waiting for his heart to stop pounding out the cold, hard truth. He was falling, and he was falling hard.

Chapter Thirty-one

The next night, the members of Ravyn's coven were gathered for the annual Lamenth celebration, a time to honor death and reincarnation, and to pay tribute to loved ones who have passed. There would be a dinner, and afterward they would perform a ritual to connect with those who'd departed.

Ravyn was sad, on edge, and the usual pleasure she took in coven dinners was severely diminished. As children, she and Sorina had dreamed of and longed for the time when they turned twenty-one and would be included in these wonderful, mysterious affairs. When she was ten and Sorina seven, they'd sneaked out of their rooms to observe. The dining-room doors had been open, and from the top of the staircase they'd had a perfect vantage point from which to watch.

Ravyn had decided that if she and her sister were caught, she would make sure Sorina wasn't blamed. Ravyn had planned to say it was her idea, even though they'd thought of it together. The adults would no doubt believe Ravyn was the instigator. After all, she was reputedly willful and incorrigible. At ten Ravyn wasn't sure exactly what those words meant, but her mother and teachers at school had used them, so she knew they must be true.

But they hadn't been caught. They'd crouched there for hours in their bare feet and pink nightgowns, peering through the railing of the staircase. They'd both been enthralled, though for different reasons. Sorina had admired the beautifully gowned women and the handsome men in their tuxedos. Ravyn had simply felt a sense of rightness, of belonging. The warm camaraderie and bonding she'd sensed between the coven members gave her a feeling of peace she hadn't yet experienced at home or school.

When Ravyn had turned twenty-one, three years before Sorina, after each dinner she had regaled her sister with the details of the evening, and Sorina had listened with rapt attention, her eyes round blue saucers of delight.

Sorina's absence tonight left a hollow feeling deep in Ravyn's belly and anguish in her heart. These dinners would never be the same without her sister's wide-eyed wonder.

Gwendyl's seat was empty, too. Where was her mother? She'd never missed a dinner. Ravyn experienced a pang of concern but pushed it aside. Whatever her mother's problem was, she'd brought it on herself.

Vanora's dining table was covered with ivory lace that was inset with tiny gold fibers. Three gold candelabras, one in the middle and one on each end, held long, tapered ivory candles. The glow from their flames increased the understated elegance of the dining room. From the kitchen wafted the delicious scents of the meal: some type of roasted meat, although Ravyn couldn't quite identify it, and the fragrance of vanilla from the undoubtedly delectable dessert that Mindy, Vanora's cook, had concocted.

As always, the dinner was a warm and elegant affair. Elsbeth was lovely and glowing in a silk lavender gown, and Aladardo sat next to her, resplendent in a black tuxedo with a lavender shirt of the same shade. Ravyn's dress was of emerald silk and floor-length, formfitting and backless. Vanora sat at the head of the table, wearing a shimmery silver dress with a fan collar that framed her fiery red hair.

Ravyn tried to keep up with the conversations around

her, but her mind went to Nick, to the kiss they'd shared. She could swear she still felt the touch of his mouth against hers and the warm imprint of his body. A flush spread through her, and she shifted in her seat.

She fought the reaction, good though it felt. This attraction to Nick was unexpected and unwanted, and she didn't know what to do about it. And yet . . . another thought made her smile: Sorina would be pleased after her initial matchmaking efforts. Sorina would be *very* pleased. She had always wanted Ravyn to find someone she could trust.

Ravyn's gaze moved to her sister's empty chair, and her heart ached with the need to see Sorina, to talk to her, to hug her just one more time. Willing away the tears that threatened, she dragged her eyes from the empty place and . . . met Vanora's piercing stare.

Vanora's eyes held . . . what? Disappointment? Anger? Ravyn wasn't sure, but the woman's expression was something other than her typical serene kindness. Ravyn felt a stirring of unease. Had Vanora learned of her activities? Did she know what had happened with the serial killer, with the pervert who had kidnapped the little boy, with Donald Moses? Ravyn's life had been touched by vermin recently. She had been acting out, trying to right her previous wrongs. The insulated cocoon of the coven thus had been compromised, and there was indeed a vile presence on the perimeter, the result, no doubt, of Ravyn breaking the coven rules.

Vanora spoke, and the chatter ceased as all eyes turned to her. She lifted a wineglass, the muted light of the candles reflected in the deep burgundy liquid. "Thank you for coming, my friends. Unfortunately, not all of our beloved are with us to share the occasion." The elder's eyes, nearly the same shade as her dress, glistened with moisture. A poignant smile touched her red-lipsticked mouth, if only briefly, before she continued. "We are not here to mourn, however, but to celebrate life—to converse, to join in fellowship with those we love."

The coven members raised their wineglasses in a toast, and the conversation recommenced along with the serving of the meal.

At last the dinner drew to a close, and the coven members, warmed and replete from the ample food and even more ample wine, rose from their seats. Vanora went to Ravyn and rested a hand on her arm. "Before the ritual, I'd like to speak with you for a moment."

Ravyn nodded, apprehension sliding over her. Vanora's desire for a private conversation could mean only one thing: Ravyn was in trouble.

The elder led her into her sitting room, extracting a slim cigar from a jewel-encrusted humidor. She touched its tip to the flame from a gold lighter, and the fragrance of cherries filled the air. Ravyn took a seat in a black easy chair and waited.

Vanora seated herself on the sofa and exhaled, giving a small sigh of satisfaction. Then the pleasure vanished from her expression and she leaned forward, retrieving a newspaper from the coffee table.

"Care to explain?" she asked, thrusting it toward Ravyn.

Ravyn glanced at the paper where it was folded back to show an article about an attempted kidnapping. Her lungs seemed to freeze for a moment as she read the headline: WOULD-BE KIDNAPPER MYSTERIOUSLY INJURED IN ALTERCATION WITH GOOD SAMARITANS.

Her heart dipped painfully into her stomach, and she swallowed loudly. "I . . . It was . . ."

"I know what it was, Ravyn. You used your powers to wound this man."

"He kidnapped a child, held a gun to his head. I had to do something."

Vanora shook her head in disgust. "You didn't *have* to. You were right to step in, to stop him. But did you have to cause him pain? Was it necessary to break his hand? You couldn't have just weakened his wrist, rendered it useless and made him drop the gun?"

Yes, she could have. But that hadn't been her first instinct. She didn't want to admit it, even to herself, but she'd *wanted* to hurt the bastard. Wanted to make him suffer for what he'd done. What he was planning on doing again. But she couldn't admit that to Vanora.

She shrugged. "I didn't think—"

"That is painfully obvious." Vanora's mouth tightened with anger. "You didn't think at all. You could be banished from the coven for this, don't you realize that?"

Ravyn couldn't speak, so she only nodded. As angry as she was over this, if Vanora knew about the Tin Man, she'd be livid. In all the time Ravyn had known Vanora, she'd never seen the woman lose her composure, and had certainly never seen her so angry with *her*. But, it was understandable. Ravyn had done wrong.

What had gotten into her? In spite of the violence she'd witnessed at home, she'd been raised with the doctrine of peace and love in the coven. She'd broken that twice recently. To be honest, she knew what the problem was: she'd gotten involved, become too close, with mortals and their world.

"I always considered you as the most probable replacement for me when the time comes to step down," Vanora was saying, her tone soft. "But now I don't know. As its high priestess, you must strictly adhere to the teachings of the coven."

"I know." A small thrill of hope wended through Ravyn. She'd always dreamed of one day becoming high priestess, but she'd never imagined Vanora would choose her. The high priestess could not be married, could not even be involved with a man. She must devote all her energy and affection to the coven. Which meant she and Nick could never . . .

But that was a good thing! She had no business becoming involved with Nick. It would be harmful in more ways than one.

As if reading her mind Vanora said, "You don't currently have a love interest, do you? I know you're young, but you don't seem interested in a relationship—not since the debacle with Kayne."

"I'm not. Not at all," Ravyn assured her.

"If that remains the case, I'll bring your name before the council when the time comes. But"—she tapped a manicured fingernail against the newspaper—"incidents like this simply cannot occur. It is bound to be a temptation, what with us being touched by the violence of the secular world, but we must resist. We cannot allow that corruption to affect our emotions, to draw us in. If one is touched by the vile, she must strive to overcome that with our teachings and not with retaliation."

Ravyn nodded reluctantly. Her mind knew what Vanora said was true, but her heart wanted to make the guilty pay—wanted to make them know the pain and suffering their victims knew. And though she was aware her desire for vengeance could destroy her chances of becoming high priestess, she knew she wouldn't stop. She *couldn't* stop. At least, not until one more monster was behind bars or dead.

A short time later Ravyn stood in the ritual place, surrounded by leafless trees and her coven. She had participated in this Lamenth ritual many times, but never had it held more meaning.

A cauldron sat on the altar, steam rising from it even though there was no fire beneath. The coven members were to stare into the smoke rising from the cauldron, and as Vanora recited their entreaty, they would perhaps see the faces of their departed loved ones. Ravyn prayed she would see Sorina, and that her sister would be somehow as happy in death as she had been in life. It seemed unlikely.

Vanora's melodic voice broke the stillness of the night. "We gather to honor our loved ones. We entreat those we love to join us once more. Though they have passed, we hope they will live again, we wish to know them in our future lives. We take these candles and light them from the candle of life."

One by one, each member of the coven stepped forward and touched the flame of their purple tapered candle to Vanora's. Purple represented the calling forth of spirits, the connection to souls who have moved on.

After they were all once more in the circle, the witches closed their eyes and waited, listening. The wind stilled, and around her Ravyn could hear the muted sounds from the deep woods: a rustling, perhaps from a small animal; a gurgle from the stream that flowed nearby; the hoot of an owl. Ravyn set her mind on Sorina, praying her sister would appear.

"We beseech thee," Vanora continued. "Goddess of the departed spirits, reveal to us now those who have passed. Those who wish to be revealed."

Ravyn opened her eyes and stared into the smoke from the iron cauldron. As she watched, the smoke moved, seeming to take on a shape and form something other than the random vapor it had been before. She held her breath, silently willing Sorina's face to appear.

So intent was her concentration, at first she didn't notice the cessation of background noise. Then, all at once, the smell of sulfur permeated the air and the ground seemed to move, undulating beneath her feet. The smoke from the cauldron was once again just smoke.

What was happening? Ravyn's heart began to pound, and she and the other coven members lifted their heads and looked around. From between the trees a hooded figure strode toward them.

Ravyn's heart shifted into overdrive as the apparition moved swiftly forward. This was not the spirit they had intended to conjure. This was something evil, and she could feel it. The tension in her body grew, and she looked to Vanora for guidance.

The high priestess's face was drawn into a grimace of distaste and . . . recognition? This was someone—some*thing*—with which Vanora was acquainted!

Ravyn returned her gaze to the figure, who now stood next to the cauldron. At his feet a swirl of leaves rose, and among them were black wisps of smoke, writhing and boiling mere inches above the ground. Ravyn sensed that within those black wisps was an evil presence. She couldn't say how she knew, only that she did.

The intruder's head was bowed, but he lifted it and threw back the hood of the robe. Ravyn's breath caught in her throat. *Kayne!* He held a hand into the steam from the cauldron, and Ravyn could smell burning flesh.

Kayne grimaced but didn't immediately withdraw his hand. After several seconds, he brought it out from the steam. The flesh was a deep red, almost black in some spots, puckered and already starting to blister. Excruciatingly painful, no doubt.

Kayne smiled and waved the hand in the air. Just like that, the flesh returned to normal; the burns disappeared. The gasps from the coven broke the strange silence that had descended.

Vanora's voice rang out, strong and unafraid. "What are you doing here? You know you're not welcome."

Kayne's gaze focused on Ravyn, but he responded to the elder. "I go where I please. I have the power to infiltrate any ritual, at any time, anywhere in the world. Your pathetic spells cannot stop me." He moved closer to Ravyn, stopping directly in front of her. "You are mine," he whispered. "One of these days you will realize that. You will rule by my side. There is nothing we cannot do together. I need you with me."

Ravyn shook her head, but her voice quavered. She lacked Vanora's strength. "You disgust me. Your evil is appalling. I will never be yours."

Fury crackled in his golden eyes. "You don't seem yet to understand my capabilities."

He whirled and strode swiftly toward Vanora. Ravyn tensed, afraid of what he might do to the older woman. But he just asked her a question, though his voice was soft and taunting. "Is it painful?"

In the dim light of the moon and the coven's candles, Ravyn could see several expressions flit across Vanora's face. First confusion, then shock, then something like despair.

"The cancer," Kayne continued. "Is it painful yet, or only a mild discomfort? It will be more painful as time goes on—you realize that, yes?"

A gasp rose from the coven members. Shock and grief slammed into Ravyn. Vanora had cancer? Surely not. But Ravyn could see the truth reflected in the elder's face.

Vanora didn't respond to him, and Kayne smiled, a slow and malevolent curl of his full lips. Then he returned to Ravyn and gazed down at her. She felt the commanding pull of his personality, his magnetic force.

"Your sister was a lesson you needed to learn. I can take anything from you. Your life, your *lover*." He spat the word with contempt. But Ravyn's concentration was on what he'd said about Sorina. Kayne had somehow been involved. Somehow he'd helped the lunatic Tin Man destroy her precious sister.

Rage and grief took hold of Ravyn, and she lunged for Kayne, but he caught her wrists in a powerful grip. "You cannot harm me. You cannot win. Come to me before all is lost."

As he stared down at her, the world around them went eerily silent. Then he released her and stepped back, lifting his arms to the sky.

Ravyn felt a scratching tickle at her bare feet, heard an unearthly scraping and looked down. Her legs went weak with fear. A multitude of scorpions, so thick she couldn't see the ground, swarmed around her. She choked out a gasp and stumbled back, kicking at the creatures, trying to free herself.

Kayne laughed—a booming, bloodcurdling sound— and waved his arms. The scorpions were gone as quickly as they had appeared. Ravyn stood there, shuddering, trying to gain control, angry at her weakness.

"I can get you and those you care about at any time, any place. Remember that, my love," Kayne said. And then he was gone.

Chapter Thirty-two

Marvin's nose was sore, and he had a black eye, but after thinking about it, what had happened a few days ago was actually pretty freakin' awesome. Maybe he hadn't done a lot to help, but he'd been in the thick of things. That was a rush like none he'd never felt before.

The office was quiet. Nick wasn't in yet. He was either running down leads or sleeping off a hangover. Either way, the guy was super cool. Everything he did was *mega* super cool. And Marvin could see there was something brewing between him and Ravyn, the lucky bastard. The chick was sort of strange—weird in a sexy, wouldn't-want-to-meet-her-in-a-dark-alley kind of way. But he'd meet her in the bedroom. She was pretty damn hot.

Marvin peeked out the front window, making sure Nick's car wasn't in the parking lot. All clear.

He opened Nick's office door and stepped inside. Settling into Nick's chair, he leaned back and propped his feet up on the desk. He picked up the phone and spoke into the receiver in his deepest, most gravelly voice. "Lassiter here. Yeah, I took care of those perps. That's right, *perps*. There were five of them. Kicked their asses clear into tomorrow. Got a little cut up, two of 'em had knives, but I stitched up my wounds with nothing but a belt of whiskey for painkiller."

He grinned and put down the receiver. Nick had promised him he could help on a case, but after the stunt with Moses, that might not happen. He *had* to, though. How cool would it be to help solve the Tin Man case? Man, that dude was one bad hombre. Marvin shuddered. It would be super cool to help, but he wouldn't want to actually *catch* the guy. What Moses had done to him would probably seem like getting bitch-slapped by Britney Spears in comparison.

Marvin got up and swaggered around the office, stopping in front of the Pete Rose photo. Pretty tight, that Nick's hero was a fuck-up like Rose. Kicked out of baseball for gambling. Shit. Lassiter liked 'em damaged, didn't he?

Marvin needed a shot of whiskey and maybe a smoke. He didn't drink, had never touched a cigarette, but what the hell. Nick sure looked cool doing it.

He went back and plopped down in the chair again. "Let's see," he murmured. "Where does he keep the hard stuff?"

He opened the top left drawer. Nothing but a notepad and a few pens. He grabbed the drawer just underneath. He wasn't sure if he heard the blast first, or felt the impact, but the explosion blew him—chair and all—through the window, bloody shattered glass falling about him like rain.

Nick was on his way to the office when his cell phone rang. It was his old captain. Nick hadn't talked to the guy since he left the force.

"I need to see you," the captain said right away. "Can you swing by?"

"Right now?" Nick asked.

"It's urgent. Extremely."

Nick's curiosity made him turn the car around and head to the precinct.

Betty was once again at the front desk, and she gave Nick a friendly smile as he waited for her to let the captain know he'd arrived. After a matter of seconds, she buzzed

Nick through, and he entered the captain's office. The blinds had been pulled down on the windows.

Captain Locke had always been a neat freak, maybe bordering on obsessive. His desk reflected that tendency, with the few stacks of paperwork on top arranged into precise piles, and a pencil holder with one capped ink pen and two recently sharpened pencils sticking out. His walls held framed commendations, each hanging ruler straight, and one photo of himself and Oklahoma country-music singers Vince Gill and Toby Keith at a celebrity golf tournament.

In the years since Nick had last seen him, Captain Locke had added a few pounds to his already large physique. With his thick dark hair and squinty eyes, he looked like a paler, more rotund version of Wayne Newton.

"Coffee?" Locke asked when Nick was seated in the chair across from him.

"I didn't like the way they made it when I worked here, and doubt if it's any better now."

"Okay. I'll get straight to the point. What do you know about witchcraft?"

Nick chuckled. "Witchcraft? You mean the religious kind, the *Bewitched* kind, or the broomstick and cauldron kind?"

Locke ignored his sarcasm. "Actual witchcraft. As in evil powers, spells and so forth."

"Nothing, except that it doesn't exist. Mind telling me why the hell you're asking?"

The captain blew out a breath and leaned forward, folding his arms on top of the desk. "Let me start from the beginning." Locke brushed a hand over his thick hair, not ruffling a strand. "A few months ago, we started hearing reports of cult activities in Wyldewood. Are you familiar with the town?"

Nick shook his head.

"It's just outside of Tulsa. Anyway, we didn't put much stock in it. Then, a few weeks ago, a woman came to us with quite a story. Wouldn't have believed a word of it, but she had video to back it up. She was a member of this cult. In the beginning she was a willing participant—she had a sexual relationship with the leader. After a while, she became suspicious he had other women, so she went to one of those online spy shops and got herself some concealed photography equipment and bugged his bedroom. What she got on tape was more than she bargained for, and it scared the bejesus out of her. So she bolted. Moved back here, came in with the tape. Now we're interested."

"What's on the tape?"

"It's something you just have to see."

"So show me."

"We'll get to that." Locke took a slurp of coffee from the "I hate Mondays" mug on his desk. "But first, I need to ask you some questions."

"Well, first let me ask you something. What does this have to do with me?"

"I'll get to that. And after I explain, I'm going to ask for your help."

Nick fought surprise. "With what?"

"We've formed an under-the-radar task force. This isn't something the general public should be aware of, at least not until we know all the details. Especially if it all turns out to be a hoax. I mean . . . we're talking about witches, for chrissakes. We'd be the laughingstock of the state—hell, the country! The task force is made up of a handful of undercovers. And we'd like you to head it up."

Nick grinned and shook his head. "You want me to head up a task force to hunt witches?"

"Put like that, it sounds crazy. But yes."

Nick leaned back and linked his hands behind his head. "Well, I'd love to help, but right now I'm busy chasing down vampires and werewolves. But I promise witches are next on the list."

The captain's face colored and he took another swig of coffee. "Always were a smart-ass," he muttered. "I know it sounds ridiculous, but if you'll hear me out . . ."

"I'm no longer on the force, yet you intend to put me in charge of a task force?"

Locke shrugged. "You know the department uses civilians from time to time. And you are a licensed PI. I'm well aware of how capable you are. I think you're the right man for the job."

"And if it goes south, your ass is covered. The blame goes on the drunken fuck-up."

A line of red climbed up Locke's neck into his face. "Not exactly a positive way of looking at it, but you got me. Pretty much the plan in a nutshell."

"Fine. Ask your questions and show your video so I can get the hell out of here."

"Does the name Kayne mean anything to you?"

Kayne? The only one he'd ever met or heard of with that name was the Fabio wannabe who'd come to see Ravyn. Nick tensed, his interest growing in spite of himself. "Why don't you just tell me exactly what this is about and what my connection is?"

"Kayne—whether that's a first or last name we have no idea, but it's all we have—is reputed to be the leader of this cult. We've had a tail on him. We know he visited the shop that belongs to the Tin Man survivor. We know you're on the Tin Man case. We know you've been hanging around the shop quite a bit. There're a lot of questions and a lot of loose ends."

Nick's relaxed pose immediately became alert, and he leaned forward in his chair. "You think I'm involved?" He clenched his fists between his knees, trying to keep a rein on his anger.

Locke gave him a sly look. "Would I ask you to head up the task force if I did?"

"I have no idea, but that sounded like an accusation. This is all so insane. I don't know where you're going with it. So just tell me what the hell is going on. Get to the point."

"I wouldn't have believed it if I hadn't seen it on tape," Locke admitted.

"Are you going to show me the goddamned thing or not?"

"I'd rather not, unless I know you're going to work with us."

"Then I guess we'll have to skip movie night." Nick stood. "Thanks for wasting my time."

"Will you at least think about it? I believe you'll see that it's to your advantage. You might say you have a personal stake in this."

Nick sighed and raked his fingers through his hair. This was getting ludicrous. "Would you just quit with your cloak-and-dagger bullshit and show me the goddamned tape? You're not going to get me otherwise."

Locke sighed and stood. He opened a desk drawer and pulled out a DVD. "Okay. Follow me."

Nick trailed behind him to the conference room. When he was settled behind the table, the captain slid the disk into a player and took a seat across the way. He pushed a button on a remote. "There are other things happening on the tape, but this is the part you'll be interested in."

The television screen filled with the image of a bedroom with a large four-poster bed and a low altarlike table in the center of the room. The table held black candles and an object that looked like a picture frame, but Nick couldn't be certain, since it was facing away from the camera.

The door opened, and a figure wearing a black hooded

robe stepped into the room. Even with the hood partially obscuring his features, Nick recognized Kayne. It was the same guy from the candle shop.

The room was in partial darkness, but when Kayne lit the candles on the altar it gave a flickering illumination to his face and to the item on the table. Kayne stepped back and pulled a long, black-handled blade from somewhere in the folds of his robe. He held the wicked-looking weapon over his head and began speaking in a coarse, booming voice that prickled the skin on the back of Nick's neck.

"I invoke thee, King of Darkness. Grant thy powers to me that mine enemy shall know no mercy. Darker than darkness, deeper than night . . . I seek thy assistance. Time is short and destruction is nigh. I implore thee that together we shall crush him, and his soul shall be mine that I might rule with strength and eternal life."

A loud crash of thunder sounded, and jagged lightning ripped across the screen. Nick tried to tell himself that it was trick photography, but the chill that rode his spine told him otherwise.

Kayne lifted the frame off the altar and held it in one hand, the dagger in the other. His head fell back and the hood slid off. Eyes closed, he hoisted both objects toward the ceiling as another round of thunder and lightning reverberated through the room. In that moment, the photo was turned toward the camera and Nick's limbs turned to jelly. He recognized the picture.

Barely breathing, he choked out the first words he'd spoken since the tape began. "The sonofabitch. That's my wife."

The captain's voice came to him as if from far away, while Nick stared, mesmerized, at his missing wedding photo.

"Now do you see?" the captain asked.

Nick nodded, still not sure exactly *what* he'd seen. It

took several seconds for him to find his voice. "What the fuck was that all about?"

The captain huffed out a breath and shook his head. "Unfortunately, we have no idea. That was just a sample of your link to this . . . madman. Whatever he is." The captain hit the remote again. "This is the part where the department becomes interested."

The same room opened up, but this time a young girl, maybe eighteen or nineteen, knelt on the bed. She was pretty, and had long blonde hair. A small diamond glinted from the side of her nose.

Kayne stood in front of her. She was naked, but Kayne again wore a robe. "You have disobeyed me," he said in a low, ominous voice.

She nodded. "I'm sorry. I just went to the mall for a little while. I didn't know—"

"You knew," he cut her off. "And now you must be punished."

She nodded slowly and bowed her head, but not before Nick saw the tears streaming down her cheeks.

Kayne's fist came up, and in it he held the dagger. The dagger came down and the girl screamed. After a few moments, she wasn't pretty anymore.

"Good God!" Nick breathed, still staring long after the screen went black.

"He didn't kill her." The captain's voice seemed to come from far away. "But apparently he keeps his followers in line with savagery and threats. Our witness is terrified."

"Why the hell haven't you brought the guy in?"

"We had a tail on him, but by the time we saw this tape we'd lost him. Will you work with us?"

Nick stood on shaky legs and walked to the door, not looking at the captain. The words trembled out of him unsteadily, like the hand that twisted the doorknob as he sought escape from the oppressive air in the room and the horror he'd witnessed that inexplicably had something to do with him. He drew in a deep breath and spoke without turning around. "Set up a meeting with the task force. I'll be there."

Chapter Thirty-three

Nick left the station, his mind nearly exploding with the images on the tape as he drove. Now that he wasn't actually looking at them, he could almost convince himself they hadn't been real. But they were. He'd seen them. In startling, spine-chilling clarity. The motherfucker had been in his house. He had to have been—he had the photo, didn't he? Unless . . .

Ravyn had been at his home. She'd had the opportunity and a history with the lunatic. Could she have . . . ? No. She wouldn't do that. Surely she wouldn't. But what did Nick really know about her? Other than his out-of-control-and-growing-stronger-every-day desire for her, what did he really know?

Deep in thought as he was, the proximity of the sirens didn't register at first. He saw the emergency vehicles before he turned onto the street where his office was located. He couldn't get within thirty feet of the building, so he stopped the car and climbed out, staring with all the other gawkers at the smoking ruins. A sick, clogging sensation filled his chest. The disaster zone was his office.

He pushed to the front of the crowd, but one of the firemen stopped him. "Hey buddy, you'll need to back away from here," the man said.

"It's my place. My office. What the hell happened?"

The fireman's expression changed to one of interest combined with sympathy. "Come with me."

He led Nick to the fire chief, Rick Furlan. Nick had

worked with the chief in the past, and he automatically stuck out his hand for the handshake Furlan offered. "I'm sorry, Lassiter. It's not good."

"Just tell me. What happened?"

"There was an explosion. We're not sure of all the details yet. Far as we can tell, only one person was in the building at the time. Does that sound right?"

Marvin. Good God. Nick nodded. "Is he . . . ?"

One of the firemen rushed up, his grimy features tense. "Chief, we've got the blaze under control and the scene secured."

Furlan wiped a hand across his face, smearing the soot and perspiration. His gaze swept the area, and he looked back at the firefighter. "Do another sweep and hang tight. I'll be right there."

When the younger man nodded and left, Furlan turned back to Nick. "They took him to Sacred Memorial. He was still alive, but it looked pretty bad."

Nick barely heard anything else. He turned and pushed through the crowd, climbed in his car and drove to the hospital with a stone of dread resting between his chest and stomach. He steeled himself for the reaction he knew he would have as he entered the building. His actions were like clips from a slide show: asking at the front desk for Marvin, punching the elevator button, exiting at the ICU.

The nurse at the desk stopped him. "Can I help you?"

"My . . . friend was brought here. I need to see him." Already the nausea was surfacing. Black shadows pushed at the edge of his vision, but he wouldn't pass out. He gave the woman Marvin's name, and her mouth turned down in what he recognized as a look of sympathy. God, this was bad.

She pointed down the hall. "Room four eighteen."

Nick hurried down the hallway and took a deep but unsteady breath outside Marvin's room. Pushing the door open, he stepped inside, and the queasiness hit him full force.

There were so many machines in the room, it looked like the set of a Star Wars movie. Marvin lay in the bed—or he supposed it was Marvin, for the person was so covered in bandages that Nick couldn't make out his features.

A pretty nurse wearing Betty Boop scrubs stood next to the bed, fiddling with tubes that snaked out of Marvin like the tentacles of an octopus. She turned and smiled at Nick. She had smooth mocha skin and large brown eyes. "Are you a family member?" she asked.

Nick shook his head. "A friend. How is he?"

"He's hanging in there. His injuries are pretty extensive, but he's lucky to be alive after what happened."

Nick nodded and made his way to the opposite side of the bed. Marvin's hand was bandaged heavily, but Nick gripped the fingertips that poked out of the white gauze. He stared down at Marvin, thinking of all the times the guy had annoyed the hell out of him, all the times Nick had wished him anywhere else. Now he'd give anything to hear one of the kid's stupid, grating comments, or hear him beg to come along on a case. The last time they'd spoken, Nick had chewed him out for his stupid-ass stunt with Moses.

"Sorry, bud. I was just trying to protect you." His voice came out as a hoarse whisper, and he knew he was close to tears.

He heard a sound at the door and turned to find a female version of Marvin entering the room. She was thin, with the same coarsely wild hair. Then he remembered. Marvin had a sister. This must be her.

He released Marvin's hand and walked over to her. "Hi. I'm Nick Lassiter."

She nodded. "I know. He talks about you all the time. I'm his sister, Ramona." Her eyes filled with tears as she looked at her brother's still form. "What happened? I mean, I know it was some kind of explosion, but how? How did it happen?"

"I'm not sure," Nick admitted. "They're investigating now."

Ramona nodded, and tears swam in her eyes. She reached out her arms, and Nick hesitated only a moment before pulling her to him in an awkward hug. She patted his shoulder, squeezing him tightly before releasing him and moving to her brother's side.

Nick left Marvin's sister to her silent vigil, still fighting the panicked queasiness clawing at his insides. Even though this was different from the usual MO, he knew in his gut the Tin Man was responsible. The Tin Man had injured, maybe killed, Marvin. Had murdered Sorina. Had almost killed Ravyn. The motherfucker was going down.

His cell phone was in the car, and he saw he'd missed a call. From Phil. He returned the call, staring up at the hospital as he waited for Phil to answer.

"I don't have anything yet," Nick told him. "But I guarantee you, before long I will."

"Why do you say that now?" Phil asked. "After all this time you haven't been sure. Why now?"

"Because." Nick started the car, gripping the steering wheel with one hand and the cell phone with the other. "Because I'm back. He's fucked with me one too many times. This guy's going down."

Ravyn answered the door to find her grandmother standing on the porch. "Yes?" she said without inviting the woman in.

The old woman smiled. "I just wanted to see you again. Just wanted to see how you're doing."

"I'm fine," Ravyn said.

"Can I come in?"

Ravyn hesitated, then stepped aside and motioned. "Please. And sit down."

Her grandmother lowered herself onto the sofa in the living room and gave another tremulous smile. "You're so beautiful. You've grown up into an amazing young woman."

Ravyn ignored the comment. "Is there something I can help you with?"

"I wondered how you're getting along. Have you gone back to work at the shop yet?"

"How do you know about the shop?"

She shrugged. "I know a lot about you, dear. You and your sister have been my life for more than twenty years. I just lived it from the sidelines." Her eyes watered and took on a faraway look. "I just wish I'd come around before Sorina . . ."

"I'm not sure that would have been a good idea. Sorina was impressionable. Your appearance in her life and your stories about our father might have really done a number on her."

"Everyone deserves the truth. Deserves to know their history." The old woman clasped her wrinkled hands together on her lap. "Do *you* know your history? Why you feel that choking sensation?"

Ravyn barely held in her gasp. How did the woman know so much? Her insides tightened with apprehension, and she felt sure she didn't want to hear any more. "You need to leave."

"I don't mean to frighten you, I just want you to understand why you feel the way you do. It's because of your past life."

Ravyn knew she'd lived before, knew she'd lived many lives. That was part of her people's teaching. But she didn't know details—and she wasn't sure she wanted to. But her grandmother pressed on, oblivious.

"You were hanged as punishment for witchcraft. That is why you fear it so deeply. When they were about to hang you, you showed no emotion, no remorse. This just convinced them of your guilt. Your refusal to give in to your emotions was part of your downfall. And you still won't let yourself feel."

"For God's sake, I'm grieving for Sorina!"

The old woman nodded. "That's easy. She was your sister, and now she's gone. You have to learn to feel for someone who can return those feelings or reject you. You have to feel real emotion. *Risky* emotion."

Ravyn looked toward the window, where the moon shifted across the gauzy crimson sheers. Trying to keep her voice level, she said, "I've gotten by fine without it so far."

"Have you? Or have you missed out on things you aren't even aware of?"

Ravyn looked back at her grandmother and shrugged. "If I'm not aware I missed out, then I guess it doesn't matter, does it?"

A smile crossed the woman's face, and Ravyn realized it was an expression of pity. "Before they hanged you, you were in love. But you wouldn't let him know. He was going off to battle, and he told you he loved you. You wouldn't tell him the same. He left and never came back. The others with him said he seemed distracted and sad, and that was why he died. He couldn't concentrate. He had no fire, no strength. When you heard the news, you went a little crazy with guilt. You were starting fires, making it storm with your powers, causing destruction. They knew then that you were a witch, and they hanged you."

Ravyn shivered. Flashes of the time to which her grandmother referred slammed into her mind. "I remember," she whispered. Her throat began to close.

"Don't let your resistance to emotion make you hard,

make you lose something you love. Don't repeat your mistake," her grandmother implored her.

Ravyn didn't speak for a moment, couldn't, until at last the sensation of asphyxiation began to recede. "I won't," she finally managed. "I know what I'm doing."

"Are you sure?" her grandmother asked.

"Of course! Besides, Nick's not going into battle, and I don't love him."

"Nick?" Her grandmother's shrewd eyes transfixed Ravyn. "Did I say anything about Nick?"

When Ravyn didn't respond, the old woman stood. "You're very strong, much stronger than me or your mother. You'll be fine. But you must try to remember your former life. I cannot tell you everything; some of it you must remember on your own."

"I don't want to remember!" Ravyn snapped.

"But knowledge is power, my dear. Even though it may be difficult, painful to think of such horrific things, sometimes facing up to them can help us gain the strength we need. And sometimes we are tested so that we can find the strength to face our pasts. And never, ever, underestimate the power of love. It's got a magic all its own, and with it, miracles can happen. One day, you'll believe. You'll learn it firsthand."

"You think so?" Ravyn's eyebrows rose skeptically.

"No, my dear. I *know* so."

Her grandmother rose without another word. She made her way to the door, and Ravyn followed, letting her out. On the porch, the woman turned back to her. "I hope someday you can forgive me. I hope one day we can be a family."

Ravyn was so intent on her grandmother's request that she hadn't heard the car pull up, but suddenly, Nick was stepping onto the porch. "Nick?" she said, confused.

"We need to talk."

Ravyn nodded and glanced at her grandmother, thinking to introduce them. "This is . . ."

"Nadine." Her grandmother extended a bony, arthritic hand. "I'm her neighbor."

"Nick Lassiter." The two shook hands, and Nadine gave Ravyn a knowing smile. Then she stepped off the porch and disappeared into the darkness.

Ravyn invited Nick inside, almost unconsciously putting a hand to her throat as she thought of what her grandmother had revealed. She'd always wondered, always wanted to know what the sensations meant. And now she knew. But what was she *not* remembering? What was she not facing? Was that just as important?

Nick waited while Ravyn closed the door. She turned and looked at him expectantly. Struggling to keep his emotions in check, he took her by the arms and pulled her toward him, brought her close enough that he could stare directly into her face. "Tell me the truth," he demanded.

Anger flashed in her eyes, and she tried to jerk away from his grip. "Let me go!"

"Not until you come clean."

Her struggles ceased, but the anger still simmered. "About what?"

"Your boyfriend, the photo. Tell me what the fuck you've done."

Her gaze searched his, and suddenly, in the silence of the room, he could hear the thumping of his heart as he waited for her answer. In spite of his suspicions, in spite of his concern for Marvin, he felt it again: that same desire, urge, whatever it was, drumming through his body as it did each time she was near. His skin felt tight on his bones, tingling with the need to touch Ravyn, to possess her, to feel her soft lips giving beneath his again.

"Let me go," she demanded. "Then I'll answer your insane accusations. But take your hands off me."

He released her and stepped back, jamming his hands in his pockets, needing to do something with them other than touch her.

"I don't have a boyfriend," she informed him. "If you're talking about Kayne, that was a long time ago. I have no idea what photo you're referring to, and no idea what the hell it has to do with Kayne."

He sighed, wanting to believe her—his instincts told him he should. But with all that had happened, he didn't know what to think anymore.

He decided to tell her the truth. Or at least half of it. "Your friend Kayne has been . . . stirring things up. Making threats. As you may recall, my wedding photo is missing. I've torn the house upside down and still haven't found it." He stopped there, damn sure he wasn't going to tell her where it had last been seen, wasn't going to tell her what he'd witnessed on the tape. "Also . . . Marvin is barely hanging on to his life after an explosion at my office."

Ravyn gasped and raised a hand to her mouth, then let it drop. "Oh, no! Is he going to be okay?"

Nick lifted a shoulder in a shrug. "He's in critical condition. They're not sure."

She stared at him, sorrow in her eyes. "I'm sorry about your photo and what happened to Marvin. And I have no idea what Kayne is up to. But why do you think these are related incidents? What kind of threats has Kayne been making?"

"Let's just say he's mentioned my name, and not in a favorable way. My wedding photo . . . Well, you're the only person who's been in my house in several weeks."

"Why on earth would I take your wedding photo?" Ravyn snapped. "You're not making any sense. I'd give anything to find and stop the maniac who killed Sorina, and who I assume hurt Marvin, but I don't know what Kayne has to do with it. I don't know what you're accusing me of, or why. Why?"

Seeing her confusion and pain, Nick sighed and shook his head. "Damn it, I don't know. I don't know."

She put a hand on his arm. "I'm sorry, Nick."

He gave her a small, humorless smile. "Sorry for what? Are you sorry that the motherfucker you were once sleeping with is a dangerous fanatic? Sorry that someone stole my wedding photo? Or are you sorry that I can't stop thinking about you, can't stop wanting you? Sorry that my desire for you is stronger than it ever was for my dead wife?" He grabbed her once more and pulled her to him. "Do you have any idea how crazy that is? How it makes me feel? I want you every second of every day. Even with people dying around me, even with the frustration and guilt of not being able to stop this murdering psychopath, I still want you."

They stood for a moment, mere inches separating them, their breaths ragged and mingled. Ravyn's lips parted and her eyes stared into his. He wasn't sure what he saw there, but he thought it was the same churning need he felt.

Before he could give in to the disastrous impulse to kiss her, his cell phone chirped. He exhaled a shaky breath and released Ravyn to answer the call. It was the fire chief.

"Lassiter, Furlan here. Our preliminary investigation shows a very small amount of explosive was used, probably the only reason your friend is still with us. The blast originated in the office on the southeast corner."

My office, Nick thought. *That was intended for me.* The Tin Man or Kayne had to have been involved. It was the only explanation. "Thanks."

"No problem. I'll let you know if I learn more."

Nick ended the call. "I need to go," he told Ravyn.

She nodded, rubbing her hands up and down her arms as if warding off a chill. "Was that news on Marvin?"

"Nothing's changed," Nick told her. It was a brusque reply, but for some reason he was reluctant to admit aloud that his tenant was clinging to life because some asshole wanted Nick dead.

Chapter Thirty-four

Ravyn paced her living room, twisting her hands together, trying to think what to do next. Nick had left some time ago, giving her time to ruminate. She'd come to a few conclusions. Kayne was a part of what had happened to Sorina. He'd somehow helped the Tin Man. She recalled snatches of the dream she'd had the night Sorina disappeared—a dream similar to the one she'd had when Nick spent the night at her place. Except they hadn't really been dreams. Kayne, in some form, had actually been in her room. Yes. Kayne's stamp was all over this whole mess. So, most likely he'd been involved with everything else.

The explosion?

Of course. Both Kayne and the Tin Man were likely behind what had happened to Marvin. Something had to be done.

Grabbing her coat, she hurried to her car and drove to Nick's office, hoping he wouldn't be angry—or that he wouldn't find out what she was doing.

Firemen and the media swarmed the area like ants on a discarded crumb. Several civilians stood just outside the crime-scene tape. The front of the building was mostly intact, but the back was severely damaged.

Parking as close as she could to the building, Ravyn looked around. When she was certain no one would notice, she hurried inside. In Nick's office she walked here and there, stepping over shards of plaster, wood and glass. She touched what remained of the inner wall and stood silent, head bowed, for several moments. There wasn't much left.

For a moment she could almost feel Marvin's pain, his terror. He'd been sitting in Nick's chair. He was happy, in a good mood—a state of mind she sensed was common with Marvin. She thought of his goofy charm, his guileless innocence, and a pang shot through her. She'd caused harm to come to him, too. When would it stop? Who else had to suffer before the Tin Man and Kayne were destroyed? Why hadn't she destroyed the murdering SOB when she first had the chance?

An impression came suddenly, and Ravyn's shoulders tensed. She saw something just on the edge of her mind's eye. *There.* It was stronger now . . . and a moment later all was clear.

Nick looked around the table at the five men handpicked by the captain. Two of them he'd worked with before, and they were good men. Two he didn't know, but the captain had the utmost confidence in their abilities. The other was Kyle Black, Scott Harris's former partner. Sonofabitch.

What the heck was the captain thinking? Black looked at Nick with seething hatred. Nick pretended not to notice, though the animosity was coming off the man in waves. He took a seat across from him.

Nick hadn't wanted to come to the meeting. It had already been a hell of a day, and this was the last thing he wanted to deal with. But he'd told the captain he'd be here. It might help take his mind off what had happened at his office—and Marvin's condition.

The task-force members filled Nick in on what they knew so far, which wasn't much. And they reminded him they'd had someone following Kayne but lost him.

Nick was in charge. "We should all work separately for the time being," he said. "The more we spread out, the more likely we are to spot him."

"I'll head to Wyldewood," volunteered Novack, one of the men Nick had worked with before.

Nick nodded. "I'll stick close to Miss Skyler. The rest of you go wherever your leads might take you. Anything comes up, anything at all, even a whiff, give the rest of us a shout. The important thing is to keep each other apprised."

"I have a question," Black said.

Nick looked at him expectantly.

"Let's say we're working the case"—his lips twisted in a sneer—"and you show up wasted off your ass. Or you pass out cold on us. What are we supposed to do then?"

One of the other men snickered, but Nick's eyes were on Black, and he wasn't sure which. He supposed it didn't matter. He was here to get things done. "Look, I know you have a problem with me, and I'm not sure why we're both here," he admitted. "But since we are, and since I'm in charge, I'm not putting up with any bullshit. We need to put our differences aside and work together, or you need to get the fuck out."

"Yeah, I got a problem with you," Black growled. "Anytime a cop stabs one of his brothers in the back I got a problem."

Nick stood and splayed his hands on top of the table, leaning forward to make it clear he wasn't afraid. "Harris may be your buddy, but he's a fucking psycho who shouldn't be on the streets. If you think it's okay for someone to abuse their power and beat up a little girl, you're as fucked as he is."

Black stood and puffed out his chest. "He didn't—"

"I was there!" Nick cut him off. "But I don't give a damn

if you believe me or not. That's not the issue here. That's old news. The issue is whether we can work together or I have to have your ass replaced."

"I'm staying," Black growled.

"Then you'll keep your goddamned opinions to yourself."

The cop opened his mouth, but before he could speak Nick's phone rang. An unfamiliar number was listed.

He flipped the phone open. "Lassiter," he barked, his gaze still on Black.

"Was Marvin from Texas?" It was Ravyn.

"What?" Nick fought confusion. "No, I don't think so."

"Are you?"

"No, why? What's going on?"

"Nothing. Never mind. Thanks."

"Wait. Where are you?" he asked. She didn't answer, but he heard the squawk of walkie-talkies and fading sirens in the background and knew. "What are you doing at my office?" he demanded.

"I need to go." She broke the connection, and he clenched the cell phone against his ear.

"We'll pick this up later," he told the task force. "Let me know if you find anything." Then Nick stalked from the room, hoping he'd find Ravyn before she once again did something that put her in danger.

When he got to his office, his heart dipped in his chest as the odor of wet, smoke-soaked wood and rubber assailed his nostrils. He even thought he could smell singed flesh, but that was probably his imagination.

The front of the building was mostly intact, but once inside he saw the gaping hole that had been his work space. He went weak with relief when he found Ravyn inside, unharmed.

"Mind telling me what the hell's going on?" he asked.

She shrugged. "I saw something. You have no connection to Texas?"

Nick shook his head. "No. Why?"

"I wonder if *he* does," she mused softly.

"What do you see, exactly?"

"An address in Garland. Just outside of Dallas."

Nick didn't know whether to believe in this intuition she claimed she had, but he had witnessed her rescue of the kidnapped boy, and he had nothing else to go on at the moment. He took her arm, steering her toward the front of the building and said, "You up for a road trip?"

The girls were fit and tan, their short cheerleader skirts flying up to reveal the matching panties beneath. Jay was far enough away that they shouldn't spot him, but close enough to hear their shrill voices squealing out their ridiculous cheers.

One of them in particular caught his eye. She was the only brunette in the group. She was different, and these days "different" appealed. She reminded him of Ravyn—a younger, more cheerful Ravyn, perhaps. He knew what he had to do. She was a little young, and not what he usually went for, but it had to be fate that he'd cruised by this school on his drive to clear his head.

It was a cool day, a bit nippy for the girls to be outside in those skimpy outfits. He could almost see the goosebumps on their firm young legs. He felt a tremble of lust work through his groin and he leaned back in his seat, hoping . . . But no, the physical desire was just an illusion. Like feeling in an amputated limb, it was a phantom sensation, and there was nothing he could do about it. Even if he had all six of those nubile young things alone, naked, at his mercy, frightened beyond their wildest nightmares . . .

He shook his head. Enticing, heart-stoppingly beautiful

and terrifying, the bitch Ravyn Skyler would pay. Her sister's life wasn't enough. He'd make her pay, make her beg and scream with fear. This brunette cheerleader would be practice, though. She'd be a prelude of things to come.

He watched for a while longer, until practice ended. Then he trailed behind as the brunette walked to a black Camaro.

Two of the other cheerleaders, both blondes, climbed inside the car with her. Damn, she was surrounded by friends. But that was no problem. Jay slid behind the wheel of his car, keeping an eye on the Camaro. The brunette had to be alone sometime, and he'd wait. He was a patient man.

Chapter Thirty-five

They arrived in Garland just before dark. Ravyn directed Nick to a neighborhood of almost identical middle-class homes with similarly manicured lawns. When he located the correct house number, he pulled over against the curb in front. Foliage with purplish berry-looking blooms clung to a small fountain that was flanked on either side by dwarf lawn ornaments. A silver Cadillac was parked in the driveway.

"It doesn't look like the home of a monster," Ravyn said quietly.

"They seldom do."

"What now?"

"You stay in the car. I'll knock on the door and check it out."

Ravyn was shaking her head before he completed the sentence. "I'm going with you. I've come this far, and I won't stop now."

Nick sighed in exasperation. "If the man who tried to carve you up is in there, I don't want to have to worry about watching out for you." He reached for the door handle. "You're staying in the car."

Ravyn grabbed his arm. "Please." He looked down at her hand on his sleeve. Even through the cloth, he could feel the burning heat of her touch. Her nearness made it difficult to concentrate, difficult to breathe. He couldn't have her with him when he faced whatever he was about to face. He had a feeling it would play out very badly if he did.

He placed his free hand over hers and looked into her eyes. "I don't know if you realize it, but I've grown to care about you." He looked down and rubbed his thumb over the soft skin just below her knuckles. "Through my mistakes I already allowed something to happen to your sister. I couldn't deal with it if"—he cleared his throat and raised his eyes back to her—"if something happened to you, too. Stay in the car."

He opened the door and without looking back approached the house. Slipping a hand down to the Beretta in its holster, he was reaching for the bell when he heard a noise behind him. He whirled, at the same time starting to draw the gun.

"Jesus, Ravyn." Shakily he let the gun slide back in place. "Don't you listen to anything? At least stay behind me."

She did, and he rang the doorbell. From inside he could hear a game show playing on a television. After a moment, a woman's voice traveled through the closed door. "Yes? Can I help you?"

"I'm a detective, ma'am. I have a few questions, if you'll please open the door." He lifted his PI badge to the peephole, hoping she wouldn't study it too closely.

The door was opened by a woman who looked to be in her early sixties. She was trim, with black frame glasses and gray hair pulled into a ponytail at the nape of her neck. She wore jeans and a long-sleeved white shirt with a green and gold plaid vest. Not knowing her name or where to start with the questioning put Nick in an awkward position. He decided to wing it.

"We're investigating a string of robberies in Oklahoma City," he told her after she'd offered both him and Ravyn a seat in an immaculate, tastefully decorated living room. "A piece of mail with this address was left at one of the scenes, but the name was obliterated. The envelope was tattered, and only the address was visible. We're chasing down anything and everything, and wondered if we could chat with you for a moment, Mrs. . . . ?"

She looked at him suspiciously. "This sounds very bizarre."

"Yes, it most definitely is," Ravyn inserted. "But we have absolutely no leads, nothing. At this point, we're grasping at straws."

The woman nodded. "I see. I'm Kay O'Connell, and I have no idea why mail with this address would be at the scene of a robbery." She laughed. "I'm a widow, I live alone, I'm sixty-five years old and I haven't robbed anyone in . . . oh, I don't know, years."

Nick smiled at the woman and cut Ravyn a look from the corner of his eye. She had to have been way off on this one. He searched his brain for something else to ask but came up blank. He was about to thank the woman and say his good-byes when Ravyn spoke again.

"How did your husband die?"

Mrs. O'Connell's eyes flew to Ravyn's. "Why?"

Ravyn shrugged. "I just want to know."

The woman cleared her throat and looked down at her clasped hands where they rested in her lap. "Three years ago, my husband was in a car accident. He died shortly after reaching the hospital." She lifted her head and her eyes were wet. "I never got to say good-bye."

"I'm sorry," Ravyn said quietly. The story was clearly not what she'd been expecting.

"He was a good man. I miss him every day. I know it's been a while, but . . ." She gave a small, bleak smile. "He was the love of my life."

"Thank you, Mrs. O'Connell." Nick stood. They'd intruded on this woman's grief long enough, and all for nothing. "We'll get out of your way now. Good-bye."

Ravyn stood also, but when the woman walked them to

the door, Ravyn turned. "Was your husband an organ donor?" she asked.

Mrs. O'Connell's startled gaze flew from Ravyn to Nick, then back again. "Why, yes. Yes he was. Why?"

Nick's pulse raced. He understood.

"Do you know the name of any of the recipients?" Ravyn asked. "Specifically, the person who received his heart?"

Mrs. O'Connell's face hardened, and her suspicious look returned. She shook her head. "That information is confidential. Please, I think you both should go."

Nick put a hand on Ravyn's lower back and guided her out the door. "Again, we're sorry, Mrs. O'Connell. Thank you for your time."

The woman nodded but said nothing more.

It was fully dark now, and in the driveway Ravyn stopped next to the Cadillac and turned to face Nick. The security light over the garage door illuminated one side of her face, while leaving the other in shadow. "That's it," she said softly. "The killer is the heart recipient. It makes sense. The medication . . . the name the Tin Man . . . my impressions. We have to find out his name. We have to get our hands on a donor list."

"That's nearly impossible," Nick muttered. At the same time, his mind was running through a list of people who owed him favors. The list was painfully short. And not one of them had access to any organ-donor registry.

Ravyn crossed her arms and shook her head. "We're so close. We can't give up now." She leaned back against Mrs. O'Donnell's car, and he could see how tense she was. Then, suddenly, she moved away from the Cadillac, staggering forward and clutching her head.

"Ravyn?" He reached out and took her shoulders, but she jerked away. Her hands moved from her head down to her neck, and she made gagging noises as if choking to death. "Ravyn!" He tried once more to touch her, but she fell to her knees, her eyes staring wildly in front of her.

"I see him!" The words burst forth from her constricted throat. "I see his name. I know . . . I know where he lives."

Her eyes turned up to him and he saw horror in their emerald depths. Her hands dropped from her neck, and in a voice radiating pure terror, she said, "He has her and we're too late. She's going to die."

Chapter Thirty-six

Nick grabbed Ravyn by the shoulders, this time not letting her jerk free as he pulled her to her feet. He shook her and stared directly into her face. "Has who? Who is *she?*"

"I don't know, but she's in danger. Terrible danger."

Nick released Ravyn abruptly and pulled his cell phone from his pocket, dialing the OCPD as he spoke. "Give me his name, the address. We'll head back that way, but it will take over three hours to get there. The cops can check it out in the meantime."

Ravyn nodded and gave him the information she had somehow gleaned.

Nick dialed as they climbed into the car and squealed off toward the highway.

"Harris," the voice on the other end of the phone stated.

Great. "Harris, it's Nick Lassiter."

"What do you want?"

"We have a lead. I need you—"

"*We* have a lead? Who the fuck you think you are? You're not a cop anymore, buddy boy."

"Goddammit, Harris, just listen to me. Someone's gonna die if you don't. I need you to check out a Jay Haleck." He gave Harris the address. "Get over there now." And then, because he thought it might feed Harris's lust for power and prompt him to hurry, he added, "Please."

"I got it," Harris said.

Nick pushed the car as fast as he dared, all the while

casting worried glances at Ravyn. She sat in the passenger seat, staring out into the blackness, her arms crossed tightly against her chest.

Half an hour later, when his cell phone shrilled in the silence, she jumped.

"We checked it out," Harris said. "Nothing. No one home. No sign of anything suspicious. We ran a check, and the guy's a doctor. Well respected. I don't know where you got your information, but he's not our guy."

Nick hung up and relayed the information to Ravyn.

She shook her head vehemently. "They're wrong. It's him. I *know* it's him, and the girl is going to die." She slammed a fist against the dash and fell back against her seat. "Hurry. If they won't do anything, we'll have to. Hurry, Nick, please."

Not knowing whether to believe her, he nevertheless increased his speed. Ravyn might be totally off base, but he'd damn sure rather be wrong and waste a little time than ignore her and waste a life.

The house Ravyn directed him to was worth twice the one they'd just left. Set back from the road and steeped in darkness, elegance and wealth emanated from the structure. Tall white columns flanked the entrance, and large bay windows stretched out over the artfully landscaped lawn.

Rather than park his car in the winding drive and announce their presence, Nick stopped at the curb. He knew Ravyn would argue with him, but he said the words anyway. "Stay here."

She pulled on the handle and was out of the car before he was. "You must be out of your mind."

As she started across the lawn, he ran to catch up with her. "What do you think you're doing?" He grabbed her arm and whirled her to face him.

She jerked away, her expression tormented as she spoke

in a hoarse whisper. "I couldn't save my sister. Maybe I can save someone else's."

She started off again, and he once more stopped her. "You can't just march up to the door and confront this guy. It's not like we're cops with a warrant. We don't have anything but a hunch. Slow down and stay behind me. I'll handle this, and maybe we can all go home happy."

"You don't believe me," she grumbled.

"What?"

"You're humoring me, but you don't really believe this is the killer, do you?"

Nick shook his head and expelled a breath. "I don't know what to believe. Still, the things I've learned lately, the things I've seen . . . Let's just say for now I'm willing to play along. But we still have to do things right. Come on." He pulled his Beretta, took her by the hand and kept her behind him as they approached the door.

The house was dark and quiet. Too quiet. The silence cast an ominous pall over everything.

Nick knocked on the door, keeping Ravyn behind him and his gun drawn. When there was no answer, he motioned for her to follow him around the side of the house, looking for another way in.

Ravyn stopped next to a basement window on the east side of the house. Nick turned back to hurry her. "Come on," he whispered. "We'll try the back door."

She shook her head and dropped to her knees. When she turned her face up to him, the moon cast slivers of light over her cheeks. "He's in there. We have to go in now."

Nick shivered, his hand holding the gun going numb. Ravyn had sensed it even before the screaming started: someone was being tortured inside.

Chapter Thirty-seven

The knees of Ravyn's pants were soaked, but she barely noticed as she tugged on the basement window. She could open it another way but was afraid of what that might precipitate. Would it so completely stun Nick that he would be less effective in saving the girl—or perhaps even careless enough to lose his own life?

She deliberated, but he reached down and lifted her to her feet. Aiming his gun at the latch, he fired, then threw open the window and hurled himself inside. Ravyn followed.

The basement was actually a converted sitting room. A television and stereo rested against one wall. On the opposite side was a forest green sofa, above which hung a life-size painting of a stern-looking, fiftyish woman in a shiny mauve pantsuit. The rest of the room was in shadow, all except the center, where a bright light shone down on a table. An operating table. A young girl covered to her neck by a blue sheet lay upon it. Her eyes were closed.

The man standing next to her looked up. His face was partially covered by a surgical mask, but Ravyn knew it was him. Her enemy. He held aloft a scalpel.

Nick aimed his gun. "Drop it and step away. Now," he ordered.

The man's eyes crinkled as if he was smiling beneath the mask. "If I step away, the girl will die. You see, not only am I her tormenter, I'm her savior."

"Step the fuck away," Nick commanded.

The doctor shook his head and didn't move. Nor did he lower the scalpel toward the girl. "I've opened her up and closed her again twice already." He glanced at a heart monitor next to him. "She's stable at the moment, but just barely. She's open right now. If I don't close her, she will die."

The girl moaned, and her eyes fluttered. Nick's gun wavered, and he muttered under his breath. "For chrissakes. Is she conscious? Can she feel what you're doing, you fucking psycho?"

The Tin Man's eyes crinkled again. "I prefer 'fucking psycho *genius*,' but have it your way." His gaze dropped to his victim. "She's not fully conscious, but she was just a moment ago. Before long the anesthesia will wear off. If you truly want to save her, you need to back away and let me finish my work. I need to close her up."

A strange glow came into those demented eyes, and a thin sheet of perspiration dotted the man's forehead. "I've had her on the brink of death and brought her back. Twice! She's been pain free most of the time, but not entirely." He shrugged. "What fun would it be if I couldn't hear her scream even a little? Of course, too much pain and she would die on me. And that can't happen. Not yet, anyway." He sighed regretfully and shook his head. "Now, with your untimely arrival, maybe not at all. But I've had my satisfaction and I, quite frankly, don't want to die. So, I'm going to do as you wish and anesthetize this young woman, sew her up and save her life. Then you can take me in so I can go through the formalities of a trial before they find me insane and lock me up to live the rest of my days ruminating over the pleasures of the past few years."

His eyes went to Ravyn. "I want you to know, my dear. You were the most exciting of all my experiments. I'd hoped to have you one last time . . . *there*." His gaze dropped to the table. "It wasn't to be. But having you here to watch my final act is almost as rewarding."

"What the hell is *wrong* with you?" Ravyn's voice was almost a whisper. She knew the question was pointless, but she asked nonetheless.

"With me?" Those eyes took on a new look, and there was a touch of bewildered innocence in the mask of depravity. "It's not *me*. I was a victim, the recipient of another's heart. I have no heart of my own, so I'm not to blame."

"Good God, you're out of your fucking mind," Nick spat. "The heart transplant had nothing to do with your evil. You blame the man who saved your life by giving you his heart? A heart that could have gone to someone worthy? Someone who deserved to live?"

The Tin Man shrugged. "We're talking semantics, I suppose. Now I must get back to my work."

He turned away, as if Nick didn't have a weapon trained on him. Picking up a syringe, he shot some clear liquid into an IV tube. The girl's eyelids stopped fluttering, and her moans ceased. The Tin Man bent over and began suturing the gaping wound in her exposed stomach.

Ravyn glanced at Nick and saw the uncertainty on his face. Take him down now and risk killing the girl? Or let him finish and still risk his killing the girl—and perhaps somehow escaping?

Ravyn ached with the urge to put an end to the murderer's reign of terror. She could attempt to end his life and save the girl, but she couldn't promise she would be successful. After all, she'd never used her powers to take another's life. What if she made a mistake and harmed the girl in her effort to save her? No. She couldn't take that chance. Her grandmother had told her to trust Nick, and she would. Nick would get them out of this alive. Mortal or not, he would save them. She had to believe.

Nick's arm was steady as he kept his gun leveled on the Tin Man. His gaze flickered back and forth between the maniac and the victim. The room was silent except for the beep of a heart monitor.

"There," the Tin Man announced, tying off the final suture. He turned to face them, and too late, Ravyn realized that although he no longer held the scalpel, his hands were not empty.

Her mind registered his weapon half a second before she saw the muzzle flash and heard the report of the bullet, which whizzed past her. She whirled, and just as Nick fell, screamed his name. Whipping back around, she saw the Tin Man lower his mask and smile widely. He was still holding his gun, and he glanced at Nick's inert body and said, "Not so tough after all, was he?"

He walked toward Ravyn slowly. "Just take it easy. I know what you're capable of, but that's not going to happen this time. I've had the assistance of an old friend of yours, and he assured me you wouldn't attack me again. He says you and your friends are too weak. And he told me I can control you with narcotics." The Tin Man pulled a syringe from the pocket of his surgical gown.

"You killed him." Ravyn's voice shook, tears of rage nearly making the words impossible to say. She began to tremble, and blood pounded through her veins. She could feel the rage taking over, knew what she was going to do and couldn't control it. She had to, though. She had to control it so her powers would stay intact and she could help Nick. Maybe he wasn't dead. Maybe she could still help him.

She used every ounce of willpower she possessed, but still her arm lifted and her splayed fingers pointed at her enemy. The Tin Man was only a few feet in front of her, and she knew what was going to happen, but she couldn't stop. He looked into her eyes, and his own widened.

"You can't!" he screeched. "He told me you can't hurt me! You did before, and you paid for it! You won't break the laws again. He promised me that you won't hurt me!"

Ravyn's glance went to the painting of the austere-looking woman. *Mother.* Jay Haleck's demon. The source of his terror. Time to put an end to his misery.

"I won't," Ravyn replied. "But *she* will."

The Tin Man lunged forward, and Ravyn whipped her arm around and pointed at the painting. Blue flames shot from her fingertips, and the room darkened, then exploded with a blinding blue light.

"You stupid, spineless little cocksucker!" A voice, female yet deep and gravelly, echoed through the room. The Tin Man whirled and a scream of agony ripped from his throat.

"No, no, no!" He backed away, moaning and whimpering as the apparition slowly stalked him, the satiny mauve pantsuit making a *swish-swish* noise with each movement. The woman held a wrinkled, bony hand out toward her son, and then she threw her head back, cackling shrilly in pleasure.

"You must be punished, you naughty boy. Too long I've waited, and you must be punished!"

It was too much for the Tin Man. Just before Ravyn turned and fell to her knees beside Nick, she saw him shove his own gun into his mouth. The echo of the weapon was more muffled this time, but the red spray on the wall behind him was proof of its deadliness.

Ravyn stared at Nick. Dark red blood ran in rivulets from his chest to the ground. She whispered his name.

His face was chalk white, but his eyelids slowly opened. "I . . . How's the girl?"

Ravyn swallowed back tears. "She's okay. She's sedated. You're the one . . ."

He shook his head. "The Tin Man?"

"He's dead." She sniffed. "Don't talk. Hold on, I'm calling nine-one-one."

His lips twitched in a smile that became a grimace. "Too late for that, baby. It's bad. You see all the blood I've lost? But we did it, Ravyn. We got him. We got the Tin Man." He coughed, and as if to confirm his prognosis, a fresh torrent of blood seeped from his wound.

"It's not too late," Ravyn insisted tearfully. "You can't die, Nick. Dammit, you *can't* die."

His eyes lifted to hers. "Dying ain't so bad. It's dying slow that's a motherfucker." His facial muscles clenched one more time before he went still.

Chapter Thirty-eight

"No!" Panic crowded Ravyn's throat, and her chest ached. She couldn't let Nick die. She couldn't lose him. She *loved* him.

Her numb fingers fumbled into his jacket pocket for his cell phone, then stopped. He wouldn't make it to the hospital. He was dying in front of her eyes. She had to help him herself. But if she did that, he would surely know what she was. Her secret would be out, and she didn't know what would happen next.

It didn't matter. She couldn't let Nick die. She'd deal with the consequences no matter what they were.

Closing her eyes, she leaned her head back and placed her fingers over his wound. She let energy flow from her mind to her heart and through her veins. Felt it pump through her like the blood that pulsed from Nick's chest. Her skin tingled, and a crackling sound filled the room. Strobes of blue light shot across the walls and the ceiling and over Nick's supine form.

Ravyn looked down at Nick, holding out her hands which were sticky with his blood. His upper body spasmed, then rose a few inches off the floor before sinking back down, but the blood began to recede, fading away as if it had never been. The hole in his chest closed, and color came back to his face.

Ravyn went limp, the tingles across her flesh turning into an aching burn. It took all her effort to pull air into her lungs as she struggled to steady the quaking in her limbs. But Nick's breathing was even, strong. He would regain consciousness any second. She had to hurry.

She pulled out his cell and dialed 911, anonymously reporting the girl's injuries and their location. Rising to her feet, Ravyn stood for a moment, willing the trembling in her legs to cease. Then she stared down at Nick and slowly backed toward the door.

"Good-bye," she whispered. Climbing back up the stairs, she fled into the night.

Nick opened his eyes, for a moment unclear on where he was. The ceiling was unfamiliar, and he couldn't think with the pain slicing through his head. He must have been knocked unconscious, must have . . .

Suddenly, he remembered and rose to a sitting position, and at the same moment he heard sirens above his head. He looked around and saw the lifeless form of the murdering psycho. The white walls behind the Tin Man and his green scrubs were splattered with blood, bone fragments and bits of grayish brain matter. Nothing was left of the top of his head.

Had Ravyn . . . ?

No. Nick saw the hand still curled around the butt of the gun and knew what had happened. But there was only Nick, the dead guy and the injured girl. Ravyn was gone.

"Freeze, police!" The pounding of feet on the basement steps merged with the squawk of walkie-talkies and the wheels of an EMT's gurney.

Nick stood and faced Carlos Mungia and Scott Harris. Kyle Black followed. The air was ripe with the stench of blood and death. A low moan came from the girl on the operating table.

"I should have known," Harris sneered. "You sorry sonofabitch. What the hell did you do?"

Nick looked at Mungia. "Call off your dog and I'll give you a statement."

Carlos put a hand out and pushed down Harris's weapon. "Cool it, Scott. You know he's not our man."

Nick shook his head and pointed. "There's your man, but he already did your work for you. Killed himself. How is she?" Nick asked the paramedics transferring the girl to the gurney.

The taller technician shrugged. "Stable at the moment. We'll see."

"Thanks." Nick turned once more to the detectives. "Let's get this over with."

"How did you know to come here?" Mungia asked.

"I had a tip. After I called Harris and gave him the info, I headed here."

"Called Harris?" Mungia shot a look at his partner. "Lassiter called you?"

Harris's face colored. "Some fucked-up story about a lead. I ran a check, found out the guy was a doctor. . . ." He swallowed, his voice fading as his gaze took in the carnage surrounding them.

"Sonofabitch," Mungia said under his breath. "What else?" he asked Nick.

Nick relayed the rest of the story, answering Mungia's questions quickly and concisely, anxious to find Ravyn. Not only did he want to know what had happened, he had to know she was okay. And he had a desperate, panicky need just to see her.

He left out the part where the Tin Man shot him. He wasn't sure it was even true, although he recalled it in vivid detail. But that was too insane, because he was obviously unscathed. He didn't want them thinking he'd been drinking. He hadn't touched a drop in days.

"You can go now," Detective Mungia told him after he'd given his statement.

"The hell he can," Harris sputtered. "You don't believe him, do you? Don't you find it a little odd that he's been right in the thick of things from the beginning of this case?" He turned to Nick and pulled out his handcuffs. "You're under arrest."

Mungia sighed. "Back off, Scott. He's been in the thick of it because he's investigating. He's a private detective, and he did what the two of us couldn't. As a matter of fact, he told you to check this guy out, and you came up empty. Nearly got this girl killed. Remember?" Mungia gave Nick a rueful look. "You might say he's a hero."

"A hero?" Harris screeched. "He's a fucking washed-up alcoholic and a goddamned murderer!" He dropped the handcuffs and pulled out his gun, pointing it at Nick. "You're not going to jail, motherfucker, you're going to *die.*"

Nick lifted his hands and faced the angry detective. "Calm down. Let's talk about this."

"Drop it, Scott." Mungia had pulled his weapon, and it was trained on his partner. "Don't make me do something I don't want to do."

"What?" Harris whirled. Spittle flew from his lips as he screamed, the cry of rage sounding like that of a wounded animal. "You'd take his side over mine? Your own partner?"

At that moment, more footsteps pounded on the stairs, and out of the corner of his eye Nick saw two uniforms appear in the basement. "What the . . . ?" one of them said.

Harris's gaze flicked to the stairs. "You're all against me? You all think he's some kind of fucking saint? He tried to have me fired. Tried to ruin my life over some little crack whore!"

Nick inched closer to Harris while the man's wild-eyed gaze roved from the uniforms to Carlos, then back again. "I'll fucking kill you all!" Arms trembling, Harris lifted the weapon toward the cops on the basement steps. Nick lunged and the weapon discharged, just missing the two uniforms, who stood in shocked stillness.

"Get off me!" Harris screamed in Nick's face, rage contorting his features. He jerked and bucked like a man in the grip of a seizure.

Detective Mungia muttered an obscenity, kneeling to slap the cuffs on his partner's wrists as Nick moved off him. He looked up at Nick. "The guy's not right. Hasn't been for a while, but I ignored it. Can't ignore it any longer." Harris thrashed beneath him, shouting curses, his face scrunched in fury.

Black spoke slowly, incredulously. "Good God. He almost killed another cop."

Nick said, "He needs help."

Mungia nodded. "Damn sure needs to be off the streets." He put his hand on Nick's shoulder. "Thanks. You saved our asses."

Nick shrugged. "Saved my own."

"Yeah, right." Mungia gave a grim smile and pulled his partner to his feet.

Harris glared at Nick. "This isn't the last of it," he seethed. "You're going down. Hard."

Black stared at his friend, shaking his head. "What the hell happened to you?"

For the first time, Harris fell silent. He dropped his head and stared at the ground, his shoulders stiff and his chest moving rapidly.

"Come on." Mungia tugged on him, and the uniforms, who were still frozen on the stairs, moved aside to let them pass.

Black stepped over to Nick and offered his hand. "Sorry, man. I had you wrong. I just heard what Scott told me and . . ." He trailed off, looking sheepish.

Nick stared at the cop's hand a moment before finally shaking it. "No problem."

"The task force?" Black asked. "You still on that?"

Nick shrugged. "I have some things I need to take care of. We'll see what happens."

Black nodded. "Just let me know."

Nick walked to the basement steps and up past the uniforms, accepting their mumbled thanks as he rushed out the door.

In spite of the fact that his driving need to find Ravyn was paramount in his mind, there was another task he needed to take care of, too. As he drove, he placed a call to Phil Bodinski.

"We got him," he said as soon as Phil answered.

"What?" Phil's voice held a hesitant elation, as if he'd been told he won the lottery but they had to check his numbers one more time. "You got the Tin Man?"

"Yeah. He's dead."

"How? Who was he?"

Nick didn't feel like going into it now. He could barely concentrate on the conversation enough to give even the smallest details. "Why don't we meet in my office next week? I'll explain everything. I just wanted you to know it's over. It's finally over."

"I don't . . ." Nick heard Phil swallow, and his voice was thick with tears when he continued. "I don't know how to thank you. Now Lindsey can finally have peace."

"You can, too, Phil."

A humorless chuckle came over the line. "Peace, yeah. Maybe not happiness, but peace is good, too."

Chapter Thirty-nine

Ravyn sank onto her sofa, her body boneless and weary, her energy spent. She let her head fall back, took deep, slow breaths. Tears threatened at the back of her eyelids, but she didn't let them fall. It was over. The psycho was dead and Nick was fine. She could go on with her life.

But it was a life without her sister and Nick. And what about Kayne? She knew he'd had a hand in this. She also knew he wasn't finished with whatever he planned. But she couldn't worry about that now. Not tonight. She was drained.

She didn't realize she'd dozed off until a pounding woke her. Someone was at the door. Kayne? No, knocking wasn't his style. Even vigorous knocking, such as the kind taking place now.

She stumbled to the door and opened it to find Nick standing on her porch. He pushed past her and she closed the door, turning to face him. She supposed she'd known he would follow her.

"What happened?" His voice was ragged, his jaw clenched against barely contained emotion.

She shrugged, unable to summon the energy to do more. "What do you mean? You were there. The Tin Man killed himself. Is the girl okay?"

"She's fine." Nick stared at her. "I mean, what happened to me? He shot me."

She gave a laugh that sounded phony even to herself. "*Shot* you? You seem fine."

"I know. That's what I don't understand. I woke up and . . ." He raked a hand through his hair. "God. I don't know. It's all so muddled."

"I can't help you, Nick. I have no idea what you're talking about."

He looked at her, but this time the distress was gone. In its place was . . . desire? Was that what she saw in the cobalt gaze? Did he desire her as much as she desired him?

He took a step toward her, and she instinctively stepped back.

"Don't," he whispered. "Don't run."

"I'm not. What do you want?" she said.

He took another step and reached out to caress her cheek. "What do I want?" He shook his head. "What I've wanted from the moment I saw you."

Ravyn's eyes drifted shut. This couldn't happen. But even as that thought crossed her mind, she swayed toward him, leaned into his touch, his strength.

"Ravyn."

Her name was a groan that came from deep within him. His hand slipped from her cheek to the back of her head. She opened her eyes. His lips were a mere hairbreadth away. His gaze locked with hers, and he must have seen the surrender in her soul. His head tilted forward, and his mouth touched hers. She moaned, and her eyes closed again as he pulled her to him.

"Nick." She breathed his name against his lips.

His kiss was firm and hot, demanding. His tongue probed, and she opened to him, shuddering with a wild, aching desire more powerful than any spell she'd ever encountered.

He stroked his hands over her back, then down to her hips, fitting her against his erection. A current of heat zipped through her, tingling over her nipples and ending in a warm, wet rush where their bodies met. She couldn't fight it anymore: she wanted him, and damn the consequences. Nothing mattered at this moment except his touch, even if it was the touch of a mortal.

She sensed a change in him, a tensing of his muscles beneath her seeking hands. He lifted his head and broke the kiss with a strangled groan. Still holding her against him, he closed his eyes, breathing harshly, the sound an echo of her pounding heart.

"What's wrong?" she whispered, feeling tremors, not knowing if they came from his body or hers.

He shook his head. "I haven't . . . not since Annie. I haven't been with . . ."

Dazed, she brushed her hair back from her face with a trembling hand. "But you . . ."

Then she understood, and it surprised her how much the knowledge hurt. In spite of releasing his guilt over his wife's death, he couldn't make love to Ravyn without feeling he was betraying her.

"You're not being unfaithful." Her voice was gentle as she put her hands on his face, and he opened his eyes and stared down at her. "She's gone, and she would want you to be happy. You're not betraying her."

He smiled and shook his head, and it was clear that she'd misunderstood. "No. It's not that. It's just . . ." Dropping his arms, he stepped away, blushing. "It's been a *very* long time." The expression on his face was tortured. "I don't want to disappoint you."

"Oh," was all Ravyn could manage. He was simply afraid of living up to what he thought she deserved. Her love for him swelled, growing inside her and filling her with equal amounts of joy and fear. It was true—she loved him. A mortal. Such feelings were dangerous and off-limits, but Nick Lassiter made her heart race in a way no other man had. He made her wonder what it would be like to wake up next to him. Made her want to please him. Made her want to dare all.

She stepped toward him and took his hand, staring up into his eyes. "You won't. I promise."

He looked at her for a long moment, then sighed and dipped his head, crushing his mouth to hers. Tangling his hands in her hair, he devoured her lips, groaning deep in his throat as her tongue thrust against his. His hand slipped from her head to her hips, caressing her bottom. He pressed her even closer. Then he pulled back and took her by the hand, leading her to the steps and up to her loft.

To her bed.

Chapter Forty

They stood staring at one another. Moonlight shone through the curtains, bathing the room in its soft light. Nick reached out a hand and brushed the hair from Ravyn's face. "I haven't wanted any woman since Annie, but I've wanted you from the moment I saw you. With Annie, it was slow and comfortable. We'd known each other in school as friends, then it grew to something else. It was good, and it was right, but with you . . ." He shook his head as if the words escaped him.

"Shhh." She put a finger over his lips. "You don't have to explain."

He gripped her fingers and pressed a kiss to them. "I want to tell you. I want you to understand that it's not just physical. With you, it's been like a clap of thunder went off in my chest, in my head. You filled me with this strange longing, this need to be with you, to know you in every way possible. I wanted to protect you, yet I was afraid of you. Afraid of how you made me feel."

She smiled and stood on tiptoe, pressing her lips to his. "That's the nicest thing anyone ever said to me," she whispered. "Now, *show* me."

He gave a shaky laugh and eased her down on the edge of the mattress, kneeling in front of her. For a moment he simply stared up into her eyes. "God, you're beautiful. I want to see all of you."

She nodded and slowly began loosening the buttons on her blouse. Nick lifted his hand and ran a finger down the skin revealed by her movements. She closed her eyes, her breath catching in her throat at the feel of his callused fingertips against her sensitive flesh.

She heard him gasp, and opened her eyes to find him staring at her breasts, which were covered only by her lacy black bra. In the dim light of the bedroom, his eyes were shimmering beacons of desire. She took his face in her hands and kissed him long and deep. She whimpered as his fingers brushed her nipples, caressing her through the lace. He grazed his hands along the flesh beneath her bra, sliding his touch around her rib cage while his mouth played with hers.

His fingers fiddled with the clasp at her back, and she felt it loosen. He slipped his hand to the front, cupping her breasts, his thumb teasing her nipple. She moaned, easing onto her back. He stayed with her, bracing himself with one hand on the bed while the other flicked and teased, making her crazy with the need to feel him inside her.

He pulled his mouth from hers, looking into her eyes. His hand left her breast and slid to the button on her slacks, deftly opening them and slipping his fingers inside.

"Yes," she said softly when his fingers found the edge of her panties. Then he was touching her, and she tensed as the moist heat gathered between her thighs. "Yes," she said again when he probed inside her. His thumb rotated firmly against her clit, and she began to move against his fingers, wanting to undress him and feel him naked beside her, but unable to stop the delicious sensations he was creating. She gripped his shoulders, feeling a wave of release move through her. Dropping her head back on the bedspread, she let out a small yelp of satisfaction as ecstasy throbbed through her, leaving her spent and utterly, gloriously satisfied.

"Wow," she said.

He laughed and placed a quick, hard kiss on her lips. "That was just the appetizer."

She gave him a slow, contented smile. "Then let's get to the main course."

Still naked from the waist up, she rose onto her knees and slipped Nick's T-shirt over his head. Straddling him, she pressed her breasts against his chest and kissed his neck, nibbling on his earlobe while she scraped her nails lightly along his forearms.

"God," he groaned. His hands moved over her shoulders, down the length of her back, massaging and caressing. "You're driving me crazy."

She nipped at his shoulder, soothing the spot with her tongue. "Then do something about it."

He flipped her over on her back, tugging at the snap on his jeans. He slipped them off, along with his underwear, and lay beside her. Tenderly he let his hands roam over her skin, caressing every inch of her with his fingers and then his lips.

Her skin tingled with renewed desire, and she felt a hot, aching urge from deep within. Reaching between them, she took him in her hands, stroking his hardness as she once more rained kisses along his chest, his shoulders, his neck.

"I'm tired of playing nice," she whispered into his ear.

"Woman." His groan was one of agony and pleasure. He gripped the waistband of her slacks and jerked them down, tossing them across the room. Hooking a finger in her panties, he removed them, then slid on top of her. "You're asking for it."

She gasped with delight as he entered her, moving against her slowly at first, increasing his strokes as she lifted her hips to meet him.

"I'm sorry," he panted. "I can't . . . I need to . . . Oh,

God." She felt a warm rush and then a throbbing inside her as he climaxed. He collapsed on top of her, using his elbows to hold some of his weight. "I'm sorry! I didn't mean to . . ."

"Shhh," she whispered, once again rocking her hips, grinding against him until she felt tremors pounding through her, moving up her thighs and her lower belly, exploding into spasms of pleasure.

"Mmmmm," she murmured against his shoulder as she held him to her. "You *so* did not forget how to do it."

He laughed and rolled off her, lying beside her and running a hand down her side and over the curve of her hip. "That was pretty good."

Playfully, she slapped him on the shoulder. "*Pretty good?*"

"*Pretty good* is a euphemism for *amazing*. Out of this world, incredible, phenomenal . . ."

She smiled. "Nice save, Lassiter."

He pulled the blankets over them both, scooting closer to her, one arm wrapped tightly around her body. His fingers caressed the skin between her breasts, then skimmed down over her belly. He stopped when he touched the burn mark from the Tin Man's knife. "I wanted to kill him for hurting you. He took that away from me."

"He can't hurt anyone ever again. That's all that matters."

Nick placed a kiss on the top of her head and sighed. "I love you," he whispered.

She froze. He *loved* her? She squeezed her eyes tightly shut, once more feeling the odd mixture of joy and fear. She loved him, too. But she couldn't say it. She couldn't tell him, because that would bind her to pursuing that love. And she couldn't. Not right now. She had to sort out her feelings first. Had to deal with the fact that she'd done the one thing she'd sworn to never do—and that wasn't just helping kill the Tin Man. No, she'd fallen for a mortal.

He didn't seem to notice her lack of response. In seconds, Ravyn felt Nick's body relax, and he was snoring softly. She laid her head on his shoulder and reached up to rest a hand on his chest. His heart thumped steadily beneath her palm, and she let her eyes drift shut, content for now just to be close to him.

Suddenly, like a runaway train, images slammed into her mind and she gasped, her eyes popping open. A task force? Nick was on a task force to hunt witches. Her throat closed and she jerked her hand from his chest. Did Nick know she was a witch? Surely not! He'd made love to her. Tender, passionate love. He couldn't know.

But that didn't matter. Because he would destroy her when he found out, her and everyone she loved. What else could a mortal policeman do?

No, he won't, she told herself. But the truth was, she was risking more than herself. Beautiful, kind Vanora, who seldom left the home she loved but welcomed others into it with warmth and kindness. Elsbeth, who was due to give birth to Adalardo's child after years of trying. Their fertility ritual had been performed monthly for the past five years, and finally, the couple had shared their joyous news. And there were the others, the peace-loving, generous people she'd grown up with. All would be destroyed when Nick exposed them as witches. They would be misunderstood. Punished.

She felt sorrow gather at the back of her throat, and this time she let her tears fall. Easing away from Nick, she took several deep breaths, willing her strangling sensation to ease. She had to think. Had to do something. But what?

A rush of cold air swept through the room, and Ravyn

shivered as Kayne's laughter rang in her ears. Looking wildly around, she could see no one. Just the same, she knew that he was there.

Nick woke abruptly, unsure for a moment where he was or what had roused him. Suddenly he remembered and reached out . . . but Ravyn was gone.

And then he heard something else, and he knew exactly what had woken him. An unearthly voice boomed through the room, and Nick's flesh froze even as his heart clenched. He was ashamed to acknowledge the feeling, but it was fear. Overwhelming, terrible fear.

Come with me, Ravyn. It's your destiny.

"You're not my destiny. You're my affliction."

A crash of thunder shook the room, and lightning snaked across the ceiling and walls. Nick bolted upright, wide-eyed, and saw Ravyn standing at the foot of the bed, one leg propped on the railing. She wore black, tight-fitting slacks and a billowy white blouse. One leg of her pants was pushed up, and she slipped an evil-looking dagger into her boot before she dropped her pant leg over it.

"Ravyn?" he said.

She whirled toward him, a look of such anguish on her face that he wanted to go to her. But he was paralyzed. Fear and shock kept him immobile. What was going on?

She shook her head, tears in her voice. "I'm sorry, Nick."

"Sorry? What the hell is happening?"

"I can't explain. I have to go. Please don't hate me."

He threw the covers back and stood, facing her, his nudity making him feel both vulnerable and foolish. "You're not going anywhere until you tell me what's going on. What happened back at the Tin Man's house, and what is happening here?"

Then it occurred to him, and a wash of chills raced up

his vertebrae to the skin of his neck, prickling his scalp with terror. The pieces began clicking into place like some horrific Rubik's Cube: her relationship to Kayne, the strange rituals, the healing of his gunshot wound, the lightning he'd thought he saw. Jesus, the confrontation with the child molester! It all made sense now, in an insane, twisted sort of way.

"You're a witch, aren't you?" The words sounded ridiculous coming from his lips, but he knew they were true. He started toward her.

She backed away, her voice thick and hoarse. "Stay away, Nick."

"I have to take you in. At least to have them talk to you." He didn't want to believe, didn't want to do this. But whatever was going on could only mean danger for everyone. They were investigating Kayne, and who knew where that would lead and how Ravyn was connected? He had to take her to the station. For her own good.

She shook her head from side to side, still backing away. "Don't make me hurt you, Nick."

A part of his mind wondered why the voice—Kayne, he now knew it to be—had gone silent. Had they been plotting all this time? Had the love and desire he'd felt for Ravyn been a spell or some sort of demonic pact? Were such things possible? Could anything be worse than serial killers like the Tin Man?

He gave a harsh laugh. "Hurt me? Good God, like you haven't already? What kind of sick game have you been playing? All this time I wanted to protect you, and you could have just waved your magic wand or whatever the hell you do and made it all go away."

"It doesn't work like that," she said. "I couldn't . . ."

"Couldn't what? Couldn't have stopped the psycho before he murdered your sister? Why didn't you stop him before that?"

A sob tore from Ravyn's chest, but no tears fell. Her body visibly quaked as she faced him, not speaking.

"What are you two planning?" Nick ground his molars, barely keeping his emotions in check. "You and Kayne. Is this about what I saw in that video?"

"What video?"

"The one of your lover and some kind of freaking ceremony . . . a ceremony with my wedding photo."

"He . . . Oh, no!" She squeezed her eyes shut. "How did you see?"

"It's a long story—and it doesn't seem so important right now. Not nearly important as *what* I saw."

Her voice was cold, determined. "It's my fault. I have to end this."

He reached for his pants and pulled the gun from its holster, pointing it at the woman he loved. He couldn't imagine her doing anything to harm him, but how stupid had he been in the past? And why wasn't she helping him make it easier on her, if she was innocent?

"Stop right there. I have to take you in," he said. But the words were hollow, weak, so faint he could almost convince himself he hadn't said them.

Ravyn shook her head, her breath a hiccup in her chest as she lifted her hands. Shock kept him frozen as a flash of blue sparks flew from her fingertips.

Chapter Forty-one

Ravyn trembled as she watched Nick stumble backward. The gun slipped from his fingers, and he fell against the edge of the bed, weakened by her spell. His eyes glared at her, his anger and sense of betrayal as strong as the love she'd seen in them earlier.

Kayne was calling to her, asking her to join him in his worship of dark forces. Wanting her to bring Nick. She would come all right, but alone—and not to join him. This was her battle, and she had to end it once and for all.

"I'm sorry, Nick."

So weak he could barely speak, he looked at her, shaking his head. "Y-you saved me . . . back there. Healed the bullet wound."

She nodded and swiped a hand across her tear-stained cheeks. "I couldn't let you die. I knew you might find out what I was, but I couldn't let you die."

He managed a bleak smile. "You should have. You should do it now. I'll come . . ." He grimaced, the words squeezing out of him as he tried to hold on to consciousness. "I'll . . . come after you. I can't let you go."

He toppled backward on the bed, insensate. Ravyn walked toward him as if in a trance. She stood over him, noting the steady rise and fall of his chest. His face was pale, but he was alive. She let out a relieved breath. He would be okay.

However, whatever wonderful thing had happened between them was now over. He'd never forgive her. But he was safe. Kayne would not get Nick's soul. And she would finish Kayne. One way or another, she would destroy him. Just as she'd destroyed the Tin Man.

Bending over, she placed a gentle kiss on Nick's motionless lips. "I'm sorry," she whispered, and left to meet Kayne.

Ravyn drove along the darkened streets, a jumble of conflicting emotions warring within her. Her body still tingled from Nick's lovemaking, but her chest was heavy with despair. Deep in her stomach, fear twisted like a serpent.

Kayne wanted Nick's soul. She couldn't let that happen, but how would she stop him? She might agree to sacrifice herself, to remain with Kayne forever, but it wouldn't stop there. Kayne wanted her, but he also wanted power, control, and he wanted to destroy Nick, the man who'd truly earned Ravyn's love. He needed Nick's soul to rejuvenate his own so that he could carry out his diabolical plan to rule . . . what? What exactly did he desire? All the world's covens, all of mankind? Whatever it was, she knew she had to prevent it.

Over the centuries many witches had gone the way of the dark side, but so far such defection had been sporadic. Their numbers had not been strong enough at any one time to band together into a new coven. If that were to happen, the results could be disastrous. Was that what was happening in Wyldewood? Was Kayne gathering enough black-magic witches to cause worldwide destruction?

The forming of a police task force indicated something odd was occurring. Ravyn wasn't sure exactly what, but she knew at the very least the anonymity of her coven was in jeopardy. The serenity and safety of those she loved most was compromised. She had to protect her coven.

And Nick. There was still Nick. If Kayne's procurement of Nick's soul was successful, Nick would most likely die. At the very least the Nick she knew and loved would be gone. After all the work Nick had done to drag himself back from the brink of the abyss, Kayne would taint his soul, bend it into an abomination, a twisted facsimile.

She couldn't defeat Kayne physically, she knew. Even though he'd most likely weakened in his continued defiance of the rules of witchcraft, she would still be no match for his strength. She could use her powers, perhaps. Before Kayne began practicing black magic, they were evenly matched. But he was using the dark forces now, which greatly diminished her odds. And if he'd transcended already . . . Well, then her odds were zero. However, it was unlikely he'd transcended. If he had, he wouldn't need Nick's soul.

Her best option was to trick him, to use his desire to lure Kayne into a situation where she could destroy him. The thought of him touching her intimately sent a spasm of nausea through her. After Nick's lovemaking, after an embrace that made her pulse race and set her nerves afire with longing, she couldn't imagine another man's caress, especially not a caress of evil.

Suddenly, all oxygen leached from the car. Ravyn gasped, barely able to breathe. Her mind reeled as, through the windshield, the lights from the passing vehicles, streetlamps and houses simply blinked out. In the next second, her hands, which had gripped the steering wheel, held nothing but air. The car evaporated, and she was falling crazily, tilting in a black void, the smell of sulfur and ammonia heavy and cloying, choking her.

She landed abruptly and painfully on a dust-covered surface. The impact crushed the air from her lungs, and black spots danced in her vision. She struggled to breathe, gasping and wheezing with the effort. It was several moments before she was able to breathe freely and her vision cleared.

Dazed, she struggled to a sitting position. She was in a large, cavernous building with a hay-covered loft above her head. A rusty tractor sat at one end, and scattered on the floor in the dust and straw were various farming tools: a pitchfork, a shovel, a gardening spade and others. Would any prove useful as weapons? Perhaps, if she could get to them before Kayne got to her.

As if her very thoughts conjured him, Kayne spoke from behind her. She scrambled to her feet and whirled to face him.

In spite of the fall chill, Kayne wore nothing but a fawn-colored loincloth. His bronze muscles gleamed in the meager light, and he seemed unaffected by the temperature. He looked powerful and confident . . . and dangerous.

"Sorry, my love, but I grew impatient. You were following the *speed limit*," he said distastefully, the same way one might say, *You were eating cockroaches*. He shook his head, a look of sympathy in his eyes. "I didn't mean to hurt you."

When he stepped closer and ran his fingers along her cheek, she shivered, trying to keep the revulsion out of her expression. His fingers were cool and smooth, where Nick's were warm and callused. Nick's touch thrilled and excited her, while Kayne's felt like that of a corpse.

"I couldn't wait to see you, to have you here," he said. "To share my plan."

"If I stay with you, will you leave Nick and the coven alone?" she asked.

Kayne's face darkened with anger. "You love him so much you would sacrifice yourself?" When she didn't respond, he continued. "I cannot grant what you wish. I need his soul to rejuvenate my body. I grow weaker and will perish without another's spirit. And once I obtain his soul, you will love me as you do him."

A spark of hope lit within her. Kayne hadn't yet transcended, and he'd clearly weakened in his physical form. His powers were probably not as focused as they should be, either. If she ever had a chance, this was it.

She shook her head. "I don't love him." The denial rang hollow, but she pushed on. "I care about him, but my main concern is my coven. Nick is a part of a task force to hunt witches. The situation has gotten out of hand, and everyone I truly love is in danger. Sorina . . ." She swallowed, willing back her sorrow. "I've already lost my sister. I can't let anything more happen to the coven. I'll do *anything.*"

"What, exactly, are you proposing?" Kayne's gaze was sharp, and she couldn't read his expression. Couldn't gauge his mood.

"I will stay with you. I will join the dark forces you gather, and together we'll rule Wyldewood. But it goes no further. You don't have to transcend, you don't need another's soul. I will be your source of power, of strength. You and I together shall be enough."

Kayne's eyes narrowed. "You would stay with me? Join my dark forces? You were so opposed before. You are too loyal to your teachings to take such a drastic step. You think to trick me."

"No!" she swore. "I've been studying *Invocations of Shadows.* I can see the value." She didn't want to push it too far; Kayne wouldn't believe she'd totally flipped sides. For that reason she said, "I admit I am not completely enamored of the dark side, but I am willing to go the way of its teachings to save those I love. It was empowering, *thrilling* to destroy the Tin Man, even if it went against the rules of the coven. I don't like how restricting our magic can be. Sometimes, it's necessary to go outside our teachings."

To demonstrate her commitment, she reached out and stroked Kayne's face, then ran her fingers down his chest. His muscles contracted beneath her hand, and he let out a gasp.

"Ravyn," he groaned. He gripped her arms and pulled her to him.

When his lips touched hers, a sudden rush of bile crowded her throat, but she fought it down. She squeezed her eyes shut and let her lips soften beneath his, pressed her body against him.

He pulled his mouth away and whispered in her ear, "Is this what you want, baby? My touch instead of his? Haven't you always wanted this? What has kept you away?"

"Mmmm," she murmured, running her fingertips over his shoulders, his back, and lower, to the waist of the loincloth.

"Oh, Ravyn." He gave a whimper as he once again claimed her lips.

She let her mind drift back to Nick, to the coven, to anything other than Kayne's vile touch. If she could distract him enough, if he became even momentarily pliant, perhaps she could get to her dagger and injure, maybe incapacitate him.

Kill him.

She forced herself to give a moan and bent her knee, rubbing her thigh along Kayne's erection. The pressure of his mouth increased against hers until he was grinding her lips against her teeth. She tasted blood, but she didn't mind. His preoccupation with his desire would eventually offer her the opportunity she needed. And she'd need every advantage she could get. Saving Nick's life had weakened her. She could feel the drain on her powers, feel it in her blood. The element of surprise and Kayne's own weakness—his desire for her—would have to be enough.

She let a hand slide off his shoulder and reached between their bodies to her bent leg, where her dagger rested inside her boot. Her fingers touched the handle, and she snatched the weapon out, clutching it tightly. But before she could plunge it into Kayne, she felt his hand twisting in her hair, his grip tight and painful. He jerked her head back, and a jolt of burning electricity shot through the hand that held the dagger. She cried out, dropping the knife as pain radiated from her fingers up through her arm.

Kayne's face filled her vision, his golden eyes burning with rage. "You lying bitch!"

He jerked her head farther back until she was staring at the ceiling. He waved his free hand, and an image appeared on the wooden beams above. It was a macabre dance of shadows that formed into a figure: a dark shape that was unmistakably a woman with a rope around her neck, feet dangling, her head canted at a grotesque angle.

Tears of anger and terror swam to Ravyn's eyes, and she tried to speak, but her neck was stretched so far back that words wouldn't form. Her bravado fled, as did all hope of defeating Kayne. Despair and apprehension for her coven, for Nick, engulfed her, and she helplessly watched the body swinging above.

In the next instant, she felt the rough strands of a rope slithering against her skin, encircling her neck. Her mind shifted from fear for those she loved to fear for herself. The scream died on her vocal cords as the rope snapped taut on her throat.

Chapter Forty-two

Nick's eyes fluttered open. He didn't know how long he'd been out, but he recalled in vivid detail what had happened before he lost consciousness. He struggled to a sitting position and looked around the room. Once more, Ravyn was gone.

Dear God. He couldn't believe what he'd seen. What he'd heard. Ravyn was a witch? She was one of the very people he was hunting—even though up until now he hadn't really believed they existed. Ravyn was one of them.

He reached for his pants, fumbling to slip them on. He didn't know where she'd gone, but somehow he had to find her. It was a calling from his heart—from his very soul.

He stopped in midmotion as he heard the dark voice of Kayne once more. *If you want her, you must come to me.*

"Who the hell are you? *What* are you?" Nick screamed in rage at his unseen enemy.

If you want to know, if you want to find her, you'll listen to me. You'll follow my instructions.

"It's not her I want, motherfucker. It's you."

The resultant laughter was evil, reaching around the room and coiling its tendrils up inside Nick. *Brave words, mortal. We shall see.*

Nick didn't respond. Instead, he listened very closely as the voice told him where to go.

Very soon he was crouched behind a fence, gun drawn,

staring at a barn. A cool wind whipped around him, and the odor of hay and animals penetrated his nostrils. From somewhere in the darkness he heard the lowing of cows, followed by the howl of . . . what? A coyote? A wolf? A frisson of apprehension slid over his spine as he glanced around. When he didn't detect a set of glowing eyes in the gloom, he turned back to the darkened barn.

Surely this couldn't be the place. The windows were boarded up and the exterior in crumbling disrepair. The structure was in the middle of nowhere. There wasn't a house within a mile, and it was obviously abandoned. Had Kayne purposely misled him? At this moment, were he and Ravyn sharing a laugh at Nick's expense? It had all been a game to her, after all. She'd lied about everything else—why wouldn't she lie about her relationship with Kayne? Was it such a stretch to believe they were in on this together?

Nick shook his head. A witch. Jesus. He was having terrible difficulty processing that fact. Everything else seemed inconsequential. Everything, that is, except the power-crazed maniac, Kayne, who also happened to be a witch. A maniac whose plan, although unclear at the moment, definitely involved him.

Nick should have called the task-force members, but he hadn't. For one, he wasn't exactly sure what he was dealing with. For another, he wasn't completely confident in their abilities.

And . . . admit it, Lassiter. You're just a little afraid of what they'll do to Ravyn.

That last thought was disturbing. He shouldn't care what happened to her, but in spite of what she was and what she'd perhaps done, the sad truth was that he did care. Too much. More than almost anything ever.

Approach the barn or go? He didn't believe for a second

they were in there, but he was here. He might as well check the building out. And then what? He didn't know. Because he had no idea how in the hell to find witches.

Making as little noise as possible, he duckwalked to the side of the building and stretched slowly to a standing position, peeking between the boards on one of the windows. He could make out very little, but he saw a glimmer of light. Someone was inside.

Sliding around to the front, he quietly lifted the board and pushed the door open. Raising his Beretta in a ready position in front of him, he stepped inside.

When his gaze took in the scene, the air left his body as if an unseen fist had pounded his chest. What he saw nearly took him to his knees.

Chapter Forty-three

Ravyn was at one end of the large room. Thick ropes bound her arms to her torso, and around her neck was a noose. When she saw Nick, she gasped and slowly shook her head.

"You shouldn't have come." Her voice was raspy and weak. Nick wanted to hold her. Wanted to save her. Wanted to be her hero, no matter what he'd thought before coming here. How could he have distrusted her?

His arms went slack for a moment, and he thought he might drop his gun, but he brought the weapon back up, whirling to aim it at Kayne, who sat in a large chair six feet or so from where Ravyn was tied up. He wore nothing but a loincloth that made him look like some evil incarnation of Tarzan. The rope around Ravyn's neck was slung over a beam in the ceiling, and the far end was wrapped around Kayne's wrist.

"Let her go, you bastard." Nick was dismayed to find the hoarse rasp of tears in his voice.

The warlock smiled, white teeth glistening in his tan face. He flicked his long blond hair off his forehead and stood, tendons jumping in his massive chest as he flexed his arms and clenched his fists. "'You bastard?' Who do you think you are? You come in and demand something of me?"

Metal flashed in Kayne's hand, and Nick recognized the dagger Ravyn had slipped into her boot while she was leaving her house. How much pain had this monster inflicted when he took it from her? The thought made Nick's stomach roil.

Easing toward Ravyn, he lifted his gun until it pointed at Kayne's chest.

"You might not want to do that," Kayne laughed. "You can't kill me. There's only one way I can die, and a bullet isn't it. But if you shoot, I will be injured. Temporarily. I will fall, thereby pulling the noose tighter around Ravyn and causing her neck to snap. If you're willing to sacrifice her to defeat me . . . well, go ahead. She betrayed you, after all."

"Do it, Nick!" Ravyn cried. "Don't worry about me. You can't kill him, but you can disable him long enough to get away."

The billowy white blouse she wore was tattered and hanging off one shoulder. Drops of blood spattered the front, and Nick noticed her lower lip was cut—more evidence of what she'd suffered at the hands of this madman. Her beautiful face was pale, drawn. Her eyes pleaded with him. He stared at her, his chest nearly exploding with love, regret, fear . . .

He didn't know exactly what they were up against, but he knew he couldn't leave her. Not willingly. Not ever. He'd left Annie and regretted it forever. He wouldn't make the same mistake twice.

He let his gun fall from nerveless fingers. It plummeted harmlessly to the dusty floor, making a small and ineffectual *thunk*. Kayne laughed, the sound roaring through the room, gathering volume.

"Do you see who's in charge, mortal?"

Nick took a step toward Ravyn.

"Stop right there," his enemy commanded. "You will obey me, or you both will die."

"I'm going to make sure she's okay," Nick vowed. His voice held more bravado than he felt.

As he walked toward Ravyn, she shook her head. "Listen to him, Nick. Do what he says, please. Find a way to save yourself."

Nick stopped, the pleading in her eyes affecting him more than any threats from Kayne.

She continued in a dazed whisper, "I'm okay, but he's drugged me and made my powers ineffectual. I can't help you. You shouldn't have come. He'll destroy you. He wants your soul. You have to go. Now!"

"My—"

"Silence!" Kayne's voice cut through their conversation. He pointed to a hard-backed chair in the center of the room. "Sit, mortal," he instructed Nick.

Nick did as he was told. For now, with Ravyn's life in this maniac's hands, literally, he had to play it cool. He had to think smart to get them out of this. Now was not the time for foolish mistakes, as if there ever had been a time for them.

Kayne tied Ravyn's rope to a beam behind him. He paced back and forth like a hungry cougar, his fingers caressing the blade of her dagger. "You will hear me out and do exactly as I say, at least if you want to keep Ravyn from harm. One false move and I will break her neck."

Nick didn't respond, just followed Kayne's movements with his eyes, waiting.

"Understand one thing. I could have disintegrated you the moment you stepped through the door. Could have reduced you to a smoldering pile of ashes—or perhaps a pile of shit would have been more fitting." Kayne's feral golden eyes gleamed with amusement. "The only reason you still exist is because I need something from you."

Nick held the male witch's gaze, even though the urge to turn away was overwhelming.

"I have acquired power beyond your feeble imagination, and I am on the brink of supremacy—*immortality*. The knowledge I have gained even allows me to defy the rules set forth in the pathetic code of witchcraft."

Nick wondered if he could somehow subdue Kayne, somehow manage to jump him when he wasn't looking. But, no. If a bullet would have no effect, a physical attack surely wouldn't.

"However, the cost has been great," Kayne continued. "My body grows weak. My soul is deteriorating."

"Is there a point to all this?" Nick interrupted.

Kayne stopped his pacing and stalked over to stand in front of him. He flung the dagger across the room. It landed with a *thunk*, well out of reach of either of them. Fists clenched at his sides, the warlock panted heavily. "You will not speak to me in such a manner. Your time will come—the time to prove your worth. But for now, you will listen."

"Kayne, leave him alone." Ravyn's voice was thready but determined. "I'll stay with you. You can recover—you don't need him," she begged.

Kayne spun and pointed a finger at her. "You *will* stay with me, but only because I've won your allegiance." The finger returned to Nick. "This insignificant insect will have the opportunity to live . . . though the odds are not in his favor."

"Let Ravyn go, and I'll give you whatever you want," Nick offered.

Kayne grinned. "Well, isn't this heartwarming? The two of you sacrificing yourselves for one another. But your words only confirm that my plan will work. Hear me out. Do not speak until I am finished."

It galled Nick to obey, made him feel useless in a manner he had never before felt, even at his lowest point. But he stayed silent, curious as to what Kayne had in mind and hoping somehow that he could get himself and Ravyn out alive. At the very least, Ravyn.

"In attaining my present state, I have overused my powers. I need a new soul. I want yours," Kayne revealed.

Nick laughed. "You want my soul? Who do you think you are, Satan?"

Kayne's eyes flashed with anger, but he emitted an amused snort. "Satan? He wishes. I am now the most powerful being in this world and beyond. With your soul, I will be reborn and can rule with unopposed authority. The world will be mine to do with as I wish."

Was he for real? There was plenty Nick wanted to say in response, but he remained silent. He doubted Kayne had any interest in a challenge of his sanity.

"Unfortunately, I cannot take your soul without permission. We have to make a deal—and so I will issue a challenge. If I am victorious, you will relinquish your soul to me, and Ravyn will be mine for eternity. Your physical form, of course, will most likely be dead. If we fight, not only do I intend to best you, but to carve your heart from your chest and present it to her as a gift. That way Ravyn will have a trinket by which to remember you. Since she loves you, once I obtain your soul she will love me. That is how this magic works."

Nick glanced at Ravyn. She loved him? Was that truly possible, given all that had happened, their mutual distrust and betrayals of each other? Why did Kayne believe it was so? And yet . . . could it be true? Could she love him as much as he loved her?

Now was not the time to think about his and Ravyn's relationship, but Nick couldn't help the tiny thrill of hope that traveled through him. He turned his attention back to Kayne, concentrating on the warlock's insane rantings, waiting for an opening to strike, any chance at all.

"If by some extremely unlikely happenstance you best me," Kayne continued, "I will lose all power and my body and soul will die. Ravyn will be spared. That is your goal, of course. However," the warlock laughed, "she will not remember you. You will be a stranger to her. She will not remember one second of your . . . association. Not a trace. So, in effect, it will be for nothing. You will rescue Ravyn, but you will lose her. You will have failed."

Kayne stared at Nick. "Do you see? There is no way to win. Either way, you lose her. At best you can only save your life. If you relinquish your soul and walk away, I shall spare you. Give in and you shall save your life—if not your soul." He laughed again, and his evil was almost palpable. The skin on Nick's arms grew cold, and heat tingled across his scalp.

"I see you are not entirely deterred, that I shall have to give you more information," Kayne said. "So be it. If you accept my challenge, we will fight like men—hand to hand, with no rules. I must say, there will be little triumph in defeating an alcoholic has-been."

Nick shook his head, trying to process everything that had been thrown at him. Was it really true that Ravyn would forget him even if he won? "Let me ask you something," he said, stalling for time. "Besides my being an alcoholic has-been, doesn't the battle seem a little unevenly matched, what with your witchy powers or whatever? How do I stand a chance?"

"You don't stand a chance, simply because I am physically superior," Kayne sneered. "However, if it eases your mind, I shall not be able to use my powers. Not in any way. I must win your soul fairly, without magic."

Nick closed his eyes and sighed. He liked these odds better than the ones he'd thought he faced, but he didn't have a lot of confidence in his ability to defeat Kayne. He was no longer as sharp as he'd once been; it had been a while since he'd been physically tested. The odds were against him, and he knew it.

"If he uses his powers to win the fight, he won't have the resources left to transfer your soul to his body," Ravyn called out, her voice weak and groggy. "But don't do it, Nick. Run!"

Nick glanced at Ravyn, then turned back to Kayne. "Give me a few minutes with Ravyn, and I'll give you an answer," he said.

The warlock held his gaze a moment, then nodded. "As you wish." He returned to his chair and motioned Nick toward Ravyn. "She will be due for another injection soon. I cannot let the narcotics wear off and take a chance she will use her powers to assist you, but before I give her the drugs, you may have a moment with her. It will be your last, either way."

Nick walked toward Ravyn, and his heart clenched at the sight of her lovely face, pale and streaked with tears. Her heavy-lidded expression was a result of the drugs. He stopped directly in front of her and reached a hand out to caress her cheek. "Hi," he whispered.

"I'm sorry, Nick. I'm so sorry about deceiving you, about bringing you into this mess, but you can't do this. You can't beat him. You have to leave while you still can."

"If I have even a chance to defeat him, I have to take it. I have to save you."

She shook her head. "No. I won't let him kill you. Just refuse the challenge, Nick, please."

"I can't leave you."

"There's so much to explain and so little time," she said, her words slurred. "But I want you to know why I deceived you, why I didn't tell you I was a witch. I was afraid to get close to a mortal, afraid that I would endanger everyone I loved. I didn't trust the authorities, didn't trust you. But I was wrong. I—"

"You don't have to explain," Nick said. "I understand." And he truly did.

"I've caused so much trouble. You wouldn't be here if it weren't for me."

Nick shook his head. "It will be okay. You must live and find a way to escape."

Her head snapped up, her eyes locking onto his. "You expect to lose? You *know* you can't win. Oh, God, Nick. Please, please don't do this." Her voice was breathless with panic. "Please, I'm begging you—"

"Shhh." Nick took her face between his palms. "Don't worry about me, I haven't given up yet. But I have a question. Mr. Demented over here said there was only one way he can be killed. You wouldn't happen to know what that is, would you?"

"I wish I did." She shook her head, clearly racking her memory. "From the book he gave me . . . The dark powers he's acquired make him almost invincible. He can only die in the same way he died in his former life. But, I have no idea what that is." She looked beaten, defeated. "I'm sorry."

Nick shrugged, trying to gather courage. "Just a thought. Who knows? Maybe I'll stumble onto it. Let's just hope he didn't die in a freak whaling accident or something." He tried to give her a smile.

"But I won't remember you!" Ravyn cried. "I don't want to live in a world where I don't know you!"

"I don't want to live in a world without you, period," he admitted. "But I have to do this, Ravyn."

He saw from the tears in her eyes, from her expression, that she didn't understand. He had to make her see. "When I met you I was existing from day to day, not really living. I was, as Kayne put it, an alcoholic has-been, hiding behind my grief and guilt, using it as an excuse not to rejoin the real world. I thought my heart had stopped beating. That my chest was a hollow void. Even more than Haleck, I was like the Tin Man from *The Wizard of Oz*. Then

I met you, and for the first time in a long while I started to care—about life, about others, about me. I fell in love with you. You gave me back my heart." He smiled and placed a kiss on her forehead. "Who would have thought I'd find my heart just in time to lose my soul?"

"No!" Her head swung from side to side. "No, please! For me! If you love me, please don't do this!"

"I *do* love you. And that's why I have to do it. Maybe someday you can understand and forgive me."

He bent his head, and for the last time, felt the softness of Ravyn's mouth yielding beneath his.

Chapter Forty-four

"Enough!" Kayne roared, rising and striding toward them.

Nick pulled away and gave Ravyn an encouraging smile, brushing a thumb down her tear-stained cheek. She lifted burning eyes to Kayne and said, "Even with Nick's soul you'll still be the same savage, heartless bastard, and I'll never love you."

Her ex-lover lifted a syringe and smiled, though his eyes flashed with rage. "We shall see, my lovely."

Ravyn felt the prick of the needle and a sting as the sedative entered her system. Her limbs began to relax, and her eyelids grew heavy. She didn't want to pass out, didn't want to wake up to the horror she knew was about to ensue. She had to watch, had to be strong. For Nick.

A hazy curtain seemed to drop over her vision, but she could see through the curtain, could see as the two men began to circle one another. Kayne's sleek muscles gleamed in the overhead light, his nearly naked body beautifully cut, every tendon and vein seeming to magnify the futility of Nick's plight. Nick, though broad-shouldered and strong, was still no match.

Kayne struck the first blow, a mighty jab into Nick's jaw. Nick stumbled backward but stayed on his feet. He circled, waiting for an opening, then charged at Kayne and pummeled the warlock's abdomen, switching at the last moment from body blows to an unexpected uppercut. Kayne fell back, shaking his head like a stunned bull.

But he came back at Nick quickly, catching him with a punch to the ribs. Nick grunted and grabbed his side, his expression one of concentrated agony, and helplessly Ravyn watched as Kayne kept attacking, over and over, barely breathing hard, minimally affected by Nick's assault. Nick was soon battered and bloody. One eye was swollen shut. She noticed that he favored his left side and wondered if he'd broken a rib.

Nick went down to one knee, but pushed himself back up, staggering forward. Ravyn let out a scream as she saw an object appear in Kayne's hand, retrieved from a shadowy corner of the barn. He aimed the shovel toward Nick's head. Nick moved just in time, and it struck his shoulder.

"No!" Ravyn yelled, but neither man turned. Nick weaved for a moment, then fell to his knees and toppled over face-first. "Nick!"

Nick lifted his head and through his one good eye squinted in Ravyn's direction. He gave her a crooked smile. She knew he was done, but hoped that some of his pain, maybe even his life, might be spared if he gave up now.

"Stay down, Nick," she cried out. "Please stay down. I love you. Kayne, spare him! I'll do whatever you want!"

Nick just winked at her and stumbled to his feet, swaying. He moved his hands in a taunting gesture at Kayne. "Let's go!"

The warlock shook his head. "We've already 'gone,' you fool. Don't you know when you're beaten?"

Nick shrugged. "Guess it must be all that alcohol. Fried my brain. Being a has-been, I don't know when to quit."

"Then I'll have to make it a little clearer." Kayne caught him with a sharp uppercut that knocked Nick back to the ground.

Panting, Nick rose once more. This time, he held the shovel he'd maneuvered to obtain. He swung it forcefully against Kayne's head.

Kayne reeled and cried out but stayed upright. He grinned as though Nick were no more than a nuisance.

"You cheated!" Ravyn shrieked. "You *are* using your powers!"

Kayne laughed at her, still keeping an eye on Nick. "Ah, did I fail to mention that I wouldn't use my powers to cause him harm, but my powers would protect me from fatal injury?" He made a *tsk*ing sound and cast his eyes downward, then back up at Nick. "I must say, it slipped my mind, but it will be nearly impossible to cause me lasting pain. Tough break, eh, mortal?"

Ravyn closed her eyes, squeezing them tight against the sorrow working its way from her chest to her throat. All she could feel was her love for Nick, a love that would soon be torn apart . . . and in her drug-induced haze, an image came to her. Suddenly, she saw it all, saw what had happened in her long-ago life. The man she loved was killed not knowing how she felt.

But it was not only her actions after his death that led to her own execution; it was another man. It had been a man who pursued her incessantly, only to be turned away time after time. He'd come to her after her lover's death, thinking she would finally succumb to his advances. But she'd refused him, sending him into an uncontrollable rage. He'd been the one to turn her over to the authorities. In the midst of one of her fits of grief, while she'd created lightning and thunder in a cloudless sky, casting a pall over the sun until the land was in darkness, they'd come for her. They'd hauled her in to stand trial for the crime of witchcraft, while the traitor watched from the back of the courtroom, a smug smile on his face.

Kayne's face.

But she also remembered something else. She had not been the only person hanged for their crimes. The execution was carried out three days after the trial—and her mother shared the scaffold with her. Not for witchcraft, but for the murder of her daughter's accuser.

Moved by the memory of her mother's love, Ravyn experienced a spike of regret. How had she never remembered that detail before? Maybe knowing how her mother had once loved her would have helped repair their current relationship. But it was too late for that now. She needed to concentrate on one other detail, the detail that could perhaps save Nick's life. She had to remember how her mother had killed Kayne.

She opened her eyes and gasped. Nick was lying facedown on the floor, his hands pressed against the ground as he struggled to stand, even though he was slipping in his own blood. Anguish ripped at her gut, formed a tight band around her heart and throat, almost as if the noose was, at this very moment, tightening around her neck.

"Nick!" She spoke, but it was no more than a whisper. He couldn't hear her, just as she couldn't help him. Not unless she could remember—and even then, would it be possible to save him? Would the instrument of Kayne's death be a means at their disposal?

Think, Ravyn, think!

In her mind's eye, her mother was standing on the platform next to her, billowing gray skirts flapping in the wind, a smile for the daughter by whose side she would perish, love shining in her beautiful blue eyes. But Ravyn had to remember more, had to remember it all, had to know how Kayne had been killed.

A shattering noise broke into her thoughts, and she raised her eyes to see Nick sliding down the wall beneath a broken window. Kayne stood over him, fists clenching and unclenching at his sides, an unholy smile spread across his features. Then another image superimposed over the one in front of Ravyn's eyes: Kayne of long ago, lying in a pool of blood, a jagged shard of glass protruding from his chest.

She couldn't have seen this! She'd been in jail at the time! And yet she knew this was how Kayne had died.

"Nick!"

Her voice was stronger now, but she didn't think he heard. He sat slumped on the floor against the wall, his head lolling on his chest, eyes closed. Was he dead? She struggled against her bindings, but it was no use. They were too tight. She couldn't free herself, couldn't do anything but watch helplessly as . . .

Suddenly, a sensation came over her, and she realized she no longer felt the effects of the drugs Kayne had given her. Somehow, they were wearing off! Was it her concern for Nick, her love for him, creating a magic that overcame all? Just as her grandmother suggested. And Kayne was so intent on his destruction of Nick that he didn't notice.

Although her arms were bound, Ravyn was able to lift her fingers enough to point toward the shattered window above Nick's head. Clenching her teeth, concentrating with all her might, she willed the current to move through her, willed the power to return, at least for this one act. She felt a tingle and almost giggled with relief. She could do this!

Kayne towered over Nick's prone form, hands on hips, a look of delight on his face. "You're finished, mortal. After the transformation, you die." He let his head fall back. Eyes closed, he began to speak, the words pouring out of him in an insanely fervent litany. "O mighty Darkness, I beseech thee. I seek another soul. I will you to transform it from this feeble husk . . ."

Ravyn felt the tingle of magic grow into a current in her veins, and blue flame charged from her fingertips. A particularly lethal-looking shard of glass jutted from a piece of the barn's wooden window frame. The makeshift weapon shook loose and fell to the floor next to Nick's splayed hand.

"Nick!" she shouted, hoping to rouse him enough that he could fight back, end Kayne's life, save himself. But he didn't move.

"Nick," she tried again, this time her voice a shriek of hopeless agony.

Kayne stopped speaking, opening his eyes and turning to her. "It's over. Soon you'll be mine and he will be vanquished. Accept it, my love. You are mine."

"I hope you rot in hell," she spat.

Kayne started to say something, but his words were cut off by a groan from Nick. Kayne looked down at him. "What was that? Are you trying to say a few last words? I suppose I can give you that."

Kayne crouched in front of Nick, hands dangling between his knees. The loincloth bulged. He reached out and slapped Nick on the side of the face, then cupped a hand behind his own ear. "Speak, mortal. This will be your last chance."

Ravyn couldn't hear the words, but she saw a look of amused confusion cross Kayne's face. "Say that again, you pathetic excuse for a man. I'm not sure I heard you correctly."

"I said"—Nick's voice was suddenly loud and strong as he opened his eyes and raised his bloodied face toward Kayne—"you should have worn more clothes!" And with that Nick brought his weapon up and into Kayne's unprotected groin. As he pulled it back out, Kayne roared and fell backward, his face twisted in pained surprise. Although she could see that the shard of glass had sliced Nick's hand, he didn't appear to notice. Seemingly imbued with renewed energy, Nick pounced on Kayne and drove the jagged glass into his chest. His enemy grunted, then fell still. Kayne was dead.

Ravyn closed her eyes, let her head fall back in relief. It was finally over.

* * *

Nick stood over Kayne's body, breathing heavily. There wasn't a part of him that didn't throb with stabbing pain, but he felt more elated, more alive than he had in years. He'd won! Ravyn was free!

He turned, but the smile on his face died as quickly as it had appeared. A coil of ropes lay like a discarded pile of snakes on the floor where Ravyn had stood. The space was empty.

He walked slowly to where she'd been only moments before, taking his time. Perhaps, miraculously, when he reached the spot, she would reappear . . . ?

It didn't happen. She was gone. He dropped to his knees and scooped the ropes up in his hands, his physical pain a mere twinge compared to the agony ripping through his heart.

"Ravyn!" The cry tore from him, echoing in the now-quiet room. He looked around wildly, as if hoping she'd just been playing a trick on him, an inappropriate and badly timed game of hide-and-seek. But she was completely, irrevocably, gone.

Tears fell, mingling with his blood to form a pinkish brine that dripped onto the dusty floor. His victory was hollow at best. He'd beaten Kayne, only to lose the woman he loved.

Chapter Forty-five

Ravyn opened her eyes and looked around, then frowned in confusion. The last thing she remembered was confronting Kayne, and now she was lying on her living-room floor. The room was dark, in wavering shadow.

She rose and rested her elbows on her knees, dropping her head into her hands. How had she gotten back home? What had happened with Kayne? She tugged on her hair, as if that could pull the memory from her mind.

She'd tracked the Tin Man to his basement. That high school girl—he'd intended to kill her. The picture of his mother, the suicide. She remembered all those things, and that when Kayne had called to her, she'd gone to a barn. She'd tried to trick him, but . . . She lifted a hand to her neck. She remembered a noose, then nothing.

What had he done to her? Slowly she stood and looked down at herself. Her clothing was a tattered mess. Red spatters marred the white of her blouse. Blood. She lifted her fingers to her lips. They were puffy, painful. But she couldn't recall exactly how it had happened.

She turned on a light, then went upstairs and took a shower, tossing away her shredded clothing and putting on a burgundy robe. She was blow-drying her hair when, over the noise of the dryer, she heard someone pounding on the front door.

Shutting off the dryer, she headed down the stairs. Halfway to the door, the pounding increased, and she heard a man shouting her name. She looked through the peephole and saw him leaning with his palms against the door. He was a mortal, tall with dark hair. She couldn't see his face well because his head was bowed, but she didn't know him. She was sure of it. He looked as if he'd been in an accident or a fight—a one-sided fight, where he'd been the loser. His dark blue shirt was spattered with blood.

"Who is it?" she asked through the closed door.

His body tensed for a split second; then he relaxed. He tilted his head back and she got a better view of his battered face. It was worse than she'd first thought.

"Ravyn?" He smiled, and the smile was incongruous with his pulverized face. "Thank God! It's Nick. Please. Let me in."

"I'm sorry. I don't know you. You need to leave."

The smile vanished from his face and he squeezed his eyes closed. "Ravyn. Please. Let me in and I'll explain. You *do* know me."

She let out a loud breath and said, "Listen, you need to leave right now, or I'll call the cops."

"No, you won't." One side of his mouth twisted in a grin. "You don't even like cops. Just let me in for five minutes, and after I've told you what I've come to say, I'll leave. I promise." He held up three fingers like a Boy Scout.

"No," she said firmly. "Just go away. I'm not interested in anything you have to say." Why was she even standing at the door arguing with this lunatic? If she ignored him, he'd eventually give up. She started to turn, but his next words caused her to freeze.

"Not even if it's about Kayne?"

She hesitated just a moment before whirling back and jerking the door open. If he meant to harm her, it wasn't like she was helpless. She stood back and let him pass, and when they were both inside she shut the door and turned to face him, wrapping her arms tightly around her middle. "What do you know about him?" she demanded.

"I know about Kayne, about Haleck . . ." And then, more quietly, "About Sorina. For God's sake, Ravyn. It's Nick. Don't tell me he won and you can't remember."

Closer up, the stranger looked even worse. His face was bruised, his lips swollen and cut. One eye was a bloodred and vibrant blue slit. The other was uninjured. The blue iris glittered at her like the surface of a sun-dappled ocean.

She clenched her teeth and said, "I don't know you, and I don't know how the hell you know me. But what do you know about Kayne? Where is he?"

"He's dead."

"How?"

He sighed and moved closer to her. "I killed him. With your help. Not even an hour ago. And just before that, you told me you loved me."

She shook her head. "You're insane."

"Maybe. Because I know what you are, and it's like nothing I've ever seen, like nothing I've ever known. Nonetheless, I'm willing to risk it."

"You know that I'm—"

"A witch? Yes. I only recently found out, and I'll admit it's hard to accept, but I was just engaged in a battle to the death with another witch to save you, so I pretty much have to accept it. Kayne said you'd be spared but would forget me. I didn't believe him, because I have to believe that our love is stronger than any curse. How can this world exist if the forces of darkness are stronger than love? I don't think I want to live in that sort of place." He gripped her arms and pulled her close, searching her face with his gaze. "You have to remember."

Through the thin silk of her robe, his touch was warm and hard. Disturbing. She tugged against it. "Let go of me. Now," she commanded in a low voice.

Pain flashed in his eyes. "You really don't remember. Not at all."

Her chin lifted, and she pulled free of his grasp. "Please, just leave. It's been a hell of a few weeks, and I don't know who you are. You're a mortal, I know that. I can't imagine that I fell in love with you. If I did . . . the truth is, I don't want to remember. I don't want to know you. I just want to be alone." Lifting a weary hand, she brushed the hair back from her face and shakily added, "Please."

He watched her intently. Suddenly, his expression softened and he seemed to come to some kind of decision, because he nodded. "So that's it then," he said, his voice dejected. He let out a long breath. "Okay. I'll go. For now. The last thing I want is for you to hate me. I'll give you some time, then we'll talk. You're alive. You're okay. That's all that matters. That's enough." He stared at her a moment longer, then said, "For now, that will have to be enough."

He turned and walked to the door. She held her breath as she waited for him to leave, and he stopped with his hand on the knob. She saw his shoulders tense, and then he turned back and growled, "The hell it's enough."

He stalked back over to her. She lifted her fingertips, pointing at him, but before she could do anything, he reached her and grabbed her hand in his. "It's *not* enough," he bit out. "I don't care how goddamned selfish that makes me—I won't lose you again. I don't know what might happen if I walk out that door, and I can't risk it. I've learned my lesson. I'll never turn my back on someone I love again. I've been hurting so long, I'd forgotten how it feels to be happy. Until you. And I know you felt the same. I won't go back to that. I won't let *you* go back to that."

She was so startled by his outburst that at first she didn't react, just let him hold her hand as the words poured forth. Somehow, she knew he wouldn't hurt her. And she no longer wanted to hurt him, mortal or not. Someone had done enough of that already.

He looked down at her imploringly and said, "You have to remember, Ravyn. You have to." His words were a whispered plea.

"I can't help you," she said, her voice gentler. "I'm sorry. I don't know you."

"You *do*." And then, more firmly, he said, "You know me." With that, he jerked her hand to his chest and held it against his heart.

Her first reaction was sudden and unexpected: pure, raw lust. Her desire was so potent that she was almost dizzy with it. She spread her fingers out against his warm, hard chest, and a small gasp escaped her lips. Her knees went weak and she looked up into his face, which was so close to hers.

Brow furrowed in confusion, she opened her mouth to speak, but then the images came. One after another. Vivid, real. Memories, not illusions.

The first time she'd seen him—his intense blue eyes, his white teeth flashing in the darkness of his beard.

Him, holding her on her kitchen floor as she wept over Sorina.

The first time they'd kissed.

The last time they'd kissed, when he'd offered himself as a sacrifice to Kayne in order to save her.

"Nick," she choked out. Tears surfaced, clogging her throat, filling her eyes.

"You remember?" he said, his voice hoarse.

One hand still on his chest, she lifted the other and ran her fingertips gently along his bruised face. "You could have walked away," she said softly. "But you fought for me. You chose me, your love for me, over your life. Over your soul." Yet Kayne had chosen evil over her love. A mortal had shown more strength of will, more strength of character, than the most powerful witch she'd ever known. Not just *a* mortal. Her mortal. Her Nick.

"Oh, God, Ravyn." He crushed her to him, her hand trapped between them as his lips came down on hers. The kiss scorched through her, sending a trail of heat down through her body. She tried to ease off, mindful of his injuries, but he was not so cautious. His lips continued to devour hers as a starving man devours a feast.

After a few moments, he lifted his head. "You're wrong about one thing. I could never have walked away. Not from you."

She moved her hand from his chest and cupped his face. "I can't believe I ever forgot you. Even for a minute. Magic or not." Her breath hiccupped in her chest. "Never again," she whispered. "I promise, never again. I love you, Nick. Forever."

"I love you, too. And I promise I'll make *sure* you never forget me again." He grinned happily at her, then kissed her once more. Ravyn allowed the thrill of it, the wonder of it, the emotion of loving him to course through her.

Somewhere in the back of her mind, she realized this would end her dream of becoming high priestess, but the thought brought no regret. This was the beginning of a whole new dream. One she hadn't even known she had . . . until she met Nick.

She thought of what Sorina had said. About love making everything better . . . about the glow inside. Finally, against all odds, Ravyn knew that now. And she knew her sister was watching. And she knew Sorina was pleased.

Epilogue

Ravyn paced the lobby of the precinct, waiting while Nick spoke to the captain. It was two days later, and all safety was gone; real life had come thundering back with a phone call. What would Nick say about everything that had taken place? Would he expose her coven? Would he be forced to take the side of mortals, despite all that they'd shared?

No! He'd promised he wouldn't. He told her he'd take care of it, not to worry. She just had to believe him.

In the time since the battle with Kayne, she and Nick had helped Marvin home from the hospital and met with Vanora—to explain why Ravyn couldn't ever replace her as high priestess. The elder had been clearly disappointed, but the sparkle in her eyes had let Ravyn know the woman was also happy for her.

Ravyn had also called her mother and grandmother and asked them to meet with her so they could talk. She wanted a chance to put all the pain, all the bitterness, behind them. Her grandmother had been the one to show her the true power of love, had convinced her to trust Nick. Gwendyl had sacrificed herself for Ravyn in another life. It was true that in this life, she was far from a perfect mother, but the three women were all that was left of a family. They could build on that. Also, if Sorina was aware of what was going on—and Ravyn believed her sister's spirit had to be—reconciliation between them all would make her almost as happy as Ravyn's finding love would.

The door opened, and Ravyn watched anxiously as Nick came toward her. In spite of her apprehension, she couldn't stop the wave of pleasure that moved through her. Although his wounds still showed, the cuts on his face and black eye, they didn't detract from his appeal. He was handsome and sexy—and hers.

Barely able to wait until Nick had steered her outside, she turned to him on the steps of the precinct. "What did you say?"

"That Kayne was demented and had some kind of un-explainable powers, but whatever they were, all danger ended with his death."

"And?"

"And what?"

Ravyn sighed in exasperation. "About me? The coven? Did you say anything about us?"

"Yeah."

Her eyes widened. "Nick—!"

He grinned. "I told them you had bewitched me, put a spell on me, and I was captivated by your charms."

A relieved laugh escaped her. "Did not."

"No. I didn't. I didn't tell him anything about you or your coven. In fact, they're disbanding the task force. I don't think they ever wanted to believe any of that 'nonsense' anyway." He laughed, then his mood turned serious as he took hold of her shoulders and gazed intently into her eyes. "You never have to worry that I'll hurt you. That I'll betray you. No matter what. You can trust me. Always."

"I know," she whispered. And she did. Above all else, she knew she'd found happiness and peace. She felt it in her heart.

"A thrill ride." —LISA JACKSON on *Ice*

Stephanie Rowe

A MAN WITH NO PAST

Luke Webber thinks he's erased his entire history. New name, new life, no paper trail. He thinks that up in the wilds of Alaska no one will find him. He's wrong.

A WOMAN WITH NO FUTURE

When Isabella shows up on his doorstep, she's got a bullet in her shoulder and all that Luke's been trying to avoid is hot on her trail. Without his help, she'll die. But helping her will mean surrendering everything—his body, his heart . . . and quite possibly his life.

CHILL

"Pulse-pounding chills and hot romance."
—JoAnn Ross on *Ice*

ISBN 13: 978-0-505-52776-9

INTERACT WITH DORCHESTER ONLINE!

Want to learn more about your favorite books and authors?
Want to talk with other readers that like to read the same books as you?
Want to see up-to-the-minute Dorchester news?

VISIT DORCHESTER AT:
DorchesterPub.com
Twitter.com/DorchesterPub
Facebook.com (Search Pages)

DISCUSS DORCHESTER'S NOVELS AT:
Dorchester Forums at DorchesterPub.com
GoodReads.com
LibraryThing.com
Myspace.com/books
Shelfari.com
WeRead.com

FALLEN ROGUE

WHAT YOU DON'T KNOW CAN KILL YOU

Harper Kane was well on her way to an Olympic gold medal in swimming. But now she'll never pass the doping test. Oh, it's not steroids. She doesn't know what exactly she was injected with—something so secret her brother died to protect it, something that's suddenly given her deadly psi abilities she can't quite control.

Special Agent Rome Lucian's instructions are clear: Find Kane and bring her in. She's a threat that needs to be terminated. What's not clear is exactly who's giving the instructions. Rome can't trust anything anymore, and his only ally is the woman he's been sent to kill, a woman who can cause massive devastation with only her mind.

It's sink or swim as the pair is caught in the murky waters of a dark conspiracy the depths of which they can't even begin to fathom.

Amy Rench

ISBN 13: 978-0-505-52812-4

☐ **YES!**

Sign me up for the Love Spell Book Club and send my
FREE BOOKS! If I choose to stay in the club, I will pay
only $8.50* each month, a savings of $6.48!

NAME: _____

ADDRESS: _____

TELEPHONE: _____

EMAIL: _____

☐ I want to pay by credit card.

☐ VISA ☐ MasterCard. ☐ DISCOVER

ACCOUNT #: _____

EXPIRATION DATE: _____

SIGNATURE: _____

Mail this page along with $2.00 shipping and handling to:

Love Spell Book Club
PO Box 6640
Wayne, PA 19087

Or fax (must include credit card information) to:

610-995-9274

You can also sign up online at **www.dorchesterpub.com**.

*Plus $2.00 for shipping. Offer open to residents of the U.S. and Canada only.
Canadian residents please call 1-800-481-9191 for pricing information.
If under 18, a parent or guardian must sign. Terms, prices and conditions subject to
change. Subscription subject to acceptance. Dorchester Publishing reserves the right
to reject any order or cancel any subscription.